Plundering the Past

Tide of Times, Volume 1

A Novel

Robert A. Tayler

Published by Robert A. Tayler, 2020

ISBN: 9781647188498

Published by BookLocker.com, Inc., St. Petersburg, Florida.

BookLocker.com, Inc.
2020

First Edition

ACKNOWLEDGMENTS

Any author will tell you that writing a book is a daunting task, no matter the genre. This novel is no different, as many people and sources conspired to help create Plundering the Past. Without the help, encouragement, and patience of my family, this book would never have been written. Likewise, there are certain individuals and sources that proved invaluable in building the world that Roger and Tom Petrie inhabit.

First, I want to thank my awesome daughter Taylor, as her love for pirates was the genesis behind this book. Her assistance in crafting this novel was invaluable.

I strove to make the historical elements of PTP as realistic as possible, and the people and speech believable. To that end, David Cordingly's book Under the Black Flag was invaluable, as was The Complete Idiot's Guide to Pirates by Gail Selinger and W. Thomas Smith. The Black Bunny: Pirate 101 on Blogspot was extremely helpful in patterning 1700's era speech.

I would like to thank the city of Sarasota simply for being itself. I had the opportunity to live there for two months in the fall of 2016, and I absolutely fell in love with it. I never tired of the beauty of the downtown area and waterfront, visiting her beaches, and basking in the awesomeness that is the Florida Suncoast. Although I have Midwestern roots, part of my heart now belongs to Sarasota.

Lastly, I want to thank you, the reader, for taking the time to peruse my book. My goal was to write a novel that would be entertaining, informative, and easy to read; I hope you find that it successfully fulfills those goals.

Robert A Tayler

LOCAL MEN RESCUED AFTER BOAT SINKS

Saturday, December 18, 2004 1:59PM EST
By: James Dawson, Indianapolis Gazette

Aguadilla, Puerto Rico – A US Coast Guard helicopter successfully rescued two local Indianapolis men Thursday after their boat sank in the eastern Caribbean Sea.

According to a Coast Guard press release, Air Station Borinquen received a vessel on fire message from a C-130J aircraft on a training mission. "Watchstanders quickly dispatched a Dauphin helicopter with a medical team on board from Aguadilla, Puerto Rico," the release stated, "after ordering the Hercules to drop supplies and mark the spot, which was approximately 400 kilometers east of Aguadilla."

The helicopter crew found the men—brothers Roger and Tom Petrie—stranded on a nearby island. They had been missing ever since their previous vessel, the MV *Belvedere*, disappeared on December 2, 2002 during a violent storm. The ship's charter company, Womack Lines out of Miami, FL, had declared her lost with all hands in early 2003.

The release further stated, "After a quick medical evaluation, the Petrie brothers were transported to Aguadilla. They were found to be in relatively good health for having been missing for two years."

"Multiple factors played a role in the survival of these individuals," said Lt. Carmen Oviella, watch commander at Borinquen. "They are experienced mariners whose quick reaction to the emergency saved their lives while making for a timely rescue operation. They were extremely fortunate; there are hundreds of uncharted islands in the area. The odds of being rescued from one without proper communications equipment are fairly remote."

Roger and Thomas are the sons of David and Christine Petrie of Fishers, IN. They declined to be interviewed for this story, other than to say they were "obviously delighted our sons have been found safe and sound, and we eagerly look forward to seeing them again."

According to Lt. Oviella the brothers have provided few details about their experiences. The mystery remains as to what exactly happened to them the two years they were missing.

ONE

"We be Freebooters sure, shackled to the allure of all things that be shiny and bright."
—Pirate Ditty

Indianapolis, IN
Sunday, June 11, 2005
6 months, 26 days since Reemergence

It was the perfect setting for a horror movie.

Late at night, dim lighting, empty building, our footsteps echoing eerily in the long, dark corridor—I would have been frightened, were I traveling with a group of witless, oversexed teenagers. Fortunately, it was just me and my older brother Tom.

"Tell me why we're here, again?" he asked, looking around warily.

"Zykes came down to fifteen thousand on the Mustang, but he'll only take cash. So, we're here to get some."

"And like most people, you store your cash in a creepy warehouse."

"Something like that," I said, un-pocketing my keys as we walked. "The interior walls are concrete block, there's 24/7 security, so it's perfect for what I need. Here it is, unit 126." I unlocked the door and rolled it up, the sound almost deafening in the empty hallway. Inside, the storage space was unremarkable; old furniture, stacked boxes and plastic totes, miscellaneous junk, all piled up around the sides and back.

"'Tis true, Roger. One man's trash is another man's treasure," Tom said. "I only hope you can find yours amidst this trash."

"You're hilarious. Help me move this stuff."

We slid boxes to the side, then pulled out a worn couch, behind which sat a distressed-looking armoire. I pulled out its bottom drawer, setting it aside. The armoire had a false wooden bottom, secured by four hidden clamps. I released the clamps, then lifted the thin sheet of plywood free. Underneath the plywood lay a one-inch sheet of foam shielding a layer of small leather bags, each tied with a leather strap. I reached in and grabbed one, hearing it clink satisfyingly.

"Let's go, Tom, we've got what we came for."

*****

We walked down to the intersection of Meridian and Market streets, entering a building on the northeast corner. An upscale precious metals broker, GS Equity Partners, had offices on the fourth floor. When we arrived, the blinds were drawn over the door, but it opened when I knocked.

"Roger Petrie?" a soft voice inquired.

"Yes, Mr. Sullivan, along with my brother, Tom."

"Come in, please," a thin, bespectacled man whispered, urgently herding us through the door. After double-checking no one had followed us, he led us to an inner office, snapping on a hooded desk lamp. "May I see the articles we spoke of, please?"

I retrieved the leather bag from my backpack, undoing the strap and pouring some of its contents on the desk before Sullivan. His eyebrows arched in surprise as five golden coins spilled onto his blotter, reflecting the lamplight with ethereal beauty.

"Oh, my!" he exclaimed. "When you said the doubloons were in excellent condition, I had no idea they would be this pristine! Wherever did you acquire such specimens?"

"As we discussed earlier, Mr. Sullivan, my grandfather bequeathed these to me last year. The details on how he got them were pretty hazy."

Tom coughed, suppressing a laugh.

"Indeed," he said, picking up a doubloon. "With your permission, Mr. Petrie, I would like to inspect them. They appear to be genuine, but we *are* discussing a sizable sum of money."

"Take whatever time you need."

He moved to a side desk, donning a jeweler's 10X loupe to inspect the coins. After a moment, he moved over to a microscope. I knew what he was looking for: bubbling, plating, or seams in the metal, indicators of forgeries or reproductions. He would not find any. He would also inspect the imprints—forgeries had fuzzy details; authentic coins would be more precise.

I was not concerned, for I knew the coins were genuine, having personally confiscated them from a pompous Spanish admiral.

After Sullivan's initial exam, he consulted several resource books and proprietary internet sites. When he was finished, he returned to his desk. "May I perform the acid test on one of these, Mr. Petrie?"

"Absolutely. I know that particular test is very accurate."

He smiled, excusing himself and walking out of sight. He reappeared shortly with the doubloon in hand, sitting down behind his desk once again.

"I'm satisfied these are authentic Spanish gold doubloons, Mr. Petrie. Their condition is quite remarkable, given that they lay under the ocean for three centuries. My references indicated they likely were recovered from a 1721 shipwreck several years ago. The *Nuestra de la Capistrano* was her name, I believe, a Spanish treasure ship reportedly lost in a hurricane."

"That's the one," I replied, giving him a wan smile. "Grandad said that was a popular opinion but insisted he had it on good authority she was attacked and sunk by a notorious pirate, the Red Raider, for aiding the British in laying a trap for him."

"Really? That would be exciting, would it not?" he said, laying fifteen crisp one thousand-dollar bills on the desk before me.

"Not for the crew of the *Capistrano*," I quipped. "It didn't turn out so well for them." I gathered the bills, securing them in my backpack. "Fifteen thousand dollars, as we agreed." I placed one more doubloon before him. "We would appreciate it if this matter was never discussed again, Mr. Sullivan."

"Of course. Discretion is a large part of my business."

As I zipped up my pack, he fixed me with a curious gaze. "You seem to be more familiar with this *Capistrano* business than one would think, Mr. Petrie."

"Aye, that I do, lad," I chuckled, standing up and turning to leave. "I be so familiar with the tale it almost be like I was there meself."

Tom snickered as we exited the office. I gave Sullivan one final glance—he was staring open-mouthed at us as we disappeared through the door.

Sarasota, FL
Saturday, October 20, 2007
2 years, 10 months, 4 days since Reemergence

Cans dragging behind my 1966 Mustang Fastback made an awful racket as I raced out of Mount Tabor Baptist Church's parking lot, heading for the Sarasota airport.

"Roger," my new wife Rebekah cooed from the passenger seat, "let's not wreck before we even start our honeymoon."

I smiled at her, drinking in the aura of this beautiful, raven-haired woman who had agreed to marry me six months earlier. "Can you blame a guy for wanting to get you alone as soon as possible?"

"Easy, tiger. You'll have your chance soon enough."

Random thoughts swirled in my head as we swung right onto University Parkway. My life had really taken off since I had moved to Sarasota. At one time, I figured I would spend my entire life at sea, but after the traumatic events following the shipwreck of MV *Belvedere* and the subsequent two-year ordeal following that, I was ready to come ashore.

Due to my nautical experience, I was hired on at a local international transport company in Indianapolis, quickly making a name for myself through hard work and a passion for customer service. My boss, David Fuentes, was hired away by TransCaribe, a respected Florida-based freight forwarding firm, in early 2007, calling for me to join him in Florida shortly thereafter.

Rebekah worked at a title company next door, captivating me with her natural good looks and the fact she was always smiling, always had something nice to say. A genuinely nice person. Gathering my nerve, I asked her to dinner, we fell in love shortly thereafter, and the rest was history.

My future seemed secure. It was my past that I was worried about.

TWO

"I wish to have no connection with any Ship that does not sail fast for I intend to go in harm's way."
—Captain John Paul Jones

Sarasota, FL
Sunday Night, October 21, 2018
13 years, 10 months, 5 days since Reemergence

"Come on, Riley, movie's over, time for bed," I said as the movie's credits rolled up our TV screen.

I had let her stay up late to watch Steven Spielberg's *Hook*, a special treat because she loved pirates, especially the classic ones from literature.

My pronouncement was met with gentle snoring. Looking over, I smiled as my nine-year-old daughter snoozed away, looking angelic with her eyes closed, long reddish-brown hair splayed over her pillow. I rousted myself from the couch, bending over to pick her up, trying not to wake her as I carried her to her room. When I kissed her forehead after tucking her in, she sighed and smiled, warming my heart as she turned over and continued sleeping.

Rebekah was a notoriously light sleeper, so I tiptoed into our bedroom as silently as I could. After changing into my pajamas, I eased the sheet back, slipping into bed beside her. The haunting French horn melody of Captain Hook's theme lulled me into unconsciousness as soon as my head hit my pillow…

*****

"This cursed fog!" the captain roared. "'Twill allow our quarry to make good her escape!"

I was serving as forward lookout, holding fast to a forestay, steadying myself as the deck heaved beneath my feet. Renegade's *prow crashed through the warm Caribbean swells, sending curtains of spray cascading over the forecastle, and me. Shaking myself off, I searched for any sign of the galleon we were pursuing. She was slow and heavy-laden with cargo, potentially Spanish silver from the Main. Her name was melodic, the* Nuestra de la Capistrano. *We had almost run her down, drawing to within ten ship-lengths and hoisting the Jolly Roger, when this blasted fog bank rolled in, obscuring our prey, and hampering our pursuit.*

"See anything, Mr. Petrie?" the quartermaster shouted. I silently cursed his stupidity; if the galleon's crew heard our shouting, 'twould aid them in evading us behind the soupy fog curtain.

I ran aft to the quarterdeck, where the captain, quartermaster, and master pilot were huddled around the ship's wheel. "Not a blasted sight of her, Mr. Vogel. Last I saw she was making for the lee of the island to port."

The captain spewed vile curses, growling, "Aye, and we can't maneuver until this bloody veil lifts, lest we run ourselves aground! Mr. Vogel, take in sail 'til we can bloody see where we be going!"

"Aye, Captain!" Vogel gave the order to shorten the fore-and-mainsails and furl the topgallants, reducing the amount of canvas exposed to the wind, slowing us down until the fog burned off.

The curtain began to lift twenty minutes later, allowing us to navigate once more. I jumped onto the mainmast shroud, binoculars in hand. Scanning the ocean off our port beam, I beheld a small islet. Barely visible above its expanse of scrub were the topgallants of a three-mast sailing ship, moving slowly to the northeast.

"Sail ho!" I shouted, pointing out the direction to the captain.

"Mr. Vogel, full sail, tighten the sheets! Mr. Slocum, hard to port once we round these rocks!"

Sailors disengaged rigging winch locks, turning their handles to tighten the halyards. The fore-and-mainsails rose fully, billowing out as they captured the wind. Renegade *began to accelerate, knifing through the azure Caribbean waters at over twice the speed the galleon was capable of. Passing the island's eastern point, Slocum threw the wheel rapidly counterclockwise.* Renegade *heeled sharply to starboard, deck yawing more than twenty degrees as she headed smartly into a left-hand turn. We all grabbed onto anything sturdy while unsecured articles skittered across the deck, either stopped by the gunwales or falling through the scuppers into the blue-green sea.*

By now the topsails were visible to all, but the galleon itself was still shrouded in fog. We charged forward as she began to emerge, first her bowsprit, then her bows. I watched uneasily; something was wrong in the ship's configuration, her paint scheme all wrong—

BOOM!

A sharp report echoed across the water, followed by a loud whistling. Spellbound, we watched as a cannonball impacted the sea, raising a majestic column of water just off our port bow. The ship fast approaching was not a ponderous Spanish galleon but a magnificent British Man-O-War, three decks of guns now clearly visible, large Union Jack flying from her stern.

Steering straight for us.

"Perdition's flames, it's an ambush!" the captain shrieked. "Hard to starboard, Mr. Slocum, get us away from here!"

Slocum threw the wheel clockwise, but our ship had slowed considerably since our last maneuver. Renegade *heeled gently to port, beginning a plodding right-hand turn. The warship was now a half-mile distant, well within range of her long nines. Tongues of flame billowed from her deck, the long-barreled, nine-pound cannon firing solid shot our way. They would probably switch to bar or chain shot when they closed the distance, to rip our rigging and knock down our masts.*

Fortunately, Renegade *began to respond to commands. Master Rigger Rasmussen and my brother Tom were furiously tightening and loosening lines and halyards, maximizing our trim. The ship slowly increased speed coming out of her turn, but the warship was now less than five hundred yards away, crossing our stern. She veered slightly to port, unmasking all her starboard batteries. Fireballs bloomed along her hull as she fired a full broadside at us. 1700s naval cannons were notoriously inaccurate beyond three hundred yards, but enough shot hit us to cause moderate damage. The air was split by sailors' screams as cannonballs smashed through our gunwales, creating deadly blizzards of splintering wood shrapnel that sliced easily through clothes and flesh.*

Our nimble ship slowly pulled away from the behemoth, but the damage had been done. Crewmen writhed in pain about the deck, crying out for help. A few appeared to be dead. Doc Loechner attended to them as quickly as possible, but the number of casualties was daunting. We clung wearily to rigging and rails, ducking every time the monstrous warship fired. A shot tore through the mainsail, another bashed our stern, then we were finally out of range.

"Captain, warship off the port beam!" someone screamed.

Everyone still on their feet rushed to see. Sure enough, a sleek Corvette was angling toward us from the east, attempting to head us off. She fired her bow guns, white puffs of smoke issuing from her barrels. Small guns, *I surmised,* much less powerful than the Man-O-War's massive cannons...

Shards flew as cannonballs hit us from both directions. Blimey, another warship to starboard! My left hip felt like it was being stung by a swarm of hornets, causing me to holler in pain. Looking down, I saw blood oozing from a dozen holes in my breeches. The blasted British were using grapeshot on us!

We steered south on a starboard beam reach, the only direction out of the trap. Fortunately, Tom had engineered our sails to efficiently provide thrust even at severe wind angles, a marked improvement over normal early eighteenth-century sailing vessels. Trimming our sails to optimum configuration, we hurtled between the two smaller warships, our four brass breech-loading cannons blasting away in response to the warships' guns. Geysers of fire blossomed as our technologically advanced, fin-stabilized high-explosive warheads impacted both Corvettes. They slewed sharply away, gouts of flame pouring from massive holes where our shells had impacted. We escaped the three-warship trap, which was Admiral Sir Alec Brannigan's latest effort to destroy Captain Craven and the Renegade.

The pain in my hip drove me to my knees, where I encountered frightening sights: Quartermaster Edward Vogel, dead from multiple wounds to his head; Bosun Patrick Carney, grievously injured and unconscious; and Captain Craven, laying against the stern rail in an ever-widening pool of blood.

Grabbing my collar, he sat up and pulled me close, rasping out what were likely his last words: "Mr. Petrie, I am fallen. But if not for ye and your brother, Renegade *would have been destroyed long before now. Seeing as me senior officers seem to be dead or dying, I be leaving her in your charge. Will you accept that charge, lad? Will you care for me ship and me crew as ye would your own?"*

"Captain, I—"

"Avast, me hearties! I will soon breathe me last, and ye be needing to vote in a new captain. What thinks ye of Roger Petrie?" he croaked loudly. A chorus of approval sang out from the remaining able-bodied seamen.

He whispered, "When we first met, Roger, I had a mind to run ye through and be done with it. I be thinking now I be glad I did not. Take care of me ship, Mr. Petrie, and if ye survive, may your prey be plentiful, your take bountiful, and the women and wine be loose and cheap, in that order..." He sighed, the death rattle sounding in his throat.

And he was gone.

*Wincing as I hoisted myself vertical, I assessed the tactical situation and it was grim indeed: torn sails, top foremast shot away, myriad holes punched in my ship (*MY ship!*), the dead and dying littering the deck. I could only imagine what it looked like below decks.*

Slocum lay slumped over the wheel, dead, his body perforated by shrapnel. Guess I needed a new pilot. First Mate Newton Berger limped up, raising a sloppy salute. "Congratulations, Captain Petrie! What be your orders, sir?"

My orders? How did it come to this? The wounded warships had resumed their pursuit, half my crew was out of action—what could I do? Where could we possibly go?

I stepped forward to begin my new command when there was a great CRACK! and the mainmast slowly toppled, stays and shrouds snapping, hurtling down right on top of me. Is this how my pirate command ends *I lamented as death rushed toward me…*

*****

I sat up abruptly, wheezing and drenched with sweat. As my eyes focused, I saw I was in bed, Rebekah at my side. Rebekah, who was staring at me in alarm.

"Roger, are you alright? You about gave me a heart attack, moving around like that! You nearly pushed me out of bed!"

Which is no small feat, considering we have a king.

"Yeah, I'm fine. Probably ate pizza too late last night, that's all."

"I don't think so, hon," she said, face etched with worry. "You used to have manic dreams when we first met, but I thought you were getting over them."

"What are you talking about? This is the first one I've had in months." I almost sounded convincing.

"Whatever. You were talking in your sleep, too," she said, an odd timbre to her voice.

"Really? Did I say anything interesting?"

"Oh, I don't know. I am wondering what the *Renegade* is, exactly."

I froze at the name of the ship. My blood ran even colder at her next sentence.

"And who the heck is Captain Craven?"

Who was Captain Craven, indeed?

THREE

"The sailor's life is at the best a life of danger."
—John Tyler

MV Belvedere Ship's Log
Master Roger M. Petrie
Monday, December 2, 2002

It was a dark and stormy night—on second thought, it was far worse than that.

Torrents of rain drummed against the windscreen, drowning out the corner stereo. I was too occupied with not wrecking my ship to care. As the ship pitched and rolled in the angry sea, I thought, *what a fabulous way to celebrate your birthday, Roger; steering a heavy-laden cargo ship through a tempest.* Atlantic hurricane season was over, but violent squalls like this one still popped up occasionally. The theme from *Gilligan's Island* played in my mind as the wheel vibrated in my hand, something about a tiny ship being tossed, then lost.

Appropriate, if you could call a three-hundred-foot-long, thirty-five-hundred-ton diesel-powered merchant vessel a "tiny ship". *Belvedere* was fitted with one large jib crane forward, positioned between two large cargo holds. The four-story superstructure, which contained the bridge where I was currently situated, was located aft of the holds, just forward of the stern. *Belvedere* was old, built in 1974, but she was *my* ship, my first command—which held a special place in the heart of any seafaring man. No matter the type of vessel, being in command was an achievement to be proud of.

We were freelance freight haulers, operating under charter to Womack Lines Shipping. Our latest cargo was a load of electrical machinery and components from Brazil, destined for Miami. Presently, *Belvedere* was steaming north, riding the Gulf Stream along the east side of the British Virgin Islands and Puerto Rico.

Tough duty, I know, but somebody has got to do it.

*****

I was startled when Jim Cable barged into the wheelhouse, water dripping from his curly red hair and bushy mustache. He brushed off his slicker, showering me with water.

"Cripes, man!" I barked, brushing off my now-soaked sweater. "If you're going to shake yourself off like a wet dog, do it away from me!" Glancing at my watch, I added, "Five minutes late, Mr. Cable. That won't do, especially in this weather."

"Sorry, Captain. Our off-duty crew was engaged in, ah, a lively debate in the mess, and I lost track of time. It won't happen again."

I slapped the back of his head a la Gibbs-style. "See that it doesn't, mister, or you'll stand half a dozen extra midnight watches."

He flashed a lopsided grin. "Aye, sir. Course heading, Captain?"

"Keep her steady on three-one-five, Jim, eighty revolutions for thirteen knots. I'm going to go grab some coffee and doughnuts."

"Copy that."

Hungry and thirsty, I pushed past him, exiting through the interior rear hatchway. Descending three floors to the mess level, I negotiated the narrow passageway leading to the galley. The air inside the ship was stale—despite modern ventilation, the atmosphere smelled faintly of paint, antiseptic, and body odor, byproducts of our constant battle with the humid tropical climate. As I drew close to the dining area, I could hear pounding and shouting. Lively debate indeed! Hustling to stop things before it turned violent, I wrenched open the mess hall door. Inside, there were eight officers and ratings (enlisted men) sitting around one of the two large tables, talking loudly, and waving their arms. The din quieted down when I entered the room.

"Evening, Captain," came a chorus of salutations.

"Evening, gents," I replied. "Don't mind me, I'm just here for coffee and doughnuts."

There was embarrassed silence, then Second Officer Vinnie Tolbert cleared his throat. "Ah, Captain, there might be a problem with that…"

"Then I suggest you fix it, Mr. Tolbert," I answered sternly. "Immediately."

Almost as one the men jumped up, scrambling to find something for me to eat and drink. Vinnie hustled to brew fresh java, Matt Samuels and Charlie Ryder searched for doughnuts, while Evan Carmichael, Doug Wolcott, and Gregg Reynolds milled around trying to look busy. It was comical, like watching a *Three Stooges* episode.

Minutes later I had my food and drink. As the men retook their places at the table, I addressed the group. "Coming down here, it sounded like there was a riot going on. Someone care to fill me in?" I said, taking a sip of steaming coffee.

"Captain, ah, we were having a very civil conversation, you know, and the subject of pirates came up, this being the Caribbean and all," Vinnie said. "We were talking about who the best…er, most successful pirate of all time was, and that started a disagreement, if you know what I mean, sir."

I did know what he meant. Life at sea could be lonely, with long stretches of boredom and monotony. Tempers tended to wear thin between ports of call. I stayed quiet, encouraging him to go on.

"Well, sir, we know you know a lot about them, more than anyone else we know. We were hoping you could settle things for us. I said Blackbeard, Charlie said Black Bart, and Wolcott voted for Captain Kidd. We'd really like your opinion, sir."

"I don't suppose there's any money riding on my opinion, Vinnie?"

He acted like I'd insulted his integrity. "Of course not, Captain! You know we don't allow gambling on board."

"That's good to hear. We can't be having fights due to gambling debts and whatnot."

"I totally agree, sir."

"I'm glad." Taking a bite of pastry, I went on, "Your nominations were quite good, famous pirates one and all. Sam Bellamy is another good one, along with Thomas Tew, Henry Morgan, and Calico Jack Rackham. Why do you suppose they were famous?"

"Well, Captain, I guess because they stole the most treasure?"

"Not a bad guess, Vinnie. Truth is most pirates didn't accumulate much wealth at all. Some barely survived day-to-day, and crews mutinied when a captain couldn't provide even basic necessities for his crew. Successful treasure hoarding was actually pretty rare."

Vinnie looked perplexed, so I took another swig of coffee and continued. "Gents, almost all the notorious pirates were caught, tried, and hung, along with their crews. Pirates like Blackbeard are famous because their behavior became public knowledge, and people became fascinated by them. Over the years we've romanticized them, but in real life they were rough, brutal characters." I paused to finish off my doughnut, wiping my mouth before continuing. "To answer your question, in my opinion the best pirates were the ones who never got caught. Someone like Henry Avery, who made off with a vast fortune."

"What kind of pirate would you have made, Captain?" Charlie asked.

Tom, our chief engineer, entered the mess for coffee and some grub. He ducked through the door to allow his tall frame to fit under the transom. He joined the fray right away. "Charlie, I'd say Roger Petrie would be closer to Stede Bonnet than anyone."

Blank stares met his statement. "He was called the 'Gentleman Pirate' because he was well-educated and well-mannered. But he was clueless about seamanship. He joined forces with Blackbeard, living on *Queen Anne's Revenge* for a time, but reports said he spent most days walking the decks in his pajamas, and reading books. That's why he reminds me of my younger brother." The crew howled while my face burned with embarrassment.

"Tell you what; if Tom Petrie was in my pirate crew, he'd be the first guy keel-hauled," I retaliated.

Tom ignored my comment. "Okay, guys, let's say Roger joined Blackbeard's crew. How long before his sarcasm would drive Blackbeard to make him walk the plank? A week? Two hours?", leading to more jeers directed at me. So much for respecting one's commanding officer.

I was preparing a snide comeback, but my thoughts were interrupted by an abrupt lurch as *Belvedere* heeled violently to port. Another jolt followed, almost feeling like we had hit something. Plates and cups fell to the deck and shattered, while boxes and bags toppled out of cupboards, adding their sounds to the din. Regaining my balance, I sprinted from the mess to the bridge, finding Cable frantically wrestling with the ship's wheel.

"Captain, I've never seen anything like it!" he cried. "We're being hit from every direction! I can't hold her steady, sir!"

Through the windscreen I could sec the ocean raging, towering waves indeed moving in several different directions at once, their crests crashing together in great explosions of white foam. *That's impossible—isn't it?*

Gregg Reynolds, a Deck Cadet, arrived on the bridge shortly after me. Turning to him, I barked, "Reynolds, sound the general alarm and get everyone to emergency stations! Secure all hatches, close all watertight doors!"

I winced as the ear-splitting chimes of the alarm commenced, finally shutting off after twenty seconds.

I stood beside Cable at the front console, gripping its brass rail tightly to steady myself. Sheets of rain blew against the windscreen, wind howling as our wipers strained to clear off the immense volume of water. *Belvedere* heaved and pitched sickeningly in the rolling seas, deluges of water crashing over the bow, washing across the forecastle. The sky was colored a putrid green, with intense flashes of lightning splitting the darkness.

In all my years at sea, I had ever experienced anything like this.

*****

My heart skipped a beat when the intercom squawked above my head, "Engineering to bridge, engineering to bridge."

It was Tom, who had dashed back to the engine room the moment the turbulence began.

I toggled a switch. "Captain here, Chief."

His voice was almost overpowered by an earsplitting whine in the background. "Captain, we've got a problem," he began ominously. "Our aftermost tunnel bearing is burning up. If it goes, we could lose the propeller. We need to stop the shaft as soon as possible so I can check it out."

That would be disastrous given current sea conditions. "Tom, we can't lose steerageway here; there are dangerous shoals around. Without the prop, we don't stand a chance of avoiding them."

"Yessir, I know. But if the bearing goes, the propeller shaft could bend or shear, and we can't repair damage of that magnitude. As it is, if we run for much longer, she'll pop the outer seals for sure, which would flood the engine room and after spaces."

That would not be good. "Copy that, Tom. Reduce speed to all ahead slow, and we'll try to find a nice, quiet spot to lay over." A crack of thunder accentuated our plight. Reducing speed in heavy seas exposed the ship to more pitch and yaw action; instead of driving through the seas, we would simply roll around, totally at the mercy of wind and waves.

"I'll try and nurse the engine," he said, "see if we can make anchorage somewhere without totally burning out the bearing."

"Roger that." I snapped off the intercom. This night was getting better and better.

Another barrage of lightning turned night into day. *There!* Off to port was a small island, uncharted, of course, but there were literally hundreds of those strewn all about the Caribbean. Checking our GPS position, I saw that we were east of Barbuda, in the Leeward Islands. If this island held true to form, there would be a horseshoe-shaped cay on the lee side, where we could anchor and ride out this storm.

"Cable, island at ten o'clock, bearing two-four-five! Aim for the lee side!"

"Aye, Captain, I see it!" He immediately steered ten degrees to port, our maneuver aided by the fact that the main trajectory of the wind and waves was to the west.

At dead slow, *Belvedere* wallowed like a drunk sow in the raging seas, making little headway toward the island. Our fathometer showed plenty of water under the keel, so I was not worried about running aground.

What worried me was turning into the cay against the force of the storm.

After a hard sixty minutes, we executed the turn to starboard. As I had hoped, there was a small bay on the lee side of the island. It was small but sported a decent amount of palm trees and conifers, which would prove an adequate refuge against both wind and waves.

"Release the storm anchors, Mr. Reynolds. Advise engineering to effect repairs immediately. Have damage control report on any storm damage we've suffered."

"Aye, Captain." He flipped a switch and I saw the bow anchor chain rattling overboard, making a cacophonous racket. The large anchor thundered into the water, *Belvedere* shuddering minutes later as it took hold. The fantail trembled as the stern anchor was similarly released.

The waters were calmer here in the protection of the cay. Things slowly returned to normal. Charlie arrived topside moments later, delivering fresh coffee and a plateful of biscuits.

"How are things in the galley, Charlie? They were a real mess a couple of hours ago."

"There were plenty of guys who helped Matt and I straighten things up, sir," he said as he handed Jim and I steaming cups of coffee. "There's a lot more to do, but we thought you could use a pick-me-up."

"Excellent thinking, Charlie, thank you," I said, appreciating the gesture as I sat in the port-side master's chair, my feet propped on the forward console.

The night's outlook was improving.

I raised my cup to Cable. "Nice work, Jim. I know it was hairy there for a mom—"

CRACK!!

A brilliant blue bolt of electrical energy struck the jackstaff on *Belvedere's* bow, nearly blinding me. Fingers of sizzling electricity swept the ship from stem to stern. Both Jim and I dropped our coffee cups, barely registering their shattering on the deck. Through the windscreen I could see a crazy white halo enveloping the entire ship. A wave of nausea washed over me and my vision blurred just as the bridge lights popped and extinguished, plunging the four of us into darkness. Emergency lights snapped on seconds later, affording limited illumination.

I found myself on my knees, my abdomen cramping painfully, my temples throbbing. As my eyes cleared, I saw a trail of blood issuing from Cable's nose, while Charlie was moaning in pain, holding his stomach.

"Is everyone all right?" I said, painfully pulling myself vertical. Since I was the first one up, I grabbed the wheel.

Everyone nodded tentatively. I activated the ship-wide intercom, grateful but curious that it was still working. "All hands, this is the captain. I need casualty and damage reports ASAP! Report any anomalies to your section officers immediately."

Reynolds picked himself off the deck. "Holy crap, Captain, what was *that*?"

"That's what I'd like to know, Gregg. I'm guessing we were struck by lightning." Straightening my jacket, I started issuing orders as my brains unscrambled. "Send Womack a message about the stern bearing burnout. Jim, get a GPS fix and relay our position to them and the Coast Guard. Also, find out from Doc Loechner if anyone was hurt. We may need medical assistance. That was one heck of a charge we absorbed."

"Aye, sir!"

The rain lessened considerably, so my view was improving. *Belvedere* appeared to be undamaged, but smoke was rising from every surface. Nothing else on deck seemed amiss.

As I fought down the bile rising in my throat, I wondered how any of us had escaped being electrocuted.

FOUR

"The sea be a wild, unforgiving and cruel mistress, never resting, never predictable."
—Anonymous

MV Belvedere Ship's Log
Tuesday, December 2, 2002

Thirty minutes later, Reynolds appeared back on the bridge. I started to issue more orders, but his grim expression gave me pause. "What is it, Mr. Reynolds?"

It was five seconds before he could respond. "I couldn't raise anyone on the radio, Captain. The Coast Guard, Navy—no one responded. No one answered, not even on International Distress frequencies!" His eyes held mine, registering real fear.

"Calm down, Gregg. Did you do a system's diagnostic? I wouldn't be surprised if most of our circuits are fried."

Reynolds shook his head. "Yes, sir, twice. I also checked the transmitter and receiver circuits, and the antenna relays and wiring. Everything is five-by-five, sir."

"Captain." The quiet urgency in Cable's voice grabbed my attention. Turning my head, I saw him fiddling with the GPS receiver.

"Have you computed our position, Jim?"

"No, sir. There's no reading at all," he said, voice cracking. I could see lights on the face of the unit, and Cable was stabbing the power button repeatedly. "It has power, and the circuits check out fine, but it's like the satellites…like they're not even there!"

"Okay, listen up!" I commanded, aggravated by my crew's loss of professionalism. "We've been through a highly unusual event, even for us. However, that is NOT an excuse to lose discipline aboard this ship! Do I make myself clear?"

Three men with sullen faces mumbled, "Yes, sir."

"Good. Gregg, what did you find out from Doc?"

He looked recovered from his earlier bout of fright. "Doc reports two sailors with fractured arms, one with a sprained shoulder, a few with bruises and scrapes. Most are complaining about nausea or headaches, though. That's about it, sir."

No electric shock victims? That was strange, given the magnitude of the bolt. Tom entered the bridge while I pondered that, giving me a short assessment of the situation down in engineering. When he finished, I said, "Tom, have your team get some rest, then effect repairs at first light." He nodded, turning to leave, but I had more to say.

"That goes for everyone. Unless you're on watch, I want you to get some rack time so we can hit this hard tomorrow morning." I thought for few seconds. "All watches are to be advised that I want flares shot off bow and stern every two hours. This is a busy shipping lane; someone is bound to see one. Also, I want someone on our radio every hour, and please activate our emergency radio beacon." I paused to let them process my orders. "Look, gentlemen, we were struck by lightning. It could have created an electromagnetic pulse that's playing havoc with our electronics. I'm surprised we have any operating circuits at all, honestly. I would expect the effects will have cleared by tomorrow morning, allowing us to contact the authorities." I glanced at Tom for confirmation. He gave an almost imperceptible nod. I knew it, too; there was no EMP effect. But what else could I say?

"Good night, gentlemen. You have your orders." Normally, we were not that formal, but I needed to grab control of a deteriorating situation. Relinquishing the wheel to Cable, I strode off the bridge, intending to get some sleep. On impulse I detoured to the radio room. What could it hurt to double-check? I powered on the unit, scanning through all the marine, military, and emergency bands. Like Reynolds before me, there was nothing, only soft static. It *did* seem like nobody was listening. Certainly, no one was responding to my repeated Maydays. I rechecked the circuits, but all I heard was stifling silence. The power was on and I was transmitting, but there was no response. No response at all.

What in the world was going on?

*****

Miles south from where *Belvedere* was anchored, a ship slipped silently through the water, a predator in search of prey. The rains had passed, and the winds and waves had calmed. Something on the northern horizon caught her commander's eye, and her course was altered to investigate this strange sight.

"There it is again, Captain!" a lookout shouted from the foremast. "Red light dead ahead!"

The captain drew his spyglass, focusing on the unusual phenomenon in the skies. *There!* A glowing red orb traveling upward in a parabolic arc, reaching its apogee, and falling slowly back to earth. It was brightly pulsating, trailing a thin plume of white smoke behind it. The captain watched until it disappeared below the horizon, then folded up and pocketed his spyglass.

The first mate joined him on the starboard bow, pointing in the direction where the flare emanated from. "What the devil was that, Captain? I've ne'er seen a ghostly light be suspended in air like that! What manner of demon be spawning such a ghastly fire?"

The captain sneered at him. "Mr. Berger, 'twas no demon that spawned yonder spectral light. 'Tis a signal of distress, I believe."

"Distress, Captain?"

"Aye, me hearty," the captain snarled, smiling wickedly. "Someone be foundering in the storm and be calling for help. I think it would be right hospitable for us to heave to and render aid, don't you?"

"Aye, Captain."

"Then set the watches, Mr. Berger, and ready me ship for action." Turning to face his crew, the captain raised his hand. "Prepare yourselves, ye salty seadogs, we be attacking at first light!"

"Aye, Captain!" rang out a throaty chorus from the assembled crew, hands thrusting weapons skyward in eager anticipation of the kill.

FIVE

"Better batten down the hatches, mate, there be rough seas ahead!"
—Anonymous

MV Belvedere Ship's Log
Wednesday, December 3, 2002

Another day in paradise.

My alarm clock clanged at six-thirty, the sound feeling like someone was driving railroad spikes into my eye sockets. I slapped it several times before it mercifully shut off. Rolling out of bed, I hoped I would feel better today. The initial signs were not encouraging as I shuffled to the bathroom attached to my quarters. Both the headache and nausea from the night before were still there, barely diminished. Shrugging off my discomfort, I showered, dressed, and hurried to the bridge.

As I opened the bridge door, I could see that the storm had passed. The previous evening's roiling black tempest had been replaced by bright sunshine and blue skies. A few high, puffy white clouds drifted overhead, the cries of gulls and terns piercing the air. Looked like it would be a pleasant day, but I would have scant time to enjoy it.

A short conversation with the watch officer confirmed my fears: no reaction all night to our flares or radio transmissions, and no response to our emergency radio beacon. Our GPS screen was still blank, even though the power button glowed green and nothing seemed amiss.

There was no explanation for that.

Engineering was proceeding with repairs, but the initial news from Tom was not good; the pivoting pads on the aftermost tunnel bearing were burnt. These pads bore the weight of the propeller shaft as it extended outside our hull. Without them, the shaft would seize, which would lead to catastrophic damage to the diesel engine. It was a major operation to replace them, and Tom doubted it could be done absent dry dock facilities. We most likely would have to be towed to port.

I fretted about the lost time. It would take two days for a tug to reach us, then a week or more to reach Miami. Since we operated freelance, we had no steady suppliers, no dedicated freight lanes. If we were delayed making port, the higher-paying loads would be snapped up, leaving us to scramble for whatever was left. In that case, exporters knew they could pay us bottom dollar to haul their goods.

I ensured the standing watches would check the radio every hour and posted lookouts to keep watch for ships and aircraft. There *had* to be someone out there that could either hear or see us!

Irritated there was nothing else I could do, I decided to visit Doc Loechner, needing relief for my headache and the uproar going on in my gut. I exited the bridge, traipsing down the stairs to level three and Sick Bay. Opening the stairway door, I was surprised to see a line of men outside our medical facilities. They cast worried glances my way, their fear palpable.

Doc was in the corridor, conducting triage on the assembled sailors. At fifty-four, he was by far the oldest member of my crew, a tall, sinewy man with graying hair and a cynical attitude. He noticed me, waving me forward. Shrugging apologetically to the men in line, I said, "Sorry, guys, Captain's privilege." They responded with grunts and groans of a decidedly displeased nature.

"Come in, Roger," Doc said, ushering me into Sick Bay. He closed the door to loud protests, motioning me to sit down. "And what ails the master of this magnificent vessel today?"

"It's strange, Doc. I felt great until last night, then suddenly, I'm trying to avoid puking my guts out, and it feels like someone's driving nails through my eye sockets."

"Um-hum," he muttered, sitting on a stool in front of me. He pulled out a penlight, checking my pupils. The intense light seared my retinas, sending sharp pulses of pain down my optic nerves. I shut my eyes and slapped his hand away.

"Dang, Doc! I told you my eyes are killing me!"

"Sorry, Roger, a painful but necessary test, I'm afraid."

"Fine, but let's complete the exam without you causing me to pass out, shall we?"

"I will endeavor to, sir," he chuckled, pocketing his penlight while unwrapping his stethoscope from around his neck. He proceeded to check my heart and lungs, then set the scope to the side.

"Nothing untoward physically, Captain, at least at first glance."

"Then why do I feel like absolute crap?"

"You and the rest of the crew, you mean, including myself," he answered. "Everyone has reported similar symptoms, either last night or this morning, and it's not the food. Near as I can tell, anyway." He laid out nausea medicine and painkillers for me to try.

I scooped up the pills. "These symptoms are ship-wide?" He nodded. "Doc, when did the crew's symptoms first appear?"

"Same as yours, I'd wager. Right after the lightning strike."

"And no one was electrocuted, or showed signs of electric shock?"

"No, which was curious," he commented. "But I found no cardiac or respiratory events, no burns, nothing that you'd expect after a massive electrical surge. Just headaches and upset stomachs. If I didn't know any better, I'd say the entire crew had suffered low-grade concussions."

"Don't you find that odd?"

"Nothing much surprises me anymore, but this…this is definitely unusual."

"I know how I felt, but what were your impressions of, uh, whatever phenomena we experienced last night?"

He fixed me with a steady gaze. "I'm glad you asked, Roger. Personally, I was frightened out of my mind, but scientifically speaking, the sensation was like being hit by a wave, almost as if we—"

"Like we passed through some sort of barrier?" I asked quietly.

"Exactly."

SIX

"Gold is a treasure, and he who possesses it does all he wishes to in this world."
—Christopher Columbus

Sarasota, FL
Saturday, November 3, 2007
2 years, 10 months, 17 days since Reemergence

"Oomph!" Tom exclaimed, stacking another wooden crate into the corner of my new storage unit. "Geez, what'd you load these things with, bricks?"

"Not exactly," I answered, shooting him a knowing look.

His eyes widened in understanding. "Is this—is this what I think it is?"

I shrugged sheepishly, continuing to unload the U-Haul truck we had rented to move the rest of my things from Indianapolis.

"You couldn't think of a more creative solution to storing your treasure?"

"Keep your voice down, someone might hear!" I hissed at him. "What am I supposed to do, bury it?"

"Worked for us the first time around."

"Sorry, I don't make it out to deserted Caribbean islands as much as I used to," I snapped, struggling to place a wood crate on top of some other boxes.

"Granted. But you could reduce the load—and the space needed—if you'd liquidate."

"And how exactly would I explain where all this came from? Being a coin collector wouldn't cut it with the police, you know. And what would Rebekah think?"

"She's going to find out sooner or later, Roger. Best if you got ahead of it, while you still can."

"When I want your opinion, I'll give it to you. Just keep stacking."

"Sure thing, Mr. Cranky. I am helping you move all this out of the goodness of my heart, you know," he complained, dragging another heavy box out of the truck.

"Yeah, you're a real hero. I'll figure something out before anyone finds out."

"You know, you can't insure this stuff. What happens if this place burns, or someone breaks in and robs you blind?"

"I chose this place very carefully, believe me, just like I did with that warehouse in Indy. It's got the latest safeguards."

We were both grimy and sweaty when we finished. I handed him a Pepsi, both of us sitting on the last crate and drinking our sodas. Tom looked around the storage space, a 10 x 20 cinder-block room with a reinforced steel roll-up door.

"FYI, I divested myself of much of my loot over the past two years, mainly to foreign buyers. Kept it low key because I didn't want to draw undue attention to myself. You should probably do the same."

"Maybe," I said, not wanting to elaborate.

He regarded me curiously. "Roger, is there something keeping you from selling? There are a couple tons of coins in here, plus a bunch of other trinkets. Why hang on to them?"

It was a question I had grappled with on many a sleepless night. At heart, I was not a bandit, so I struggled to enjoy the spoils of my labor knowing I had stolen them from someone else. Initially, Tom had struggled with the same problem; at some point, he had made his peace with it. I had not.

"I don't know, Tom. I want to, but something's holding me back."

"You know, you keep talking about making a future with Rebekah, and I think she's great. But it's going to be tough moving ahead if your past is weighing you down."

"Thank you, Dr. Freud."

"Just saying." He checked his watch, then jumped off the crate. "Hey, we need to return the truck before they charge us an extra day."

"Okay, let's call it a night. This stuff will still be here in the morning."

"You hope, anyway."

I whopped him on the shoulder as we pulled down the heavy entrance door and padlocked it. Tom turned to me as we climbed into the truck's cab.

"One last thing, Roger."

"What's that?" I asked, turning the key to start the engine.

"I really like Sarasota. I wanted you to be the first to know I'm thinking of moving down here myself."

"What?"

"Yep, this is a great area. Lots of sunshine, close to the sea, close to your family. All the things I need."

"There goes the neighborhood," I grumbled, putting the truck in gear as Tom bent over laughing.

SEVEN

"Where there is a sea there are pirates."
—Greek Proverb

MV Belvedere Ship's Log
Wednesday, December 3, 2002

Time to figure out what the heck was going on.

After consuming my meds, I returned to the bridge. Consulting the watch officer, our status was unchanged, and the prognosis for repairing *Belvedere* and resuming normal operations had not improved. Frustrated, I plopped into the pilot's chair, knowing I could do nothing to speed up the process.

My thoughts were interrupted by an urgent yell from outside.

"Cap'n, come quick! You gotta look at this, sir!" port lookout Steve Durham cried. He stood on the port wing, gesturing excitedly to something astern. Grabbing my marine binoculars, I rushed to the railing and focused in the direction he was indicating. A vessel swam into view, approaching leisurely from the southwest about eight miles distant. That was not unexpected; we were anchored astride busy sea lanes, so chances of spotting another ship were good.

It was the *type* of ship that captured my attention.

I mentally cataloged some details: sailing ship, twenty-foot beam, two masts, three flying jibs out front, British flag flying from her topmast. A wooden schooner, making around six knots and heading straight for us. Were they answering our distress calls?

Durham was thinking along the same lines as me. Lowering his glasses, he yelled, “Hey, Cap’n, maybe they saw our flares, or heard our Mayday!”

I chewed my lower lip, considering the possibility. If they had heard our SOS, why hadn’t they radioed back? I saw nothing to indicate she had communications equipment aboard. An uneasy feeling was forming in the pit of my stomach, my imagination running wild after all the recent talk about pirates. *Quit being an idiot!* I told myself. It was probably one of those sailing excursions where passengers paid exorbitant fees to spend a few days on a “real” sailing ship. Durham and I watched the schooner grow nearer, and other *Belvedere* crew members gathered topside, taking pictures of her.

After an hour, the schooner was a mile away. “Cap’n, she’s lowered her colors, and it looks like she’s raising another flag…” Bewildered, Durham looked at me and exclaimed, “Criminelly, it’s the Jolly Roger, sir!”

I had to laugh. Pirates, here in the Caribbean, circa 2002? The thought was preposterous, but I raised my glasses to verify his claim. To my amazement, I could see they *were* raising a flag, a white skull over two crossed swords set against a black backdrop. I felt a pang of anxiety, for I had seen that flag before—the flag flown by Calico Jack Rackham, a notorious eighteenth-century Caribbean pirate.

What was it doing flying from this ship here in the twenty-first century?

Most of my crew had abandoned their duty stations by now, lining the deck rails to gawk at the sight of a ship flying a pirate flag. I continued to focus on the schooner as she closed the distance. Numerous sailors gathered on her deck, all looking at us. Their clothing was comical, like something out of a bad buccaneer movie. Many held muskets, flintlock pistols, and swords. There were men standing on spars and booms of both masts, while others were hanging on her shrouds, all brandishing weapons. I looked around for cameras, because someone must be pranking us, or making a movie. But I saw nothing, and the schooner was the only other ship in sight. Maybe—

BOOM!!

What the…? We looked on incredulously as a cannon on her bow fired, the detonation echoing across the water. Seconds later there was a faint whistling sound, followed by a splash three hundred yards astern.

"Captain, they're firing at us!" Reynolds exclaimed.

I stood stupefied at the spectacle unfolding before me. My Third Mate, Clayton Smythe, appeared beside me. "Captain," he whispered, "as stupid as this sounds, there might be some real danger here. Should I unlock the gun cabinet?"

Being hijacked at sea was something I had never considered, not in these busy waters. Piracy had been virtually eradicated from the Caribbean in the 1800s. In areas like off Somalia, where piracy still occurred, merchant ships were well armed, and might even have a security detachment on board.

Belvedere had no such defenses.

"What inventory are we carrying, Mr. Smythe?" I inquired quietly.

"A couple of shotguns and four forty-fives, sir, with four extra clips per pistol, and ten boxes of shells." Not enough against a boatload of rowdy buccaneers. There were numerous firearms visible on the schooner, not to mention they evidently carried cannons.

We appeared to be seriously outgunned.

"Stand down, Mr. Smythe. If these are real pirates—I can't believe I'm saying that—four guns won't be enough to repel boarders. If we had any heavy weapons, it'd be a different story. If you have a .50 caliber machine gun or some Uzis stored aboard, I'm all ears. But I won't risk the lives of my crew mounting a pitiful defense."

Ryder excitedly asked, "Captain, maybe we're going to be in a movie! That's got to be what this is, right?"

"Perhaps you're right, Charlie. I'll be right back." I retraced my steps back to the bridge and switched on the intercom. "Bridge to engineering. Bridge to engineering. Come in, Tom." No time for formalities at this point.

"Engineering to bridge, Tom here. Say, I can't effect repairs—"

"Shut up and listen! Remember in *The Wrath of Khan* when Kirk told Scotty, 'Scotty, I need warp speed in three minutes or we're all dead'?"

"Sure, but—"

"Same scenario, Tom. I need full engine power ASAP or something very bad is going to happen to this ship."

"What the heck are you talking about, Roger?"

BOOM!!

"What was that?" he shouted.

"The something bad I was talking about. Now, what about our engine?"

His dejected tone told me everything, unfortunately. "Sorry, Roger, but we've got the tunnel bearing torn apart. It'd take hours to get things in even partial working condition."

"Not your fault, Tom. It was worth a shot."

"Speaking of shots, it sounded like a cannon firing outside. Are we under attack?" I could hear the disbelief in his voice.

"Yes, apparently by a group of pirates. You'd better bring your team up on deck. Bridge out." I cut the intercom before he could respond; if he could not get us moving, there was not anything else he could do to help.

Back on deck, I watched as another shot impacted the ocean. They were not trying to hit us, just frighten us into surrendering. From the facial expressions of my crew, mission accomplished.

My mind was working furiously, but I could not concentrate. Did Womack have a pirate boarding protocol in their operating procedures? Probably, buried in the immense volume of its text, with plans that would do me no good anyway. Besides, no one had responded to our previous distress calls—they were not likely to start now.

I returned to the deck. "Sorry, Charlie, but I don't think these guys are acting." His face fell, the implication of my statement clear. Swinging around to Smythe, I said calmly, "Stand down, Clayton. They're firing warning shots because our ensign is still flying."

The US flag was waving from our stern; if we did not lower it, the pirates would assume we wanted to fight them. Which we did not. Speaking so everyone could hear, I declared, "Men, I believe these people are serious and intend to board us. Do NOT resist, and please don't say anything stupid. Leave the talking to me. Jackson, please lower our flag. Reynolds, get everyone up on deck."

Smythe was furious now, bellowing, "Captain, please! If these *are* real pirates, we could barricade ourselves in the engine room, or forward hold! They could never break through the watertight doors! And there's no way that ship has guns big enough to punch a hole in our hull!" There were murmurs of agreement from other crewmen.

"Mr. Smythe, does your maritime expertise include piracy?" I answered calmly. "No? Well, mine does. Do you have any idea what pirates used to do to ships' crews that resisted? They slaughtered them, with extreme prejudice." I paused to let that sink in. "While our hull is probably too thick for their cannons, are you willing to bet our lives on that?"

He shook his head sullenly. I went on, "Look, guys, they may not have the guns of a battleship, but I'll bet they're carrying enough pitch and gunpowder to either blow our watertight doors or burn us to a cinder. We'd be trapped in our own spaces. As Master of the *Belvedere* I must do whatever I can to protect your lives. Much as I'd like to muster our guns and give these guys the what-for, I can't take that risk. I'm sorry."

My crew was crestfallen. They wanted to fight, but I knew they did not fully understand the risks. If we surrendered peacefully, we might get out of this alive. If we resisted and failed, everyone on board would end up dead. Something in the way this ship was approaching led me to believe this was not a harmless prank, and the lives of everyone on board depended on my actions.

Jackson lowered our ensign while the crew watched gloomily, some still believing this was a joke, others staring in disbelief. I empathized with them, but I was convinced I was doing the right thing.

I summoned my bosun's mate, Evan Carmichael, with one last order: "Evan, get the emergency kit and bring up the Satphone. See if you can raise the Coast Guard or the Navy." He immediately left, and I stood there, the eyes of the crew upon me, clinging to a sliver of hope. I held out no such hope. Our GPS, which operated via satellite, was not functioning, so there was little chance the phone would work. Still, I felt better issuing orders than standing around doing nothing.

As she drew nigh, some of the schooner's sailors hefted long gaffing hooks and pikes; others carried large axes, while a few held grappling hooks and lines. They meant to board us. My crew looked to me for guidance, but I stood there numbly, the unfolding events so nonsensical that I could not rationally process them.

I spotted a tall man standing by the ship's wheel, excitedly observing the progression of events. He sported shoulder length, jet-black hair which covered his head and face, his long beard hanging disheveled and wild. He wore a long blue coat, what appeared to be a white ruffled shirt, knee-length tan pants, and white hose. The most striking thing was his hat: it was a large, blue, cavalier-type affair with a large brim pinned to the crown on one side, decorated with a large white feather. An undeniably garish outfit, one that probably identified him as the captain.

The schooner drew to within a hundred yards, her sails reefed, main boom swung out wide. I was impressed with the seamanship; whoever was handling her knew what he was doing. The sails were backed to the wind, her speed reduced to bare steerageway.

I surveyed my shipmates lining the main deck starboard rail, mentally doing a roster check. Everyone seemed to be present, except for—

Bang! Bang! Bang! Three shots rang out in quick succession from somewhere above. We all involuntarily ducked below the gunwale. There was a scream and then a splash. Our gunman must have picked off an unlucky sailor from the schooner. *That will not please its commander,* I thought unhappily. I squinted up at the superstructure, straining to draw a bead on the shooter.

"There, sir, aft of the bridge!" someone yelled. I spotted the flash suppressor of an automatic rifle resting on the bridge roof railing. Puffs of smoke spewed forth, accompanied by sharp reports as the gunner rapidly squeezed off several more rounds. There were more yelps of pain from the schooner, as well as a great deal of shouting and cursing. Our mystery gunman evidently was a decent marksman.

It must be Tompkins! He was the only man missing from my muster. He was an avid hunter, and reputedly owned a large cache of high-powered weapons. If he had snuck one on board, I figured there would be spare ammo magazines with him as well.

A surge of hope welled up within me. If he could lay down effective suppressive fire, he might drive our attackers under cover long enough for us to gather our ship's firearms and defend our ship in earnest. I looked around for officers to give the orders to—

BLAM!!

A small rail-mounted gun fired from the schooner's bow. A hail of lead shot whanged off *Belvedere's* upper superstructure, shattering windows, raining debris on the deck. Immediately afterward, the pirates unleashed a withering volley of musket fire, forty or more flintlocks firing in ragged unison. The schooner was momentarily obscured by smoke as they took aim at Tompkins' perch. Screams of agony pierced the air, and Tompkins, gravely wounded and covered in blood, stood up and fell head-first over the railing into the water below. A chorus of cheers erupted from the schooner, and dozens of sailors held swords, pistols, and muskets aloft as they celebrated the demise of our shipmate. I looked up and down my muster, holding their wide-eyed gazes.

Any doubts this situation was deadly serious dissipated with Tompkins' death.

EIGHT

"Let's jump on board and cut them to pieces."
—Blackbeard

From the Personal Journal of Roger M. Petrie
December 3, ???

"Captain?" Charlie implored, voice quivering with fear.

"Stand strong, Charlie, and let me do the talking," I said with a confidence I did not feel. My headache had returned full force, which made matters worse. "God willing, we'll survive this and have a heck of a story to tell our grandchildren."

"Yes, sir," he replied as the schooner's bow slid next to ours. Deck hands tossed out fenders to protect their ship, while others reached out with gaff hooks or threw grappling hooks, which wrapped around our gunwale railings with a raucous clanging. As they pulled the two ships together, *Belvedere's* bow was riding eight feet taller than the schooner's, so they tied off their ropes and ran out a couple of three-foot-wide boarding planks. Hordes of sailors scrambled up them, deftly landing on our bows and separating into several groups. Sweeping aft, some circled around our position, while others headed further aft. I caught them occasionally touching the strange surfaces of our vessel or gawking at our cargo handling equipment.

The captain boarded and made directly for us. He stood over six feet tall, walking lightly on the balls of his feet. A dangerous man, I surmised. His countenance became more frightening as he drew closer. There was a palpable air of menace about him; his thin lips were drawn back in a sneer, cheeks leathery and hollow. His nose was wide and flat, and a prominent white scar that ran from the left side of his nose to over his left ear. His brown hair was long and unkempt, fluttering wildly about his face. His left eye was larger than his right—the left was open and inquisitive, while the right was hidden in a squint. He marched forward confidently, chin held high, and he wore cruelty and brutality like a cloak. A thick leather belt was slung across his right breast, from which hung a variety of pistols and daggers, culminating in a cutlass scabbard hanging at his left hip. Two more small pistols were tucked into his waist belt.

A dozen hard-looking men accompanied him, all in short-sleeve shirts, bandanas tied around their heads and necks. They approached from upwind, and their stench washed over us as they got nearer, a nauseating mixture of unwashed bodies, filthy clothes, and dirty weapons. It was difficult maintaining stoic faces against such foulness.

The group strode purposefully to where we were standing. "Who be the master of this ship?" the captain demanded, his deep, resonating voice tinged with an English accent.

"Who's asking? And what is the meaning of boarding our ship?" Smythe replied angrily, stepping forward before I could stop him.

The man frowned, displeased at this interruption. Looking Smythe up and down, he smoothly drew a flintlock pistol from his belt and pulled the trigger. The gun's discharge was loud, jarring. The ball smashed Smythe in the chest, knocking him backwards over the railing. His spinning body slapped into the bay, joining Tompkins' in the depths. The acrid smoke from the pistol hung in the air, stinging my eyes.

Replacing the pistol, he repeated harshly, "Who be master of this ship?"

I stepped forward, hoping to forestall any further violence. "I am the master of this vessel, sir. Roger Petrie, of MV *Belvedere*."

He gazed at me contemptuously. "Is that so? Well, Mr. Petrie, I am Captain Benjamin Craven, commander of the *Renegade*." I remained stoic as he continued. "I hereby claim your vessel as me own. Do ye peaceably surrender, Mr. Petrie?" He motioned to the side where Tompkins and Smythe had fallen. "Two lads were not so agreeable, eh? I trust there won't be others." It was not a question.

I had never heard of a Benjamin Craven or *Renegade,* but that meant nothing. Thousands of pirates had operated in the Caribbean at one time or another.

"No, Captain Craven. We will cooperate with you fully. In exchange, I'd ask that you give quarter to my crew."

He placed a hand on his sword hilt. "Do ye, now? From where I be standing, Mr. Petrie, ye not be in position to be requesting anything." The men behind him sneered appreciatively at his swagger.

Sweat started dribbling down my forehead. "That's true, Captain, but I swear as master of this ship there will be no further violence committed against you or your men."

He seemed pleased with that. "That be excellent news, Mr. Petrie. 'Twould be a welcome respite, if ye speak truthfully." He paused, then said, "I be curious, what manner of weapon didst your scurvy sot be wielding? Never in me life be I witnessing such a display!"

"It's called a semi-automatic rifle, captain," I explained.

"Would that be so? Be there other such weapons in your arsenal, that we not be aware of?"

I shook my head, after which he stepped closer, his voice low and menacing. "Good. Now, Mr. Petrie, to the task. Where be your valuables? That's what we be wanting from your scurvy ship."

My anxiety deepened. I had read David Cordingly's opus on Caribbean pirates, *Under the Black Flag*, and I knew what Craven, if he was a real pirate, was after. But *Belvedere* carried no cash, no jewelry, nor any precious metals. Our cargo of electric motors and generators would be of little value, nor would our personal gear be of much use for his own ship. We carried no containers of alcoholic beverages, or drinkable liquids of any kind; we de-salinized our water from the sea, a process *Renegade* could not duplicate. About the only thing of value was prepackaged foodstuff, though I doubted he would be jubilant over landing a haul of pastries and crackers.

"Captain, everything our ship holds is yours. We will cooperate with you fully," I stalled.

"Fine words, Mr. Petrie, but not quite addressing me demands, are they? Would ye care to know how I be convincing the last captain who first refused me request?" Pirates behind him snickered, grinning evilly. "Let me illumine ye, lad. I lashed him to his ship's bowsprit, then burned his eyes with matches until he be confessing where his treasure lay. Afterward, I hacked his officers to pieces for his reluctance!"

The pirates erupted in coarse laughter, slapping each other's backs. What disturbed me most was how he related this episode like someone would describe scoring the winning touchdown in a big game.

Seeing my expression, he laughed scornfully. "Have I offended your sensibilities, Mr. Petrie? That cursed captain was a tyrant. His officers abetted his cruelty. Indeed, former members of his crew be going a pirating with *us* now." Several "Ayes!" sounded in confirmation. "Before I be consigning ye to a similar fate, ye might reconsider and enlighten me to the whereabouts of your bounty." The band of ruffians pressed in closer, the threat to my life visceral and real. I noticed my crew were likewise terrified. I had to protect them, because if Craven killed me, he likely would show them no mercy, either.

"I'll show you, Captain, but you need to understand something about my ship first," I said as bravely as I dared, hoping his curiosity would win out. He agreed to hear me out, which was a huge relief.

"Your ship doth be a mystery, Mr. Petrie. She seems to be wholly metal, with nary a sail in sight. After we be done plundering, I be appreciating a better understanding of this behemoth."

Having said that, he moved left several steps. "However, there be a matter to settle forthwith. Gather round, ye mangy swabs, and lend me your ears." Heavily armed pirates herded my crew into a semi-circle in front of him. He grabbed my upper right arm, then shouted, "To the task, then! One thing we never abide be a scabrous dog of a man commanding any ship we encounter. Too many men who fancy themselves gods sail these waters. So, men of *Belvedere*, what kind of master be Roger Petrie? Does he command justly, or be he a tyrant fit to be fed to the sharks? What say ye?"

My shipmates were shocked by this unexpected turn of events. I know I sure was. Cordingly had described this sort of behavior but experiencing it firsthand was terrifying. When the shock wore off, Tom spoke first. "Mr. Petrie is a good man, Captain, a fair man. He always treats everyone with respect. It's been my honor to serve with him."

Craven glowered at the rest of the *Belvedere* crew. "Anyone else? Speak up—or has he removed from ye your tongues?"

Gregg Reynolds stepped forward. "I echo what Tom said, Captain. Roger Petrie has been a fair master of this ship. He's never done anything to cause me to doubt his judgment." He stepped back, giving me a quick upward flick of his head in encouragement. Other crewmen mumbled their agreement.

Craven smirked at me. "Well, Mr. Petrie, it appears ye be passing the test. For now."

"What test is that, Captain?"

He cackled, an unseemly, disturbing sound. "We be testing the character of the captains of every ship we vanquish. There be far too many tyrants plying these waters, who delight in violence and cruelty. Had ye been found thusly, we'd be obliged to slit your throat and dump ye like flotsam. Be thankful, Mr. Petrie, your men be coming to the defense of your honor." It seemed ironic that the man who had shot Smythe so callously would talk about putting down tyrants, but this day was proving to be full of unpleasant surprises.

I feared it held one more.

"Captain, if you'll allow me one final question; your ship appears to belong to our ancient history. I have to know, sir—what year do you believe it to be?"

He gazed at me critically. "'Tis a right strange request, Mr. Petrie, but thus far ye have acted honorably. In that spirit, I give ye my answer—for us, it be December of the year 1720."

My crew gasped; the thought impossible to comprehend.

"Is that a fact?" I asked dispassionately, though my head was aching.

"That be fact. Whether ye choose to believe it be your concern, not mine." He looked up, shading his face from the sun. "Let's repair to cooler spaces, Mr. Petrie, where the sun not be burning our skulls to ash."

It would take a while to get used to his colloquialisms.

"Certainly, Captain, why don't we go up to the bridge, where I think all your questions will be answered."

"Lead the way, lad." He barked instructions to the fifty-odd sailors who had boarded us. Some would serve guard duty; others would pillage our cargo spaces. Tom, Reynolds, and I headed for the bridge; Craven followed, with his first mate and bodyguards in tow.

Once on the bridge, we stood against the rear bulkhead while Craven and his minions inspected the instrumentation. They regarded the dials and displays on the main console with wonder, running their hands over the various buttons and switches. A diagram and model of *Belvedere* was situated in one corner, which attracted much attention. I moved over to the diagram, carefully watched by two thugs. I pointed to the stern while Craven looked on.

"Our ship is not driven by wind, Captain, but by a diesel engine. It burns fuel inside, which turns the propeller shaft. The propeller turns rapidly, creating backward thrust. This drives *Belvedere* forward, her speed depending on how fast we turn the propeller."

He stood, fascinated. "By thunder, I've never seen the likes of this! Ye be needing no canvas at all?"

"No, sir. The engine and propeller do all the work."

He ran his hands over the bulkheads, control console, doors, windows—all materials and textures that were foreign to his touch. "How was it we found ye at anchor?"

"We experienced mechanical difficulties due to last night's storm, so we laid up here to attempt repairs."

He glanced at me, uneasy. "Repairs, ye say? Be this ship seaworthy?"

"No, Captain, not without the engine, I'm afraid."

"I see. That be most unfortunate." He paused, then went on, "How do ye sail this leviathan with such a wee crew?"

"Many of our systems are heavily automated, Captain, so we can operate with a minimum of personnel."

"Aye, that sounds right impressive, though beyond me understanding," he said, cocking an eyebrow.

"It simply means hcr engines, anchors, and systems were designed to be operated by a minimum number of personnel. Saves the company money that way."

"Ah, merchant sailors of the world, always protecting the interests of the company and its well-heeled benefactors, eh?" he scoffed. I was shocked at his level of comprehension. He saw that recognition on my face, adding, "Why ye be surprised at me understanding, Mr. Petrie? It be the way of the world, no? It's why we be choosing to be gentlemen of fortune, though our Letter of Marque be not duly recognized by the sovereign powers that be." Seeing my confusion, he chortled, "I mean that we be privateering for ourselves, lad. We owe no allegiance or tribute to any man, company, or government."

I grunted an acknowledgment, momentarily lost in thought. If Craven was correct about the year being 1720, we had landed smack-dab in the middle of the Golden Age of Piracy in the Caribbean.

An age that Captain Craven, the *Renegade*, and this band of malodorous hooligans belonged in, but we most assuredly did not.

NINE

"Your brother be babbling on about 'time-dilation' and 'quantum gravity' to explain your presence here; truly it be making me head hurt something fierce."
—Edward Vogel

Sarasota, FL
Saturday, February 23, 2019
14 years, 2 months, 7 days since Reemergence

"Everyone, it's time," my wife Rebekah said, beckoning our family to gather in the living room.

Saturday night was Movie Night at our house, where Rebekah, me, and our two children Riley and Drake camped out on our sleeper-sofa, ate popcorn, and watched videos. We used to play games, but my competitiveness usually ruined them for the kids. I explained I was toughening them up for the real world. They did not appreciate this explanation.

Tom came by, Rebekah brought in bowls of popcorn and some sweet tea, and we settled in to watch *Timeline*, a flick based on the Michael Crichton novel. I had read the book several times—it featured history students who were sent back in time to medieval France to rescue their professor. I loved the book, and hoped the movie lived up to it.

*****

I awoke to Rebekah poking me in the ribs. "Hon, the movie's over."

"Already?" I rubbed my aching eyes. Sharp pains behind them were becoming more frequent, a troubling development from days long past.

"Yeah, Dad," six-year old Drake rebuked. "You were snoring so loud we couldn't hear the show sometimes."

"Sorry about that," I mumbled. "Did everything turn out all right?"

"Yeah, it was neat. Uncle Tom, Riley, and I were talking about how cool it would be to go back in time and be pirates!"

"Is that so?" I asked, shooting Tom a scathing glance.

"Dad, has anyone ever gone back in time, for real?"

My gut clenched at his question because I could not give him an honest reply. "Um, well, Drake, uh, as far as I know, no one has ever travelled back in time. No one who ever made it back, anyway." I threw that last part in, to ease the crushing disappointment written on his face.

"Aww, that stinks. I was hoping I could go back with Uncle Tom."

"Go back with Uncle Tom where?"

"To his pirate ship. I want to help him fight against Admiral Brannigan!" Drake responded eagerly.

I flinched at the name of our greatest adversary. "Well, that would be cool, I guess, but seeing as time travel is science fiction and *not* science fact, that's probably not going to happen."

"Are you sure, Dad?" Riley chimed in. "Uncle Tom's gone back to the 1700's, he told us so!"

"Sweetie, Uncle Tom's stories, while entertaining, are just that, stories. Neither he nor anyone we know has travelled through time. You can Google that if you want, but it's true."

Tom harrumphed but said nothing.

"Well, me hearties, we can still pretend, can we not?" I growled in my best pirate voice, trying to cheer them up. "Now, off to bed with ye, ye mangy swabs!" I swatted their behinds as they scampered to their bedrooms.

After they had disappeared around the corner, I turned on Tom, hissing, "So, now *you're* going back in time to be a pirate, eh?"

He grinned sheepishly. "Yeah, I know, but—"

"AND you told them about Admiral Brannigan! What happened to you just making stuff up? Your stories have to be personal now, relating actual events?"

"I was running out of material," he chortled. "Plus, truth is much more interesting than fiction, don't you think?"

I could only shake my head as he opened the front door and walked out into the night.

TEN

"Any commander who fails to exceed his authority is not of much use to his subordinates."
—Admiral Arleigh Burke

From the Personal Journal of Roger M. Petrie
December 3, ???

Captain Craven turned to leave the bridge.

"Mr. Petrie, I be needing to attend more important matters. Be staying here so I knowst where to find ye." He pointed to Tom and Gregg. "Lead me to your holds, gents." Craven, Tom, Reynolds, and four of the bodyguards moved out in search of wares to plunder, leaving me alone with two smelly, scary-looking men.

Working in tandem, one would shadow me while the other played with the equipment. We were operating on emergency power, so they could not cause too many problems. They would grunt at each other every so often, then sneer and scowl at me.

If their plan were to scare me, it was working.

Time crawled as I watched them gawking at the instrumentation, discussing what each thought this knob or that switch did. Had conditions been different it would have been hilarious to watch. Their clothes were plainer and dirtier than Craven's or his officers; short-sleeved shirts, baggy crew-length pants, white stockings or hose, and black slip-on shoes. The clothes looked—and smelled—like they had not been washed in ages, tattered, torn, a rancid mixture of body odor, tar, and the sea. They adorned these plain outfits with colorful sashes around their waists and heads, and both sported gold hoop earrings in their left ears.

Their dress may have been cartoonish, but they were heavily muscled and carried a variety of weapons. They moved fluidly, looking very much like men accustomed to violence.

I stood against the back bulkhead, not knowing what to do. Had Carmichael succeeded in raising the authorities via the Satphone? Was help even now speeding on the way? What I would not give to see the looks on these jokers' faces when an *Arleigh Burke*-class destroyer came charging over the horizon! Or better yet, if a squadron of F-14s came screaming out of the clouds and bombed their wretched boat to kingdom come! But as the minutes passed and I did not hear the whop-whop of a passing chopper or the roar of high-performance jet engines, my hopes began to dim.

There was a commotion outside, and angry steps were clanking up the stairs. Craven burst through the wheelhouse door, angrily shoving his two cohorts aside and accosting me. He stuck a dagger he had drawn from his weapons-laden baldric into the underside of my chin, his breath putrid and foul.

"Mr. Petrie, I need ye to be explaining things right quick. This be a cargo vessel, is it not? Yet I beheld nothing that be useful or profitable to me. Where be your valuables, Petrie? Be quick about it, lad, for I'll not be caught like a drowned rat like Rackham. There be too many warships patrolling these waters."

He twitched his dagger for emphasis.

"*Belvedere* is a merchant ship, Captain, but she's unlike anything you've ever encountered. The cargo we're carrying is likely useless to you."

He frowned, a frightful expression on his pock-marked features. "Why would ye be saying that, Mr. Petrie?" he growled.

"Well, Captain, if you're correct about what year this is, it's likely our cargo would be useless to you."

The dagger twitched again, drawing blood. He leaned close, snarling, "I not be a patient man, Mr. Petrie, so ye best be explaining yourself quickly, or by thunder I'll hang ye from the yardarm!"

Swallowing hard—not easy to do with a dagger to my chin—I tried to explain. "Captain, my ship and crew are not from your time. The year 1720 is a long way in the past to us, before our country was even founded. For us, yesterday was December 2, 2002, two hundred and eighty-two years in your future. How we got here, I haven't a clue, but here we are."

He took a step back and lowered the dagger, his eyes wide, his mouth opening and closing but producing no sound. Eventually, he found his tongue.

"Be ye touched in the head, Petrie? I have little patience to be suffering fools!" He feigned moving forward, then stopped, eyeing me suspiciously. "If ye be mad, I'll run ye through soon enough. But 'tis true, Petrie, here ye be, and that be presenting me a conundrum. What am I to do with your ship, as by your witness she be damaged? What about your crew? If your cargo be useless to me, most likely the mangy sots be manning this ship would be, too." There were growls of affirmation from the other pirates gathered.

His attitude put us in a dangerous predicament. Pirates often commandeered captured vessels for their own use, either to augment their "fleet" or as an upgrade from their current vessel. *Belvedere* was neither; she was inoperative without major engine repairs, so Craven could not take her with him. My crew was trained to operate a diesel-powered vessel, so bringing them aboard *Renegade* would likely be pointless. He would not be inclined to let us live, for we could give testimony about *Renegade* to the authorities, which might aid in her capture. Our lives hung in the balance, and as *Belvedere's* commander, it was my duty to save my crew.

I had to choose my words carefully; they did not call pirate captains "cutthroats" for nothing. "Captain, I realize *Belvedere's* cargo itself may be of little use to you. But there is equipment on board that could be useful to you, and my crew is skilled in the operation of such. If incorporated onto *Renegade,* her performance, not to mention her comfort, could be enhanced considerably."

He looked disinterested, not a good sign.

I forged on. "Captain, being an avid student of maritime history, I've read quite a bit about pirate activities in the Caribbean."

"Is that so?" he sneered cynically. "And what have ye learned?"

"First, I know there are certain persons who are highly regarded on board a pirate ship—people like a surgeon, a master carpenter, or a skilled tradesman—who can keep both the ship and its crew in good health."

He perked up. "Aye, 'tis true, Mr. Petrie. Ye have such artisans amongst your crew?"

"I do," I affirmed. "We also have people like Tom and me, who can solve engineering problems and install equipment that will make life aboard your ship more enjoyable, while improving her performance."

I hoped I was not talking over his head, but he was proving to be quite intelligent. “So ye be proposing, if I spare your crew, you would labor to prosper me?”

“Yes. We can rig lights below, so you don’t stumble around in the dark, maybe ventilation fans to cool the ship, things like that. I understand that pirate ships usually had a rat problem—”

“Aye, the little devils be infesting every dark corner of the ship! Oft times they eat better than me crew, they do,” he grumbled. “Ye can fix that?”

“We can. We have traps and poisons on board that will eradicate your rats. We have storage containers that keep food from rotting, and we might even be able to formulate fresh water from saltwater.”

“What kind of magic be that, Petrie?”

“Not magic, Captain. Chemicals,” I replied.

“Is that the truth of it? If so, ’twould indeed be valuable for our voyages,” he answered.

“We can do a lot of things for you, Captain, in return for our lives.”

He appraised me steadily. “That all sounds right agreeable, Mr. Petrie, but a thought be nagging me. Why be ye so eager to be aiding a man who killed members of your crew but moments ago?”

It was a valid question, one that I would probably wrestle with for years to come. “Because, Captain, as commander of this vessel, my first duty is the safety of my crew. I’m willing to help you if that saves their lives in the process. I do not care for the alternative.”

He nodded approvingly. “Aye, there be conviction to your speech. Very well, we’ll canvass your crew to see who be worthy. If there be surgeons or carpenters amongst ye, we be keen to bring them aboard.”

“That’s all I can ask from you, Captain,” I said, an exceedingly sour taste in my mouth.

*****

Now, the lives of my crew rested on the "canvass" of their skills and talents. It was nerve-wracking, watching each remaining *Belvedere* crew member step up and be grilled by Craven and his officers. HR departments everywhere would have been offended by some of the questions put to my charges, questions of a very personal nature, or questions intended to measure the amount of violence one felt himself capable of visiting upon others.

In the end, Craven impressed three men who had no choice in the matter: Doc Loechner, Chief Cook Mark Samuels, and Engineering Mate Quentin Riley, who was also a skilled carpenter. They would either join him or die. Seven others who were deemed to have transferable skills were offered the chance to join and had accepted: me, Tom, Reynolds, Cable, Charlie, Carmichael, and Wolcott. The other nine men either were not asked or had refused outright. After some cajoling, Craven agreed to give them a *Belvedere* lifeboat. He ordered them to travel to the island opposite the one in whose lee we were anchored, several miles distant. We sent as much food and supplies as the boat would hold, along with tarps and ropes so they could make shelters. With those, they might be able to construct some way of getting off the island. Though, if it were 1720, where could they go?

I addressed Vinnie, the most senior officer not joining *Renegade*. "Mr. Tolbert, I assign this detail to you. I charge you with doing your utmost to ensure their safety and prosperity." I choked out the last words, emotion constricting my throat.

"Prosperity, sir? We're being condemned to a desert island—" he began bitterly.

"You would prefer the alternative, Mr. Tolbert?" I snapped.

He shook his head. "No, sir, I reckon not."

"Good." In a lower voice I added, "Vinnie, I've left you two forty-fives with spare ammo. Use them wisely."

"Thank you, sir. But why are you joining them, after what they did to Tompkins and Smythe?"

"I've asked myself that question a thousand times, believe me." I looked down the deck at Tom, who was busy supervising the loading of some equipment on a pallet. Motioning in his direction, I said, "As much as I'd like to stay with you, that's why. He's my brother, the only family I have in this part of the world. I can't leave him to his own devices, Vinnie. He may be a genius, but he's also rash and impulsive, and I've got to look out for him." I shrugged helplessly; there was nothing else to say.

"Aye, sir, I understand. Good luck, sir, you're going to need it sailing with that madman."

"Thanks, Vinnie. Take care of yourself and the crew. If I ever get the chance, I'll come back for you."

We both knew there was scant chance of that.

ELEVEN

"We must free ourselves of the hope that the sea will ever rest. We must learn to sail in high winds."
—Aristotle Onassis

Clearwater Beach, FL
Sunday, February 24, 2019
14 years, 2 months, 8 days since Reemergence

It was an unseasonably warm day on the Suncoast.

With the mercury hitting eighty-five degrees, my family decided to drive up to Clearwater after church. Rebekah packed a picnic lunch, and Tom joined our party. It looked like it would be a beautiful afternoon.

After eating, I walked into the ocean, standing in surf up to my knees. To me, the water was too chilly to swim in—though a few hardy souls were frolicking in deeper water. I was thoroughly fatigued. A pounding headache had made sleep difficult, and I woke up tired and depressed. Shading my eyes, I spied the red-and-black pirate ship from Captain Jack's in Tampa, meandering north along the horizon with a boatload of tourists. My melancholy deepened as I watched her, memories of my first foray helming a sailing ship springing forth unbidden…

My mind was troubled as I lashed one of our Rigid-hulled Inflatable Boats (RIBs) to Renegade's *stern. During the capture of the* Cantabria, *I had witnessed the torture of several Spanish officers by Captain Craven, Teodoro, and Khamisi. Most appalling was how much they seemed to enjoy it.*

I was tying the last knot when Craven clomped up beside me. "Mr. Petrie, ye helmed that metal beast of yours," he growled. "Would ye care to take a turn with me ship?"

I fumbled for an answer, unprepared for this challenge and not wanting to be in Craven's company. "I, ah…well, helming a large ship like Belvedere *is a different animal…"*

"On the wheel, Mr. Petrie!" he ordered. "Let's see what ye be made of."

"Aye, Captain." I dutifully complied, grasping the polished wooden handles of Renegade's *wheel.*

Steering a sailing ship was different than helming a diesel-powered merchantman. Renegade *was thirty times lighter than* Belvedere, *her propulsion depending entirely on wind and waves. It was a gusty day, and she surged with each blast of air. The wind direction was forward of the port beam, making* Renegade *want to turn on her center of mass into the wind. She heeled to starboard as she cruised, deck only a few feet above the waves. It was far more difficult to maintain a constant heading if she was not running parallel to the waves, due to her relative lightness and shallow draft.*

The value of a good pilot became more apparent the longer I manned the wheel.

Craven stood behind me. Looking skyward, he ordered, "Twenty points to starboard, Mr. Petrie, a favorable wind is a'borning."

"Aye, Captain," I answered. The only navigational instrument visible was an old magnetic compass set before the wheel. I guesstimated that twenty points meant twenty degrees, so I spun the wheel clockwise to begin a starboard turn. Too fast! As the bow swiftly swung right, the wind caught the mainsail, swinging the main boom overhead.

"Boom about!" someone shouted, and I ducked reflexively. Worse, the mainsail was full out, and a powerful gust of wind blew Renegade *sharply over, sending sailors and anything not secured tumbling to port.*

Craven screamed at me, "Petrie, ye mangy milksop, ye be capsizing me ship!" He turned to yell at others, his face beet-red. "Mr. Roesh, on the wheel! Mr. Rasmussen, reef the sheets and furl the topsails, quickly now!"

Roesh shoved me out of the way and gripped the wheel as riggers reduced the amount of canvas exposed to the wind. Renegade *righted herself, still listing slightly to port as her sails were trimmed.*

Craven clasped my right arm painfully and threw me to the deck, still furious. "Back below deck with ye, Petrie, ye feckless puppy, 'til ye learn proper seamanship!" Evidently, my part in saving his neck from pirate hunters was long forgotten. He continued to glare at me with malevolent eyes, and I did not lower mine.

He drew his cutlass, the blade ringing in response. Taking two quick steps, he held the point of his blade between my eyes.

"Ye be fixing me with a right hateful gaze, Petrie! Would that be a challenge?" he roared.

I lowered my eyes. "No, Captain, I meant no disrespect."

He did not immediately answer, his cutlass floating before my face. I started making amends to my Maker, thinking I had gone too far, my death assured.

Tom scurried up, pleading his case on my behalf. "Captain Craven, you'll have to forgive my brother. He's still struggling to assimilate to this life, but back at Tortola he proved his worth to you, did he not?"

Craven bared his teeth, and for a moment I feared my stupidity had killed us both. After a pause, he relented from running me through, returning his blade to its scabbard. He waved us both away.

"Remove this son of a harlot from me sight, Tom, 'efore I skewer his gizzard!"

"Aye, Captain," Tom responded, grabbing my arm, ushering me out of Craven's presence. I felt the eyes of the crew upon us as he half-dragged me forward, simultaneously enraged and ashamed as I stumbled along.

"What was that, bro?" Tom hissed as we arrived at the bow. "Are you trying to get yourself killed?" He grabbed a forestay to steady himself, eyeballing me angrily. "That was stupid, Roger. You may not realize this, but you're the glue that's holding our Belvedere group together. If he kills you, it would probably mean the end of us all." He wanted to say more but fell silent.

I fidgeted with a line, answering, "I'm sorry, Tom, but I couldn't help it. I hate that man, for what he did to Smythe and what he continues to do to everyone we meet."

Tom looked around in alarm, then faced me, whispering fiercely, "You have got to stop saying things like that out loud! We don't stand a chance of getting back to our time if you keep acting this way! I don't like him any more than you do, Roger, but there's nothing we can do about that now!"

"I know."

"Act like it, then!" Straightening up, he muttered, "Let's get back to work, before Craven finds another reason to want to kill you."

*****

Shaking the memory off, I fished a coin out of my shorts pocket—something I had found the day before—playing with it as the ship passed by. I did not react as Tom splashed up beside me. I am considered tall at six-two, but at six feet five, with a head full of curly black hair, he managed to tower over me.

"Reminiscing?" he teased, pointing to the pirate ship.

"Something like that," I said, massaging my temples.

"Still with the headaches, huh? Mine are fairly mild when I get them. Time travel's not for the timid, right?"

I grunted in reply, perturbed he was so cheerful.

Ignoring my moodiness, he noticed the coin. "Whatcha got there, Roger?" he asked, reaching for it.

"Something I found in the attic yesterday." It was a silver coin, comparable in size and weight to a quarter, but much older and more valuable.

He inspected it closely, turning it over several times. "Ah, an excellent specimen! Real de a ocho, minted in 1716, that would make it from the—"

"*Cantabria*," I finished for him.

"*Cantabria*, yes! Our first open-ocean capture. That was quite a day, right?" he enthused, slapping my back

I sighed heavily. "Yeah, it was a swell day for us. For her crew, not so much."

"Yeah, it was a real scrum for a while. I don't know why such a small crew thought they could resist us. But we handled the situation without much problem."

“Not much problem, huh?” I snorted. “When I got on deck, the first thing I saw were bodies lying in pools of blood, and there was Craven, digging his dagger underneath the captain’s clavicle and twisting it, laughing the whole time. I’ll never forget the look on that poor man’s face as long as I live.”

“That was regrettable,” he said somberly. Brightening, he added, “But we subdued the rest of the crew and found the loot without any more casualties.”

“Besides the ones already lying dead, you mean.”

“That happened before we boarded, you know that. Khamisi, Bartlett, and Teodoro, always eager to prove their prowess with a blade.”

“And we were right there with them.”

“Until you deftly removed them,” he chuckled. “That was a nice piece of work.”

“Is that the modern convention used to describe sending men to their deaths?”

Tom exhaled loudly. “You know, Roger, sometimes talking to you is a serious buzzkill. Don’t you ever get tired of shouldering the weight of the world? We were conscripted into a life we didn’t ask for, operated under the most extreme conditions, and came out alive. What else do you want?” He flipped the coin back to me. “And we made out pretty good in the process.”

“And that justifies everything we did?”

He shrugged, looking out to sea as the pirate ship came about and headed south. “Maybe, maybe not, who’s to say? Besides, that was a long time ago. Why worry about it now?”

“If it was so long ago, why do the scars in my mind seem so fresh?”

TWELVE

"Being a swarthy buccaneer be the best life t'be contrived, so climb aboard our pirate ship, 'tis grand, if ye survive!"
—Pirate ditty

From the Personal Journal of Roger M. Petrie
December 3, 1720?

The day finished with plenty of backbreaking work.

Our crew used *Belvedere's* jib crane to lift machinery, equipment, and foodstuff from her cargo holds, setting them onto the forward deck. Craven was preparing to careen *Renegade,* which entailed emptying her of everything not securely fastened down. With that in mind, everything we were intending to install aboard her would be held here on *Belvedere's* deck. Once careening was completed, it would all be transferred over to *Renegade.*

Craven was concerned about how much weight the *Belvedere* equipment would add to his ship. Tom assured him that when he was done retro-engineering, *Renegade's* performance would be enhanced, not degraded. We brought up wires, cables, winches, pulleys, PVC piping, batteries, lights, food, and anything else Tom and his engineering mates could think of that would be of use. It took hours to accomplish this, with Craven ranting about the time it was taking, but we eventually scrounged together almost everything on Tom's wish list. Whatever was not already on *Belvedere's* deck would be hauled up in the morning. With the day's work completed, we shut off all power generation and *Belvedere* went dark.

There would be much more to do tomorrow.

*****

Each man joining *Renegade* was allowed a small ditty bag with some personal effects and a change of clothes. I stuck in toiletries, my Ozark hikers, a pair of khakis, extra underwear, socks, and t-shirts, as much as would fit in a small canvas duffle. We left most of our personal gear behind.

Before we climbed aboard *Renegade*, Doc distributed more medications to the crew. Travelling backwards in time was proving to be rough on the human body. I spotted Tom walking toward the boarding ramp and pulled him aside.

"Can you tell me why you're sticking with Craven and not going ashore?" I demanded.

"Why are you?" he shot back.

"I asked you first, and I really need to know."

He exhaled heavily. "Well, remember *Gilligan's Island*?" I nodded, curious where this was going. "They were all stuck on that stupid island for years, right, despite the best efforts of the Professor, and somewhat modern resources? So, I figure I…I mean, *we,* have a better chance to see a ship or plane while out at sea than we would being stuck on that heap of sand."

"Are you telling me you're basing your whole survival plan on the plot of a 60s television show?" I asked in disbelief.

"Yep, that's my plan. Do I want to join a criminal enterprise? Not really. But I figure we can find a way out once we hit the trade routes, or we can gradually take down Craven and his cronies from within. Either way, we're better off at sea. We gave Tolbert plenty of food and water, but realistically, how long is that going to last? A month, maybe two? Will they be able to build reliable transport off the island? Doubtful. So, I'm playing the percentages, bro, going with the more survivable option." He climbed over the rail onto *Renegade's* deck, leaving me to stew in my own doubts.

If the year was 2002, the better option was to stay on the island.

Gilligan notwithstanding, the odds of being spotted and picked up were good in this part of the world. But if it was 1720, going to the island was a certain death sentence, no matter if we were twenty-first-century men or not. It was a question of resources, and the island offered few.

Though I still hoped this was some mass hallucination or nightmare, it sure did not feel like one.

The sun was setting behind *Renegade*, sky ablaze with orange light. The visual effect of the sun's dying rays on her sails was breathtaking, making it appear like the sails themselves were alight. *Renegade* had clean lines, her hull dark brown, weather deck level from stem to stern. She looked to be ninety feet long, not counting her bowsprit, which jutted out another twenty feet. Her foremast was set aft of her bows, behind two wooden gun carriages. Various lines ran between the two masts; forestays to the bow, backstays to the stern, along with side stays fastened to her gunwales. Two large rope ladders, called shrouds, ran from the gunwales to the topmasts on either side. Myriad other rope lines, some attached to pulleys, others to block-and-tackle rigs, spider-webbed through the rigging. Three square sails were draped from her foremast spars, flapping limply in the gentle evening breeze.

There were three cannons spaced several feet apart directly amidships, their muzzles dark and menacing in the fading light. Midway between the foremast and stern rose her mainmast, the great mainsail lashed to a large boom which was tied up parallel to the ship's keel. Somewhere in the recesses of my mind, I knew this type of rigging was called brigantine.

I hated to admit it, but *Renegade* was a beautiful ship.

*****

Once on *Renegade's* main deck, Craven lined us up by the mainmast, surrounded by his crew. He passed a piece of paper to me and said, "Gents, here be the Articles of this ship. Ye lubbers be on probation until you've proved your worth. Once we be satisfied, you'll sign your own copy, and be treated to an equal share of plunder. By your oath you'll be bound by the terms therein, come life or death. But before ye sign, ye need to be clear about what we be purposing."

He passed in front of us, fixing each with a cold stare. Turning, he said, "Gents, we be gentlemen of fortune, taking whate'er we please, with no apology. We live hard, lads, because buccaneering be a dangerous affair. We plunder under the black flag, and if any sailors deign to resist, we give 'em no quarter. We use whate'er means be necessary to relieve captains of their booty, understand?" This elicited some evil cackles from his crew. "'Tis likely foreign to your present inclinations, but we've no time for moralizing. We be under sentence of death, for to be caught is to swing from a rope, so we live merry and free whilst we can. If ye can abide by that, welcome aboard. If ye can't, join your shipmates on yonder island. If ye stay aboard and find ye can't abide, well, *Renegade* 'tain't no ferry. You'll be marooned or shot, at me discretion." He scanned our faces intently. "Are ye agreeable to these terms? If so, stay where you be. If not, step forward, and take your leave of me ship."

We glanced at each other nervously, each weighing his options. I felt a powerful pull to join Tolbert and the others, but I did not want to end up marooned with little recourse. Only Charlie stepped forward. He was a gentle soul, not cut out for this kind of life. He shook all our hands, then set out to join Tolbert in the lifeboat. It was powered by a small outboard motor, and Tolbert waved as they began the laborious task of navigating a small boat through the open ocean.

It saddened me to think I likely would never see any of them again.

Craven then introduced us to his officers and important men on the ship, the masters. There was Quartermaster Edward Vogel, a powerfully-built fireplug of a man; First Mate Newton Berger, also squat but kinder-looking, with graying hair and sideburns; Boatswain Patrick Carney, tall and wiry; Master Gunner Noah Spenser, another stout, muscular man; Master Pilot Henry Slocum, a slim, dour-looking man with a long beard and longer ponytail; Master Rigger Shane Rasmussen, a big, shaggy red-head; Master Carpenter Kyne Tolliver, a large, freckly, bespectacled man with bulging forearms; and Ship's Cooper Khamisi, a former slave, as tall as Tom, with huge hands and a chiseled physique. Last was Bodie, the chief cook and by far the oldest amongst the pirate crew, who all looked to be in their twenties. Bodie was in his forties, a rotund man with long, straggly gray hair and a perpetual limp. He was the friendliest man we were introduced to. The officers greeted us cordially but with suspicion.

Among the regular crew, which numbered sixty, there were seven blacks, former slaves known as Cimarrons; two Arawak Indians, E'twan and Lonii, who were 'strikers', men adept at catching large fish, sea turtles, and marine mammals; two Spaniards, Armando and Gael; and one Frenchman, Alain. The rest were mainly Welsh, with a smattering of English and Scots. Most of the men were former merchant sailors, many of them were orphans who had gone to sea at an early age, and a few were deserters from the various navies that patrolled these waters. There were no women aboard, which was not unusual; many superstitious old-time sailors viewed women on board as bad luck.

Women's suffrage had a long way to go in this era.

After this formal introduction, we were instructed to read the Articles of the ship. I had read of pirates like Bartholomew Roberts having a sort of "code" governing the operations of their ships. As I perused the Articles, I marveled at the democratic ideals contained within them. No doubt some of the reasons why these sailors risked death every day were contained in these words:

1. **Every man shall have an equal vote in affairs of the ship.**
2. **If any man robs another, he shall have his nose and ears slit and be put ashore.**
3. **There will be no gambling on board, in any form.**
4. **No women are allowed on board.**
5. **No fighting on board. Two men fighting must end their quarrel by sword on shore.**
6. **Any man that deserts the ship during battle shall be put to death.**
7. **Every man who shall become crippled or lose a limb shall receive eight hundred pieces of eight and proportionate amounts for lesser wounds.**

8. **The captain, quartermaster, and first mate shall each receive two shares of a prize, the masters and bosun one and one-half shares, and seamen one share each.**

We prepared for a toast to our new life, and large metal cups (called 'Black Jacks') brimming with clear liquid were passed out. Craven raised a cup and bellowed out a hearty, "Well, me lads, welcome aboard the *Renegade*! I raise a toast to ye new members of our merry band! May our prey be plentiful, our take bountiful, and women and wine be loose and cheap, in that order!"

The regular crew cheered lustily, and we all were obliged to take a swig. It was molasses-based rum, sweet to the taste but caustic to my throat and stomach. Berger told me to get used to drinking rum, because water fouled aboard ship after a few days. When I said my workplace had a strict non-alcoholic beverage policy during working hours, he looked at me like I was crazy.

After the events of the day, I doubted it would be long before *crazy* proved an apt description of me.

Several seamen sat amidships, playing weathered fiddles and guitars. They started singing a ditty, and we contemporary sailors realized with a start their song was directed at us:

Lend us yer ears, ye newbie crew, ye interlopers aboard our ship,
Ahoy, me hearties, 'ave a taste of rum, raise a Black Jack to yer lips!
We be freebooters, sure, shackled to the allure of all things that be shiny and bright,
We scour the seas, takin' whate'er we please, always spoilin' for a fight!
Captain Craven be bold, a rowdy buccaneer, the scourge of the Spanish Main!

British warships galore, and scurvy privateers, 'ave all pursued him naught in vain.
So, hoist the colors, mates! We sail from dawn's first light, standin' watch 'til after dark,
Avast ye now, lads, better pull yer weight, lest we feed ye to the sharks!

Well, that song was full of warm sentiments. The crew howled in delight; no doubt spurred on by our looks of dismay. Not a great welcome, but these men were real pirates, not movie caricatures or fictional creations. I would be wise to remember that.

It was well after dark before the evening's festivities waned. I noticed that the regular crew generally avoided us new recruits, but a few deigned to speak with us. I asked Khamisi what a Cooper was; he was good-natured about it, explaining that he built and maintained all the barrels, trunks, and other storage vessels on board. He seemed okay, but another seaman, James, said one of Khamisi's favorite methods of killing people was to squeeze their necks until their eyes fell out. He was not joking. I gave Khamisi a wide berth after that.

Craven came over to give us some parting advice. "Sleep well, me hearties, for we careen the ship tomorrow. We've much to do, so rest your bones and be fit by morning. Remember, ye be on probation for now, lads, so I would be showing me regular crew your willingness to bend your backs, if I were ye."

I wanted to spend the night in my cabin on *Belvedere*, but Craven wanted us *probies* on board *Renegade* to begin the acclimation process. Sleeping accommodations on board a crowded pirate ship with no ventilation or internal plumbing left a lot to be desired. The air below decks was sickeningly foul. I quickly discovered why: First, bathroom facilities were primitive; two holes cut in the beak served as toilets, pots and pails were set out for urination. Second, all the spills and leaks aboard ship seeped down to the bilge. The stench from this drainage cesspool wafted upwards, fouling the air below the open-air main deck. Third, both the pirates and their clothing smelled awful. With no fans or windows to provide air movement, the noxious odors hung in the atmosphere like a poisonous fog.

No one seemed to care.

There were numerous hammocks hung haphazardly throughout the second deck for sleeping, but this ship was built for a crew of eighteen, not seventy. Space was at a premium, and some the hammocks were hung mere inches from each other. I got the impression that the stronger, more intimidating members of the crew got their choice of sleeping arrangements, and the rest fended for themselves. Not wanting to get into a fight my first night aboard, I decided to brave it outdoors, curling up in the prow of the ship under some canvas. At least the gentle rocking of the ship might lull me to sleep, and I would not dry heave through the night due to the smell, like I would below. Other sailors found sleeping niches on the main deck. The Hilton it was not, but I needed to make the best of it, or else suffer the same fate as Tompkins and Smythe.

And a good night to you too, Captain Craven, you bastard! was my final conscious thought before drifting off into a fitful and dreamless sleep.

THIRTEEN

"Now and then we had a hope that if we lived and were good, God would permit us to be pirates."
—Mark Twain

Kinnan Elementary School - Sarasota, FL
Thursday, March 7, 2019
14 years, 2 months, 19 days since Reemergence

As we approached Riley's school, I understood why my parents had hated being asked to meet with my teachers.

Rebekah and I entered Riley's third-grade classroom at 6:55 pm. It was a typical elementary school room: large whiteboard in front, colorful posters ringing the walls displaying math problems and cursive writing, a long bookcase along the length of the room on one side, and students' desks placed in the middle of the room in groups of four. Riley's teacher, Mrs. Megan Truitt, was sitting behind her desk grading papers. She was a handsome older woman, her black hair pulled back severely in a bun. She greeted us warmly as we took seats in front of her.

"Mr. and Mrs. Petrie, good evening! Thank you for coming."

"This *is* unprecedented," I said. "Two parent-teacher conferences in one semester."

"Believe me, I'm just as surprised. Riley is an excellent student, and she's a main reason I'm making it through this year." Seeing our questioning looks, she laughed. "My class this year is…challenging, so having a student as pleasant as Riley makes it worthwhile."

"We're happy to hear that," Rebekah replied, "though I'm more mystified than ever why we're here."

Megan straightened up. "Ah, that. Third grade is the last year we engage in show-and-tell. Riley loves to participate, which happens often due to her active imagination." I groaned, eliciting a chuckle from her. "Yes, Mr. Petrie, we were all entertained by her vivid recounting of how you served with the Special Forces in Afghanistan but flew home on weekends. Then there was the scar she has on her forehead, from a dog bite, I believe? That one turned into a safari trip in which a lion swiped her head with its claws, and you arrived in the nick of time to save her."

Yes, Riley had quite the imagination.

"Mrs. Truitt, has Riley done something recently that troubles you?" Rebekah asked.

Megan turned to me. "Mr. Petrie—"

"Roger, please."

She smiled wanly. "Of course. May I ask, Roger—have you ever been a pirate?"

I flinched involuntarily, causing her to eye me curiously. She could not possibly know, right? "A pirate, me? I…I don't think so. Why do you ask?"

To my consternation, Rebekah burst out laughing. "That's the most ridiculous thing I've ever heard!" She doubled over, grabbing my left arm. "Roger Petrie, a pirate! I'm sorry, honey, but that's hilarious! You're so even-keeled, deliberate, and logical, the thought of you attacking anything other than a juicy ribeye is really funny!"

I shot her a rebuking look. "Thank you, Rebekah, but I could be a rogue if I needed to."

I had a cache of riches that attested to that.

"Of course, you could, honey," she replied sweetly. "I wasn't knocking your manly prowess."

Megan coughed; no doubt thrilled by the tack this conversation was taking. "Getting back to Riley—she loves pirates, which is why I asked you that, Roger. She talks about them constantly, but this semester her stories have gotten more, ah, outlandish, especially in the last three weeks. She now insists you and your brother Tom were real pirates back in the 1700s and regales the class with your escapades. What's become a problem is how defensive she's getting when other children question the truthfulness of her stories. I believe Tom is the source of these stories, yes? Well, she takes the criticism as attacks on his integrity."

I sighed inwardly. Tom was two years my elder, a gregarious bear of a man. He was highly intelligent, with a mischievous streak a mile long. We were both seafaring men, having served in the Navy and merchant marine. Through a bizarre set of circumstances, we had also served aboard the *Renegade*, an ancient pirate ship. Lately, he had been filling Riley's head with *our* actual exploits, and apparently was now adding me to his anecdotes. He loved our buccaneering experiences with a passion, a passion he had poured into Riley, which was now getting her into trouble.

"Riley and Tom do spend a lot of time together talking about pirates," I said," though I wasn't aware he's been including me now."

"Is that becoming a problem, Mrs. Truitt?" Rebekah added.

Megan opened her front drawer and removed a small object, laying it in front of us. It was a golden, misshapen coin just over an inch in diameter. I reached out to examine it; it was slightly heavier than a quarter, with the Hapsburg shield imprinted on one side and a deep-struck Jerusalem cross bordered by four arcs on the other side. I was momentarily transfixed by the ethereal beauty of it, for I knew immediately what it was.

"Wow, it's heavy. Is this real gold?" Rebekah asked, taking the golden coin from my hand. "Did Riley bring this to class?"

"Yes, last Friday," Megan confirmed. "She said Tom gave it to her. To her, it proves everything he's told her of your adventures as pirates, Roger. She claims this is a real doubloon recovered from a Spanish treasure galleon. And by recovered, I mean she told the class you and Tom attacked the galleon in your pirate ship and stole many coins like this from it. She even named the galleon…" She shuffled some papers. "The *Nuestra de la Capistrano*. Does that name mean anything to you?"

I flinched again at the ship's name. Dang those involuntary responses! I *did* recognize the ship, and plunder it we did, but I was not about to tell her and Rebekah that. Retrieving the coin, my mind started to wander…

"Roger, we may have found something," Tom's voice squawked over the radio.

Pulse pounding, I left Admiral de Oquendo by the mainmast under guard and hurried to the forward hatch. Tom was two levels beneath me, scouring the dark, dank depths of the Capistrano's *holds, searching for the elusive treasure we suspected was hidden there.*

"On my way, Tom."

I took the ladder two steps at a time, landing heavily on the gun deck. The grapeshot recently buried in my left hip sent shocks of pain coursing through my body, knocking me to my knees. The deck smelled of gunpowder, mildew, sweat, and urine, a noxious mixture that stung my eyes. Gathering myself, I swung around to descend the next ladder to the cargo deck, taking care to hit the deck more gently.

My entire crew was ragged and exhausted, having spent the last few hours under steady fire from British warships, and witnessing shipmates being wounded or killed. I was astonished they had voted to pursue Capistrano *after the pounding we had suffered.*

Only a bounteous amount of plunder would make all that worth it.

I turned aft, attracted by the display of lights playing off the wooden bulkheads. Tom, Berger, Carney, and Reynolds were shining their flashlights in my direction, beckoning me to join them. I jogged to where they were gathered, a section of the aft hold where the crew's luggage was stored. Nondescript trunks, crates, and bags were piled there, lashed to beams and rafters. Some of the lashings were cut away, and various storage vessels lay in a heap to one side.

"Take a gander at this, Captain," Tom said, pointing to a small door, four feet tall and three feet wide, hidden behind the luggage. Taking a hammer and chisel, he gave the brass lock four solid blows, the lock finally giving way with a loud clang. Wrenching the door open, Tom and I shined our lights inside.

The harsh white light exposed stacked wooden trunks with metal corners, bracing, and latches. We pulled one out, marveling at how heavy it was. Setting it on the deck, we exchanged hopeful glances as clinking sounds emanated from inside. Tom bashed the latch repeatedly with a chisel until it broke. More crewmen pressed in behind us, drawn in by the hammering. Lifting the lid, the walls around us sparkled with golden stars as reflections played off the contents of the trunk. Inside lay a mass of freshly minted Spanish doubloons. Taking a knee, I reached in and pulled out a single coin, shining my flashlight upon it. It was a cob, slightly misshapen, heavy...

The purest gold I had ever laid eyes on.

Standing up, I addressed my crew. "Gents, people everywhere are captivated by stories of buried treasure and pirate legends." Holding up the doubloon for all to see, I exclaimed, "Well, me hearties, after today, it looks like the most captivating legends of all will be told about us!"

*****

Rebekah was shaking me. "Roger, are you paying attention? Mrs. Truitt asked you a question."

I needed this conversation to change direction. Time to display the even-keeled, deliberate, and logical Roger Petrie. "No, I've never heard of that particular ship, but I do know many galleons were lost off Florida's east coast back in the early 1700s." I held the doubloon up, adding, "I doubt this is the genuine article. Tom collects all kinds of pirate artifacts and paraphernalia, with most being replicas and reproductions. I'm sure that's what this is." It was not, but I needed to douse their curiosity.

"Oh, that's good to know," Megan said, relieved. "Riley was quite vehement about the doubloon's authenticity. She's normally so good-natured, but she got so defensive after her last two presentations that it caused major classroom disruptions."

My eyebrows shot up at that. "*Riley* caused classroom disruptions? That doesn't sound like her at all."

"And it's not. She's usually so quiet, completes her work regardless of the environment. She tends to avoid conflict, so these outbursts are startling, really. I'm concerned, because I think she's internalized these pirate stories to the point that she believes them to be truth. I don't want this situation to affect her scholastically." She thoughtfully studied the coin I still held. "It is beautiful, isn't it? It looks too perfect to be hundreds of years old."

"Yes, it's quite stunning, which is caveat numero uno," I said matter-of-factly. "If it looks too good to be true, it probably is. That's why I judge this to be a facsimile. If you don't mind, I'll return this to Tom, and we'll have a nice chat about it." I pocketed it quickly; the less said about this doubloon, the better.

"Mrs. Truitt, what do you suggest?" Rebekah implored. "We don't want to quash Riley's imagination, but we can't have her causing disturbances, either."

"I suggest helping her find other positive outlets for her passions. For now, I can't allow her to participate in show-and-tell, and she is not to bring in any more pirate paraphernalia. Much as I love her, I can't tolerate any more conflict in my class, not if I'm going to retain my sanity to the end of the year."

Rebekah was chagrined to hear all this. I was just glad we did not delve deeper into the doubloon mystery. I did not need her poking around my secrets, secrets that needed to stay dead and buried.

*****

When the meeting was over, we walked to our car. She was somber, the news about Riley quite a blow.

"Honey, don't worry, we'll get this fixed," I said, hoping to buoy her mood as we buckled up.

She nodded gloomily, staring out the window. Finally, she turned and said, "There is one other thing that's bothering me."

"And what is that?" I asked as we pulled out onto Tallevast Road.

She hesitated, then said, "Why do you think Tom is including *you* in his pirate fantasies now?"

"I'm wondering that myself," I said, desperate to allay her suspicions. "Obviously, I was such a great captain on the *Belvedere* that it's only natural he'd want to include me at some point." Logical, right?

"I guess so," Rebekah mumbled. She got that look on her face, the look that said she did not fully believe me and would dig around until she found the truth.

Better batten down the hatches, mate, I thought to myself, *there be rough seas ahead.*

FOURTEEN

"A ship in harbor is safe. But that is not what ships are made for."
—John A. Shedd

Sarasota, FL
Thursday Night, March 7, 2019
14 years, 2 months, 19 days since Reemergence

I drove the mile to Tom's condo, stewing about what to say.

It was late, but he was still up and dressed when I arrived. He grabbed two diet sodas and led me outside. It was a warm evening—frogs were thrumming, and the occasional fish splashed in the pond behind his place. We stood for a moment, then I whirled on him, holding out the doubloon.

"Dude, why the heck would you give something like this to Riley?" I demanded. "*And* you gave her the name of the galleon!

What if someone decides to do a little research and traces things back to us?"

"Bro, you worry too much. What if they did? Evidence *might* lead them to *Renegade*, but it'd be difficult to connect her to us. Riley was helping me clean, and she found it buried under some papers in my desk. It wasn't a big deal, and I didn't know she'd take it to school. But look, given Riley's reputation for exaggeration, no one's going to take this seriously."

"That's not the point, Tom!" I countered. "You've been more vocal about our actual exploits recently, and I want to know why."

Tom threw a stick into the lake, watching the ripples radiate outward. "I don't know why, really. It naturally progressed from telling pirate tales to telling *our* pirate tales. All those memories came flooding back, man, and I realized how much I loved it. I'm tired of suppressing the truth about some of the best times of my life." He glanced at me. "You know, maybe it's high time we reconciled with our past and moved on."

I stared at him, dumbfounded. "Are you insane? We'd be harassed to the ends of the earth by every pirate fanatic alive! How would we ever explain that to anyone—let alone our family—without being labeled as stark, raving mad?"

He shook his head. "I'm not saying we come out publicly. I'm talking about telling our family the truth. The truth always comes out, Roger. Think about it: would you want them to learn the truth from us, or some academic who stumbled across it?"

"You just said no one could tie us to anything!"

"Yeah, I did." He shrugged again. "I did some work for Schraeger Salvage in Ft. Myers last year; did you know they found the *Capistrano*? The chances are remote, but someday a salvaged wreck may eventually lead to *Renegade,* or a clever scholar will connect the dots. Are you prepared for that?"

I kicked a rock into the pond. "No, because it's not going to happen. Not in our lifetimes, anyway. Who'd ever believe that you and I were involved in piratical activities so long ago? But some discretion on your part would go a *long* way to stifling this problem with my daughter." Shifting toward the villa, I took my leave. "Listen, I need to help Rebekah put the kids to bed. Can you at least promise me you'll cool it with the pirate fantasies?"

"Fantasies," he scoffed. "It's like you're trying to deny it ever happened."

"We didn't have much choice!"

"Perhaps not, but you came to embrace buccaneering life, man, and you were good at it. What puzzles me is why you're trying so hard to distance yourself from it now. All I can say is that I loved it, bro."

"I know you did, but as a husband and father I have responsibilities you can't fathom, Tom. Dragging our past into that would be a disaster for all concerned. All I'm asking is you tone down the rhetoric and stop trying to convince my daughter you and I were pirates."

"Sounds like I need to convince you, not her," he observed. "But I hear you. I'll see what can be done." He checked his watch. "Tell Rebekah I said good night." We walked back to his condo, him to his bed and me to my car.

One situation handled. Time to deal with the second one.

*****

The kids were already in bed when I returned. I kissed Drake good night, then turned my attention to Riley.

Rebekah was already sitting on Riley's bed when I entered her room. Riley was sitting up, arms wrapped around her legs. Her eyes were red and puffy from crying, mortified that she had gotten in trouble with Mrs. Truitt.

Rebekah stroked Riley's long, brown hair soothingly. "Sweetie, Daddy and I aren't upset with you," she said. "You've never been in trouble at school before, so this is new for us all. Mrs. Truitt isn't mad, either, but she does need control of her class. Do you agree with that?" Riley nodded through her tears. "We just want to know why you're getting so upset at show-and-tell. Doesn't everyone understand this pirate talk is all make-believe?"

"But's it's not make-believe; don't you understand?" she exploded. "They're calling me a liar, and that makes Uncle Tom a liar, and he wouldn't lie to me about this!"

I tried my hand. "Riley, we know Uncle Tom means well, and you two share a love of pirates. But you do know, deep down, that he's making these stories up, right?"

"No, he's not, Daddy, and you should know that better than anyone! You were right there with him! Didn't you see the doubloon?"

"Sweetie, take a good look at your dad," Rebekah said. "He would have to be hundreds of years old to have attacked a 1700s treasure galleon, right? Does he look that old to you?" I hoped she did not answer that question. "Uncle Tom is a very free-spirited man, we know that. He loves you to death, but these pirate tales are fantasies, nothing more. He's taken what happened to real pirates and projected those adventures onto himself and your dad."

"Really, Mommy? But he talks as if what he and Daddy did actually happened…"

I squeezed her hand. "Honey, Caribbean pirates lived a long time ago. I know Uncle Tom likes to pretend that was us, and it's fun to imagine being a pirate, right?" Honestly, it had been enjoyable overall, but there were many times piracy was boring or terrifying, too. "I spoke to him tonight, and I think he'll be clearing things up with you shortly, okay?"

She sniffled, wiping her nose on her sleeve. "I guess so. I don't know how I'll face everybody tomorrow. I'll never be able to show my face in my class again!"

"It'll be tough, but be honest, own up to your mistakes, and go on. Your true friends will understand and forgive you." Wow, that was profound. *And your magic numbers are…*

We comforted her for a few more minutes, then got up to leave. I looked back and she met my eyes, her dejection piercing me like a rapier. I wished I could sweep her up into my arms and confess the whole thing to her: Yes, Uncle Tom is telling you the truth; yes, the stories are real; yes, the doubloon is genuine; and yes, Tom and I "recovered" it from the *Capistrano*. But who would ever believe that? Would I lose my family, my job? Would I be locked up for being crazy?

To me, the ramifications would be too terrible to bear, so for now I had to leave my daughter suffering and alone in the darkness of her bedroom, unable to give her what she truly craved from me:

The Truth.

FIFTEEN

"Avast ye now, lads, better pull yer weight, lest we feed ye to the sharks!"
—Pirate ditty

From the Personal Journal of Roger M. Petrie
Aboard the Renegade
December 4, 1720

I awoke to someone kicking me in the shins.

Bleary-eyed, I struggled to get my bearings. Sharp pains coursed through my head, and my tongue stuck to the roof of my mouth. *Too much rum last night* I thought ruefully. My damp clothing clung to every part of my body as I attempted to sit up. The bundle of canvas I had slept on was still beneath me, clammy to the touch and stinking of mildew.

My eyes cleared, allowing me to see my tormentor. He was a short, burly man with coarse black hair pulled back in a ponytail. About his neck was a blue satin bandana, and he was wearing a white linen shirt under a black vest, black pants gathered at the knee, white hose, and black leather slip-on shoes with big silver buckles. His left hand held a Black Jack, clear liquid sloshing over its rim. I foggily observed that his clothes were markedly different than standard navy or merchant marine issue, for officers or enlisted men.

"Show a leg, Petrie, you slugabed!" he scolded me, his low voice imbued with a slight Germanic accent.

"I'm sure we met yesterday, but your name escapes me, sir."

I added the sir because his clothing indicated he was an officer. Better to render respect than not. I remembered an episode aboard the guided-missile cruiser USS *Richmond K. Turner* when a buddy and I were standing on the port rail. Someone came up on our right, and when I glimpsed scrambled eggs on his cap, I snapped off a salute. My buddy did not, and the person turned out to be our XO. He spent the next thirty minutes standing at attention in front of the XO's desk as they reviewed when and where to salute.

"Sir?" he chuckled. "Blimey, Petrie, we're not in the bloody navy!" He took a seat opposite me on a crate of coiled rope. "I be First Mate Newton Berger. I know your memory likely be foggy, given what all happened yesterday." *That is the understatement of the year*. "May I formally welcome you aboard the good ship *Renegade*, commanded by Captain Benjamin Craven."

Good ship Renegade, I reflected bitterly, trying to process the previous twenty-four hours. Was it only yesterday I had been in command of a cargo ship bound for Miami? Looking up, I beheld three square sails hanging from their spars, rigging rustling in the breeze; this was not a delusion, and yesterday's events were terrifyingly real.

He snickered at my distress. "Why so glum, Mr. Petrie? A beautiful day be dawning."

"I was hoping this was a nightmare and I'd wake up in my bunk in 2002."

"I sympathize, lad, but your wishes be for naught. I fear ye still be with us here in 1720. Better get used to it." He took a hearty swig of rum, then continued, "As Captain Craven bespoke last night, we be sailors of fortune, Mr. Petrie, beholden to no one, accountable only to ourselves."

He cocked his head at my sour expression. "Perhaps you feel piracy be a contemptible vocation, but 'tis better than what else be available to us. Aye, a pirate's life be the only life fit for a man of any spirit." He paused. "You strike me as being a reasonable man, Mr. Petrie, but reasonable men can be driven to unreasonable actions by unpropitious circumstances. I be needing to know; can you sail under the command of Benjamin Craven?"

I nodded numbly, causing him to break into a wide grin. "An excellent decision, Mr. Petrie. The captain be tough but fair, so ye have little to fear from him if you abide by the Articles." He turned to leave, then added a final comment. "This promises to be a fortuitous day! We'll begin to careen the ship, and that tall bloke of yours, Tom, has promised to be making changes that be making *Renegade* the deadliest vessel plying these waters. He also spoke of dealing with our foul water and food. That be agreeable to the captain, so we shall see what transpires, eh?"

He started to walk away when a commotion arose on the aft end of the ship. I strained to see what was happening. Craven appeared by the helm from below decks, accompanied by Vogel and Khamisi, who were holding a squirming, greasy-haired sailor named Nigel between them. Sailors working on deck stopped to watch what was happening.

Craven addressed the assembly, pointing a crooked finger in Nigel's face. "Gents, shares be parceled out last week, but Mr. Courson here evidently be feeling his stake be unsatisfactory. He be caught dead to rights pilfering another man's property." This triggered a fusillade of cursing from the crew, who shook various weapons at Nigel. Craven held his hand up for quiet, the uproar subsiding as he continued. "Now, his punishment be what the Articles stipulate for stealing from a shipmate."

The mob yelled their hearty approval, while Nigel looked pitiful as he strained to break free from the grip of his captors. Vogel and Khamisi led him to the port rail, with Craven following close behind. They pinned his back against it, his eyes wide as Craven, smiling diabolically, drew a dagger from his baldric. He raised the blade to eye level, cackling in Nigel's face.:

"Ye scurvy whelp, ye signed the Articles, now be consigned to your appointed fate!" He slashed at Nigel's face with strokes quicker than I could follow. Nigel shrieked pitifully, and when Craven withdrew, I could see blood streaming from his ears and nose.

Recalling the Articles, I remembered:

2. If any man robs another, he shall have his nose and ears slit and be put ashore.

"I hope ye can swim, ye mangy mongrel!" Craven growled.

"C-C-Captain, the Articles state I b-be put ashore!"

"Aye, 'tis true," Craven mused, "but they not be signifying *how* I be accomplishing that!" Turning to his henchmen, he ordered, "Scupper this bilge-sucking buffoon, 'efore I remove his limbs as well!" Vogel and Khamisi heaved the now-screeching Nigel over the rail, his body splashing awkwardly into the water below. He surfaced, thrashing about and yowling like a cat being tortured.

"Why is he screaming like that?" I asked Berger, turning from the spectacle. "It's a short swim; even a poor swimmer could make it with little problem."

He chuckled. "Mr. Petrie, nearly all these scurvy sots be poor swimmers. Most can't swim a lick, even to save their lives."

"What!" I cried, drawing glances from those around me. Lowering my voice, I said, "But they're all veteran sailors! How can they not know how to swim?"

"Just because one crews a ship not be meaning one can swim, lad." Boy, was he destroying my preconceived childhood notions about pirates.

"So, you don't swim with daggers in your mouths, attacking unsuspecting ships at night?"

"Neptune's blood, no!" he guffawed. "Wherever did you get a notion like that?"

"From movies and tele…never mind. Still, even with dog-paddling he should make it."

"Perhaps, lad, but there be more to the swim than meets the eye." Seeing my confusion, he elaborated, "Mr. Petrie, we be dumping our refuse overboard. That be proving mighty tasty to some of the nasty ocean critters be haunting these waters."

Nigel screamed again, more urgently, and I hastened to the rail to see why. He was splashing chaotically fifteen feet from our hull, eyes and mouth open wide in terror. There was a flash of gray from below, and his body was jerked underwater like a fishing bobber. More shadows converged beneath him, striking with shocking speed at his flailing legs. Caribbean or Black Tip Reef sharks, I speculated, maybe a Bull shark or two. The blood from his head was now mixing with blood from his appendages, spreading out across the water's surface in a red slick. I watched spellbound as the swooping shadows danced under and around the terrified sailor, occasionally breaking ranks to race in and bite off a small chunk of his flesh.

No one on *Renegade* showed the slightest compulsion to help him.

Nigel continued to dog-paddle furiously in the direction of the island with the small sharks nipping at his heels. His yowling was enough to curdle my blood; none of the pirates seemed to mind at all. Finally, he pulled his torn, bleeding body up on shore, alternating between shouting vile curses in our direction and slumping his head on the sand.

Craven turned from the rail, a look of fury on his face. "What ye be gawking at, ye scurvy salts? Mark me words, he that ceases toil makes an enemy of me! Back to work, 'efore I scupper the lot of ye!" He stormed forward as sailors scattered to resume their tasks. He threw me a glance as he drew near, about giving me a heart attack. His hair whipped wildly about his face, left eye wide open, and he flashed me a toothy grimace. His gums were black, teeth yellowed or brown. He laughed deeply, the sound dissonant and disturbing.

It was one of the most frightening things I had ever witnessed, shark attack included.

Berger shrugged, turning to attend to other duties. "See, Mr. Petrie? Ye have little to fear from the captain, if ye abide the Articles," he said, irony dripping from his voice.

SIXTEEN

"*It is not that life ashore is distasteful to me. But life at sea is better.*"
—Sir Francis Drake

From the Personal Journal of Roger M. Petrie
Aboard the Renegade
December 4, 1720

After Berger left, I returned to the prow, which was still damp.

Renegade rode low in the water, her main deck only six feet above the ocean surface. Waves and spray would assure the forecastle would remain perpetually wet, meaning my sleeping quarters would likely be cold and damp at sea. Not ideal, but it still beat sleeping below amidst the stink and rancor of the crew.

I was still getting used to the change in atmosphere from *Belvedere* to *Renegade.* Aboard a modern cargo vessel, the smell of oil and machinery permeates everything, and background noise is constant. Aboard *Renegade*, machinery smells were replaced with natural ones—fresh sea air, rich wood of the hull and deck, wet rope and canvas, all competing with the ripe odors of the live animals on board, and the unwashed state of the crew and their clothing.

Several of my former shipmates shuffled toward me, heads down and shoulders slouched. They would never last if they carried themselves that way. Cable, Carmichael, Wolcott, and Reynolds joined me, all peering around tentatively at our new environs.

They looked awful—hollow-eyed, gaunt, defeated.

"Gentlemen, like it or not, this is our new home. We'd all better get used to it, and act accordingly. Skulking around like frightened rabbits is not the way to ingratiate yourselves to Captain Craven." I scanned the deck. "Where are the others?"

Cable replied, "Tom and Riley are aft with that Vogel fellow, and I believe Doc and Samuels are below."

Reynolds stepped close, hissing fearfully, "Did you see what they did to that poor sailor, Captain—"

I quickly clapped my hand over his mouth.

"Listen to me, gentlemen. From now on, do not call me 'Captain', EVER!" I whispered urgently. "I do not command this vessel, and I doubt Captain Craven would appreciate my being addressed as such. Relax, gentlemen. You're all experienced seamen, so let's show these shipmates of ours what we can do."

"But Cap…sir, er, Roger," Cable fumbled, "like Gregg said, did you see what they did? They threw that poor guy to the sharks, while they all laughed! What have we gotten ourselves into?"

"This isn't a cruise ship, Jim," I said. "These are real pirates, and they don't suffer fools. Like Craven told us yesterday, they live hard, and they die hard. Nigel violated the Articles of his own accord and paid the price. From here on out, everyone be quick to listen, slow to talk, and do whatever is asked of you."

"What if I'm asked to throw someone overboard, or shoot someone Craven is angry at?" Reynolds asked, trembling.

"Gregg, we'll deal with situations as they arise," I said. "Now, go get some food, and for crying out loud, carry yourselves like sailors!"

As they glumly departed, a flapping sound caught my attention. Looking up, I saw the Skull and Crossed Swords still flew from the topmast. Was this an actual pirate ship? Piracy had been wiped out in the Caribbean by the early 1800s. If, by chance, we had not traveled backward in time, what was *Renegade* doing here in 2002? They surely could not think they could avoid air patrols in this ship or outrun military vessels. Sailing schooners topped out at ten to fifteen knots, with the average speed being closer to six knots. Even the slowest modern cutter or destroyer could attain twenty-five knots easily, so there was scant hope *Renegade* could escape any pursuer. And she would be seriously outgunned by any US Navy warship, which were armed with powerful radar-guided guns and surface-to-surface missiles.

To port, I was relieved to see *Belvedere*, set far enough away to allow both ships to swing at anchor without crashing into one another. She was a known landmark for me to pin my sanity to; I wondered what would become of her once we left. Even though she was an unremarkable vessel, she had been *my* ship, and the thought of never setting foot on her again filled me with inconsolable sadness. My first command, ending in a hostile takeover by ancient pirates!

Ripley's Believe it or Not had nothing on this situation.

I stood there, uncertain as to what I should be doing. On board a naval vessel, you belonged to a section, and the section chief would call a muster at 0745 and lay out the work for the day. I had no idea who I was to report to, or what was expected of me here. This was a pirate ship, and it was immediately apparent the rhythm of duties was different. No one seemed to be in a hurry to get anything accomplished.

I noted with surprise that most sailors were barefoot. The ships I had crewed were all metal, even their decks, so strolling around sans shoes under a tropical sun was never advisable aboard any one of them. My uncle had served on the carrier *USS Lexington* during the Battle of the Coral Sea in 1942. When I could coax him to talk about the ordeal, he spoke of sailors abandoning the *Lexington* as she sank, taking off their shoes before jumping overboard. He was a strong swimmer so kept his shoes on. The *Lex's* flight deck was made of wood, but the destroyers picking up the survivors had steel decks, and temperature on deck was over a hundred and twenty degrees. Sailors pulled from the sea screamed as their uncovered feet hit the sizzling steel.

Uncle Clyde was thankful he had kept his shoes on. I wondered if I would feel the same after a few months aboard the *Renegade.*

SEVENTEEN

"You can't sail across the ocean if you don't possess the courage to lose sight of the shore."
—Anonymous

Sarasota, FL
Monday, April 1, 2019
14 years, 3 months, 16 days since Reemergence

Happy April Fool's Day to me.

I opened our lanai drapes, letting the rays of the rising sun warm my tired, aching body. I had not gotten much sleep—a headache hammered behind my eyes, and any sleep I had gotten was haunted by dreams of battle and death. I sipped some orange juice as I observed the vista outside. Our community, Palm Pointe, was meticulously landscaped, the green lawns finely manicured. To me, it was a veritable Garden of Eden of lush tropical flora and fauna. I loved it dearly.

Turning from our back windows, I ruminated on Tom's warning. Was he right? Were scholars, historians, or treasure hunters even now piecing together the clues, discovering threads of evidence that would connect us to events long ago? We had been back for over fourteen years, thinking the threat of our secret being revealed waned with each passing year. But if revelation were nigh, what would that do to my family? I was blessed with a gorgeous wife and two terrific children. Plus, we lived in Sarasota, a beautiful city with abundant amenities, world-class beaches only minutes away.

What would the truth of my past being divulged do to all that?

I closed my eyes as the sun's warmth enveloped me. Warmth was a familiar sensation here in tropical latitudes…

Sweat poured down our bodies as the five of us labored through the night, each wielding a shovel, displacing great swatches of sand and soil with every thrust. We were digging at the base of a two-trunked palm, the very place Tom had marked a year earlier, before the Coast Guard whisked us off this island. Each of us carried weapons, and Riley and Wolcott stood guard, in case anyone got too curious.

THUNK! Tom's shovel struck something solid, causing the other four to immediately stop and look. He excitedly cleared off a patch of sand, and I reached in to help him drag the heavy trunk out from the three-foot hole. Brushing it off, Tom unlocked the latch and threw the top open. Inside lay tightly packed leather pouches; he picked one up and untied it, pouring some of the contents into his hand. The coins clinked into his hand, reflecting our flashlight beams with golden brilliance.

"Avast, me hearties!" he crowed. "Looks like our booty remains! No toiling into our twilight years for us!" Doc, Cable, Berger, Riley, Wolcott, and I exchanged satisfied looks, glad we had not come out here to get drenched with sweat for nothing.

Doc smiled broadly; of all of us Belvedere *survivors, he had enjoyed pirating the least.*

"What are you going to do with your share, Doc?" I asked.

"Way back when, you mentioned retiring to Tahiti," he replied. "That sounds pretty good to me right now. What about you?"

I did not answer, for I was still conflicted about the methods we had used to acquire this wealth, and if it was within my rights to spend these ill-gotten gains.

*****

Rebekah padded softly up behind me, interrupting my reverie. She wrapped her arms around my waist, peeking around my right shoulder. She was a green-eyed, brown-haired beauty, possessing an angelic character and a selfless attitude I had never witnessed before, in anyone. We had promised before God and men twelve years ago to honor, cherish, and stand by one another, no matter what. Would she forgive me for keeping my pirate past hidden from her all this time?

"Are you okay, honey? Those must have been some dreams. You haven't rolled around like that in months."

I rubbed my eyes. "Oh, just dreams about an angry ocean. I'm fine now." Even I did not believe that.

"If you say so. By the way, you're taking Riley to work with you today, remember?"

Holy cow, I had not. She was supposed to job-shadow with me today for a school project. In my exhausted state, I would be wonderful company.

"Of course, I remember, honey! I'm probably looking forward to it more than she is."

"Riiiiight," she said, turning to get dressed.

I followed her to our spacious master bath. Rebekah was prettying herself in front of one of our vanities, though she did not need to, in my opinion. I studied my own reflection in the mirror; my dark brown hair was thinning and graying, hairline receding somewhat. I kept it short, but there was a time when it had grown rangy and long. That was long ago; these days, my body was considerably paler and flabbier than it had been in my sailing days.

After we dressed, we sat down to breakfast at a glass-topped table in the lanai. We loved sitting out there; the glass doors rolled back to form a screened-in porch. Palm Pointe was set in a secluded section of Four Palms Country Club, five miles east of the Sarasota airport. Our villa backed up against one of the community's many lakes, which I appreciated because the bass fishing was spectacular. As we dined, a sand hill crane poked around outside, shrieking its peculiar call, and I could see the lake's resident alligator sunning himself on the opposite shore.

"Ready for your big day today, sweetie?" Rebekah asked as Riley joined us. She wore twin braids in her hair, which looked adorable. Fortunately, she got her looks from her mom.

"Yep, she finally gets to see her old man in action!"

Riley made a face at me while picking up a piece of toast.

I chomped on a breakfast bar, noticing several bags piled in the corner. "What's all this stuff?"

"Riley's birthday party is Friday night, remember? That's all the trappings for it."

"No kidding. What's the theme this year?" I asked, as if I did not know.

"PIRATES!" Riley shrieked, nearly bursting my eardrums.

"What a shock. This is my surprised face!" I gaped at her, my eyes and mouth wide open.

"That's gross, Dad," she huffed, stomping off to brush her teeth.

After she left, I regarded Rebekah cynically. "Pirates, seriously? Is that a good idea, given our visit with Mrs. Truitt last month?"

"I know, but it's her day and that's what she wanted."

"I was just wondering why you had to buy new supplies. Isn't Pirates the theme every year?"

"Hahaha, you're hilarious. Make sure you are home in time for the party and leave the details to me."

"It frightens me to do that, but you're the boss." Striking a more somber tone, I added, "I suppose Tom is going to be here."

Ah, Tom, the free-wheeling engineering genius who had moved to Sarasota a year after us. He had bought a swanky condo nearby in another Four Palms community called Palm Isles. Working from home allowed him lots of free time, as did the fact he was still single. He spent a large portion of that time hanging out at our place. Talking with Riley about pirates.

That had not bothered me before, but now he was telling her about what we had actually done back then, which was a problem. We had left that life long ago, and in my mind the past should remain dead and buried. Most pirates were not dashing anti-heroes as portrayed in the media; our crew had been a profane, bloodthirsty bunch.

"Of course, Tom's going to be here," Rebekah said, breaking my train of thought.

"It's just goofy, hon. We ask him to tone things down then invite him to a pirate-themed party. We're practically goading him into doing what we asked him not to. Doesn't make sense to me."

“What do you suggest, Roger? Riley loves that he loves pirates, too. Most of her relatives live far away, and he’s literally around the corner.”

“He lives close so he can torment me,” I fumed.

“Oh, for Pete’s sake! Why are you being so ridiculous?”

“Because he’s doing it on purpose. He could live anywhere in the world, yet he chose to live here, practically in our laps. All because he loved being a stupid pirate…” I stopped, realizing I had said too much.

She regarded me quizzically. “Now why would you say a thing like that?”

“Oh, nothing. I’m burned out on pirates, that’s all.” Looking at my watch, I feigned surprise. “Good grief, we need to get going! Goodbye, my darling, love you!”

“Bye, dear. Love you! And remember what I said about keeping Riley interested today. And fed!” she added with a wink.

“Yes, dear,” I humbly responded as Riley and I climbed into our Ford Edge Titanium.

The drive to my office down Whitworth Ave to Highway 301, took about fifteen minutes. To pass the time, Riley pulled out a notebook and pen. “What exactly do you do, Daddy? I need some background information for my assignment.”

I smiled down at her. “Let’s see, I’m Logistics Director for a transportation company called TransCaribe.” I handed her my business card, so she would have the correct spelling and title. “We move cargo throughout the Caribbean and South America, mostly by ship.” I paused, chuckling as she scribbled like mad. She finished with an emphatic tap of her pen, then looked up, ready for more. “I run the day-to-day activity of the office, and I’m responsible for the overall profits of our station.” Seeing her befuddlement, I said,

"That means I'm responsible for how much money we make, sweetie."

"Oh, I get it. You're in charge of the treasure!" she clapped happily. "Uncle Tom talks a lot about pirate treasure."

"Yes, I'm sure he does," I sighed. "Managing profits isn't exactly like hoarding treasure, but I guess that's close enough for now." She looked pleased, humming the theme of *Pirates of the Caribbean.* I silently cursed books, movies, and television for making piracy look so romantic to her.

Of all people on earth, Tom and I were the only ones who knew how real pirates had lived and behaved. And he embellished the truth for Riley's sake.

A *lot.*

EIGHTEEN

"Give me freedom or give me the rope. For I shall not take the shackles that subjugate the poor to uphold the rich."
—John Goldenwolf (American pirate)

From the Personal Journal of Roger M. Petrie
Aboard the Renegade
December 4, 1720

I straightened myself up because Tom and Vogel were heading my way.

Tom comically towered over the Quartermaster, who was wearing a "uniform" like Berger's. Instead of a vest he wore a short blue jacket, with a brown tricorn hat gracing his head. His stringy blond hair hung freely about his shoulders. Per the crew's reaction to him, he was an important man.

"Ah, Roger, how fares your day?" he said cheerfully, as if he had not participated in Nigel's murder moments ago.

"As well as could be after losing my ship, I suppose." Anger flashed across his features, and I regretted being so flippant. This was not the merchant marine. There, my sarcasm might be met with a one-fingered salute. Here, it might get my throat slit.

A humbler response was called for.

"Begging your pardon, Mr. Vogel. I didn't sleep well at all. I suppose it will take time to get used to my new quarters." I swept my hand toward my makeshift canvas bed.

"Aye, I suppose it will!" he chuckled. "I'm sure you be used to more luxurious accommodations. Perhaps if you ascend to the captaincy, you'll have quarters more in keeping with what you once had."

"Wouldn't that be something," I mused, wisely not adding what I was thinking—*I* was *a ship's captain before you came along, you moron!*

No need to enrage the powers-that-be my first day aboard.

He eyed me up and down. "Your crew be in need of proper freebooting clothes, Mr. Petrie. I'm mystified by your present cloaking." My present ensemble may not pass for proper sailing garb in 1720, but I was comfortable in my cotton button-down shirt, Wrangler jeans, and black Puma low-tops.

"These have served me well over the years."

"Aye, perhaps they sufficed before, but I be doubtful they'd strike fear into any prey we come across."

"Is that our goal, to strike fear into everyone we meet?"

He looked at me like I had lost my mind. "Of course, it is, Petrie! This be a ship of fortune—captains won't lower their flags and heave to if they fear us not! You'll need proper attire to accomplish said goal. When you've proved your loyalty, I'll issue you proper weapons as well."

That was something to look forward to. "So, Mr. Vogel, you are quartermaster of the *Renegade,* is that correct, sir?" I asked.

"Sir? No need to be so bloody formal, Petrie." I guess that was a thing with the officers, not wanting to emulate the hated naval rules of etiquette. It was ironic how they dressed like the very men they purported to hate. "But yes, I am the quartermaster."

"Is it true that the quartermaster is just below the captain in the chain-of-command on pirate ships?"

"'Tis true, Roger. I be second-in-command to Captain Craven, though if he were incapacitated, the crew would vote on his successor. We were elected by them, and they could vote us out, if they so desired."

Recalling Cordingly's book, I recollected many pirate ships operated more democratically than the merchant or military vessels of the day. The captain and top officers were elected positions, and they could be voted out if they failed to deliver enough plunder.

Although I could not imagine anyone trying to impeach Blackbeard.

"It strikes me that our boarding ceremony last night was wholly incomplete," Vogel said. "Would you care to join us for a short tour, Roger?"

"Thank you, Mr. Vogel, I would like that very much."

"Excellent. As for *Renegade*, Captain Craven was given her by his former captain, Calico Jack, after a raid on Vera Cruz. She was new, Jamaican-built, and used as a shallow-water cargo runner by the Spanish. We mount two six-pound cannons fore and aft as chase guns, and three eight-pounders on either side."

We turned to head aft. The main deck teemed with people and material preparing for careening. Large upright barrels holding water and rum were spaced throughout the deck, which men were liberally dipping into, even this early in the morning. There was a steady stream of crewmen bringing stores up from below, causing us to move out of their way frequently. Open lanes through the myriad stacks of crates, boxes, and barrels were carefully kept clear, so that you could run unhindered from one end of the deck to the other without tripping over something.

Other sailors had opened the large lattice doors to the cargo bay shaft, and were hauling large nets up filled with trunks, barrels, and crates from the hold. Thc rigging swarmed with men tightly lashing the sails to their spars, securing lines so they would not be damaged during the careening operation.

Amidst all this gear, chickens, goats, and pigs ran free. The menagerie of sights, sounds, and smells emanating from all this was truly amazing.

We ambled toward the foremast. I gauged it to be eighty feet high, with two sections; one held three spars, to which the foresails were attached, and a smaller section atop which held the topgallant. The mainmast was about twenty feet taller, I reckoned.

Pointing to the main topmast, I asked, “Mr. Vogel, isn’t that the flag of Calico Jack Rackham?”

He shot me a suspicious look. “How in tarnation do you know that, Roger? ’Tis the very one, but I be curious how you acquired that knowledge.”

I spoke quickly to tame his suspicions. “In a book I have about Caribbean pirates, that’s all. It seemed most ships had their own colors.”

“Captain Craven served under Calico Jack, who had a fearsome reputation in these parts. When sailors see the skull and swords, they normally heave to right quick.”

"Makes sense," I said, as we continued walking. "What are these smaller guns on the railing?" I pointed to guns set in iron brackets bolted to the railing on either side. The guns themselves were about two feet long and eight inches in diameter.

"Ah, those be our swivel guns," he expounded. "They can swing through a fairly good-sized arc. Not heavy shot, but effective at close range." *As Tompkins could attest to,* I thought glumly.

Amidships, just forward of the mainmast, I saw the three large, black muzzle-loading cannons I had seen last night, with three others on the opposite side of the ship. They were mounted on sturdy wooden carriages, each one attached to the railing on either side with two-inch hemp ropes wound around block-and-tackle rigs. They were fired by touching a lighted match to touchholes bored in the top of their breeches. A work detail was engaged in disconnecting all that, so the guns could be offloaded.

I compared these ancient cannons to modern breech-loaded naval guns, which were loaded, aimed, and fired electronically. Back in the 1700s, a good gun crew could fire two to three times inside of five minutes. A US Navy 5"/54 gun could fire once every two seconds, while a Phalanx twenty-millimeter close-in weapon fired 4,500 rounds per minute.

I imagined Tom would seek ways to upgrade our firepower.

"You must have been a seafaring man before *Renegade*, Mr. Vogel," I said conversationally. "Did you serve in the Royal Navy?"

"No, I never served with those cursed dredges!" he proclaimed. "I was a privateer, first serving with Charles Vane. Some of our crew is ex-navy, but most served on merchant ships, or are former slaves. As you might think, Roger, freebooting be dangerous work, so we be in constant need of fresh blood to replace those injured or killed. Our crew…we either pick them up in port or from ships we capture." He hoisted his cup and remarked loudly, "These days we serve ourselves. A plague on anyone who serves at His Majesty's bequest!" He took a swig of rum to accentuate his point.

"Who would you pick up in port?" I wondered.

"Sailors that be out of work, lad," he said. "After Queen Anne's War ended, crews recruited to man navy ships and privateers no longer be needed, and all the Letters of Marque were revoked." He stared off, deep in remembrance. "Aye, it had been grand, having free reign to capture enemy vessels and keep a portion of the plunder."

"But that didn't last…" I remarked.

"Indeed, it didn't. When the war ended in 1713, thousands of sailors were discharged. There be no need for a large fleet now that the European powers be great friends, right?" He snorted derisively. "Those sailors flooded the islands, with few good job prospects. Many of us went from privateering to freebooting. We knew nothing else, and we could keep all that we plundered."

"And you're okay with choosing a lifestyle—piracy—where you're automatically branded an outlaw, and where the penalty if you're caught is death?"

Vogel smiled. "Aye, there always be a trade-off, eh? Remember, there were no seafaring jobs to be had, so our choices for making an 'honest' living were slim. Many of us would've been reduced to begging in the streets. No man with pride and a spine could abide that, Roger. Men who work for the merchants be no better than slaves. No, 'tis better to live as free men, loosed from the shackles of aristocrats, bureaucrats, and tyrants. Aye, we know most of us may hang one day, but we'd rather endeavor to enrich ourselves than someone else."

"That sounds a little melodramatic, Mr. Vogel," I opined.

"Does it now, lad? Remember what Roberts said: 'In honest work, the food is bad, the wages are low, and the work is hard. In piracy there's plenty of loot, it's fun and easy, and we are free and powerful. Who, when presented with this choice, would not choose piracy? The worst that can happen is you can be hanged. No, a merry life and a short one shall be my motto.' That be what we aspire to."

Interesting. Changing subjects, I asked, "Do you still insist this is the year 1720?"

"I insist on nothing, lad," he replied. "It is what it is."

"I still don't see how that's possible. Einstein clearly postulated that time travel is impossible."

"Who?" He scratched his head. "Your brother be babbling on about 'time-dilation' and 'quantum gravity' to explain your presence here; truly it be making me head hurt something fierce. I neither understand nor care about such things, for they have no bearing on where me next meal be coming from. All I be knowing is, we be here, and we need to careen quickly and be gone. No man ever got rich laying at anchor!" he roared, punching my shoulder.

Looking out over the guns, I beheld two dark-skinned men paddling a shallow skiff. They were Lonii and E'twan, the Arawak *strikers* I had met previously. The skiff itself was a hollowed-out conifer trunk, with small platforms fore and aft. As we watched, Lonii used his paddle to stop the skiff, then leaned all the way back, distributing his weight. E'twan climbed on the front platform. He was a compact, powerfully built man, a couple of inches over five feet tall. He held a four-foot long spear, front end pointed with a barb, back end tied to the skiff with thin rope.

E'twan stood still as a statue for over three minutes, holding the spear in his right hand, right arm cocked. Lonii was throwing out small pieces of bisket and meat. There was a swirl to E'twan's right, causing him to turn slightly and sling the spear down with incredible speed. Something thrashed in the water, and E'twan pulled the line in, effortlessly flipping a small blacktip shark into the middle of the skiff. Lonii sat up as E'twan jumped down, dispatching the shark with a few deft strokes of his knife. Prize secured, they set out for different spots, taking turns being the spearman.

As Tom, Vogel, and I watched, they filled their skiff with fish over the next hour, with Lonii once jumping overboard to snag a sea turtle. Once done, they paddled back to the other side of the *Renegade*, where a built-in ladder aided them in boarding the ship.

Vogel nodded approvingly at their approach, clapping us both on the back. "There be fine dining tonight, gents!" he crowed.

As I stood there digesting everything I had seen, Vogel slapped my arm, mistaking my thinking for something else. He laughed at my imagined discomfort.

"By the Eternal, from the look on your face I'd swear you'd seen a ghost!" He leaned toward me, his voice low and ominous. "Well, this ain't no ghost ship, nor will you find the captain a mere apparition should ye violate the Articles! You've had your respite, now there's work to be done." Tom gave me a quick thumbs-up as he and Vogel prepared to walk away.

"Aye, sir," I answered, preparing to leave.

"Blimey, Petrie, I told you we're not in the bloody navy, you picaroon!" What on earth was a picaroon? I probably did not want to know. "Report to Mr. Saunders for duty. Our holds are still not empty, and I need you to help get things squared away."

I fumbled with an awful salute, which only made Vogel laugh harder.

*****

I found Saunders, a squat, rotund man, standing by the aft hatchway. He had also recruited Carmichael and Wolcott, so at least I would be working with familiar faces. They handed me breakfast: smoked meat and fish; hardtack, which were square biscuits made of flour, water, and salt that were barely palatable; and a power bar from the *Belvedere*, which was not much of an improvement. There was rum to wash it all down, heavily sugared, and flavored with nutmeg. After eating, our little troupe headed down to the hold of the ship, joined by three *Renegade* sailors. We were tasked with organizing and storing all the equipment and supplies transferred from *Belvedere*. As we traversed the ladders down to deck three, we tried to ignore the stares, gestures, and remarks from the regular crew. It was not easy.

One thing was certain; this ship stank, and I mean bad. I had read that hygiene was not a top priority on pirate vessels, but holy cow! The lack of bathing water and indoor plumbing, combined with the smell of rotting food, animal feces, and vomit, added up to a stench that assaulted my olfactory senses like nothing I had ever experienced. My fellow contemporary mates had similar reactions to the pungent aroma.

Saunders noticed our displeasure at the unhygienic conditions. He crowed, "You'll get used to it, me little bilge rats! It's one of the joys of serving down below!" He was still laughing when we arrived on deck three, which sat above the bilges and was only six feet high. The bilges smelled worse than the second deck. Saunders spurred us on. "Now, forget about your sensitive noses and be getting these supplies up on deck, or you'll be kissing the gunner's daughter!"

We contemporary sailors stared at him, ignorant of what the heck that meant. Saunders growled, "Was that not plain enough? I be meaning we'll lean ye over the cannons and flog some sense into ye, ye scurvy knaves!"

Oh, yeah, pirating was proving to be a real blast.

NINETEEN

"Ahoy, me lads, we welcome ye aboard our mighty ship. Grab a line, hoist up the sails, as we embark upon our trip."
—Pirate ditty

From the Personal Journal of Roger M. Petrie
Aboard the Renegade
December 5, 1720

I was hoping to sleep in today. No such luck.

As the sun peeked above the eastern horizon, a cock crowed right next to my head. After my ears stopped ringing, I lunged, wanting to wring its scrawny neck. The rooster scampered out of harm's way, clucking madly. Sitting up, I threw off my canvas covering and stretched my legs, my head throbbing madly. Hopefully, time would mitigate the pain, but I worried that this would prove to be a permanent symptom of crossing the threshold of the time-space continuum.

My head was not the only part of my body smarting this morning. My arm, leg, and shoulder muscles burned from all the activity in the hold yesterday, moving, lifting, and stacking various storage vessels. I wearily rolled out of my erstwhile bed, clothes damp, feeling grimy and gross. What I would not give for a decent shower! Walking aft, I rubbed my gritty teeth with my finger as I went looking for some breakfast.

My modern contemporaries were already up. They were huddled around a barrel of water as Samuels parceled out smoked fish and hardtack to each. I joined the group, gratefully accepting my portion from Matt. The barrel water was still clean, so we dipped Black Jacks into it to slake our thirst.

Vogel walked up, slapping me on the back as he addressed our gathering.

"Top 'o the morning, gents! How is everyone feeling today?"

I wondered if he was joking because we all looked like death warmed over. "A little on the sore side, Mr. Vogel, but we'll survive," I said as jovially as I could.

He laughed. "Well, I'm afraid that will get a tad worse before it gets better, lads." We exchanged worried glances. "Yesterday's labor served to ready the ship for careening today."

"What does careening entail, Mr. Vogel?" I asked for the group.

"Ah, it be an onerous but necessary task, Roger, to keep *Renegade's* hull in good repair, and perform vital maintenance."

He went on to explain the process. Any hope I had about getting some rest today was thoroughly dashed. I was not familiar with this process—modern ships put into dry dock, and any maintenance was done by contractors—but from Vogel's explanation, it was going to be time-consuming and labor-intensive. Pirates did not have access to proper port facilities, so careening was done on out-of-the-way beaches. I sighed, swallowing my food without tasting it, steeling myself for the physical exertion that was sure to come.

After breakfast, we finished unloading the *Renegade*. Lighter material was piled into longboats and rowed ashore. Heavier items were palletized and winched over to *Belvedere's* deck with the jib crane. I hated to think how hard careening would have been without *Belvedere's* modern cargo-handling implements.

Next, Craven beached *Renegade* at low tide, using thick ropes and pulleys to pull her onto shore. We affixed a halyard from the mainmast around a large palm trunk and pulled her over onto her side. Once done, we commenced with cleaning and repairing her hull. Some of us scraped off barnacles and other sea junk that were attached, while others repaired spots of dry rot and damage caused by Teredo worms, which burrowed into wood and caused it to weaken. Inside, other crewmen re-caulked the keel and repaired damaged portions of wood. Still others worked at repairing and mending rigging and canvas. We pulled her over first on her starboard side and then her port, working as fast as we could.

It was hot, tiring work. Craven wanted to be underway the next day, so he drove us mercilessly to complete the work. According to Berger, Bahamian waters had become decidedly less pirate-friendly ever since Woodes Rogers became Governor in 1718. Rogers had offered pardons to anyone who disavowed piracy, but he also hired pirate hunters to aid the Royal Navy in capturing anyone who refused his pardon. The longer we sat here, the greater the chances we would be spotted and attacked. *Renegade* might be a formidable opponent on the open ocean but sitting on the beach she was helpless and vulnerable.

For the regular pirates, this careen was proving to be much different than previous ones, thanks to Tom's ingenuity and the advent of power tools. We ran power cables from *Belvedere* over to *Renegade,* using our diesel generator for electricity. The tools were a source of fear to *Renegade's* crew, who at first likened them to a witch's wand. They gradually gained a healthy respect for them, and as the day progressed it was not uncommon to hear Master Carpenter Tolliver exclaim, "Why, what I won't be able to do with this _____!" naming whatever tool Tom, Riley, or Wolcott was training him on.

For the hull, Tom devised a more effective coating than the pitch normally used. It consisted of various chemicals poached from *Belvedere*, combined with copper. His team first caulked *Renegade's* keel with advanced silicone, then coated it inside and out with this elixir. Tom explained to Craven that, with regular applications, the hull should stop leaking. It would also resist adhesion of barnacles and other ocean detritus, making the ship faster. In theory.

Tom envisaged other improvements as well, but Craven wanted to forestall those for now. I suspect he was waiting to see if the first batch of renovations proved viable or not. Tom's credibility, and likely his life, depended on the results. Thus, I was praying that the elixir congealing on *Renegade's* keel proved astoundingly successful.

As I helped lash a longboat into our rigging, Berger walked by. I waved him over, wanting to speak with him again.

"Mr. Berger, why the urgency to be underway? We still have a lot of work to do, by the looks of it."

He scratched his chin, saying, "Ah, Captain Craven has good cause to be vexed, Mr. Petrie. Two weeks past we be informed new Royal Navy ships be showing up in Port Royal. Some scurvy admiral named Sir Alec Brannigan be purposing to stamp out piracy all by himself, and his efforts already be meeting with some success. He be capturing freebooters all around Jamaica and Hispaniola. Word is he transports the poor sots back to Port Royal, to be tried in Admiralty Court. Soon after, the lot of 'em be swinging at Gallows Point. The captain wants to be afloat so as not to be caught as Rackham was." He quickly left to attend to other duties.

As time in this bay wore on, the crew became more anxious. Tempers flared, and several fights almost broke out below decks. The whole crew was on edge, and there was not much to be done about it. Music and singing did little to lighten the mood, and the copious amounts of rum consumed served only to make men surly. As Berger put it, "There's nothing like the demon rum to be bringing out the devil in a man."

We needed to be gone from this place. Hopefully, come morning we would be ready to set sail and resume normal shipboard operations.

Hopefully.

*****

Dawn brought with it hope, as repairs and resupply were almost complete. We had refurbished the cargo hold, incorporating heavy-duty racking, strapping, and storage containers cannibalized from *Belvedere*, keeping Khamisi busy integrating these modern implements. We now could carry twice the cargo than before, and that cargo would be secure and less likely to shift at sea. This also provided a greater ability to keep perishable items fresh and safe from vermin.

Carpenters cut a boom and gaff from island conifers and rigged the foremast like the mainmast, changing the rigging style from brigantine to fore-and-aft. With this style we would be swifter, especially in littoral waters. Tom replaced some of the rope lines with metal cables, rigging the two masts and bowsprit with cabling connected to manual winches, so that the sails could be drawn tight or loosened from four stations, weaving in twenty-first-century technology wherever he could. Craven was impressed with that bit of engineering.

I grudgingly assisted in this work, wary about aiding and abetting a piratical enterprise. But since I had bargained for my crew's lives with this new tech, I could not renege on my oath or sabotage the enhancement process without risking all our lives. I had been made aware a small cadre of *Renegade* veterans were not happy to have our help, evidently worried our successes would cause them to lose influence and power. We avoided them whenever possible, but on a small ship it was inevitable we would cross paths eventually.

*****

Later that morning, Tom and I were laboring in the dark confines of the cargo deck, installing cabling for solar-powered fans and lights. Tom's imposing size kept most from challenging him, but a former merchant seaman named Quigley was spoiling for a fight with him, according to Plue. Running cabling forward, we encountered a huddle of sailors pretending to work by the front hatch. As we approached, they turned to face us, Quigley in the middle.

"Behold, it be Thomas and Roger, the mangy whelps who'd depose *Renegade's* rightful crew!" he spat. "Ye'll both rue the day your mother spawned ye!" He drew an evil-looking dagger while two henchmen rushed me and pushed me down. Brandishing the blade in his right hand, a crooked smile on his lips, Quigley advanced, swinging the knife at Tom in great, slashing arcs.

"Come close, ye bloody giant, and I'll free yer evil soul by incision of steel!" he threatened. He made a sudden thrust, but Tom was ready, catching his wrist easily. Tom applied pressure to Quigley's nai-shoko, the nerve cluster on the wrist's underside. He cried out in pain and dropped the knife, which I kicked out of the way, having regained my footing.

One of Quigley's minions came at me, throwing a big, looping right-handed punch at my head. I inverted my right hand, avoiding the punch and catching his forearm. I clamped my left hand on his right elbow, pushing up and twisting his arm painfully. When another man rushed me, I threw him forward, the top of his skull plunging into the second man's solar plexus. They both crashed into the far bulkhead, temporarily out of action.

Meanwhile, Tom cocked his right arm to throw a palm heel punch at Quigley's head, but one of his cronies grabbed it, preventing Tom from pressing his attack. Quigley recovered quickly and moved in like a boxer, holding his fists out in front. Tom grabbed a rafter with his left hand and jumped, lashing out with his left foot in a vicious kick to Quigley's face, causing him to drop in a heap.

Tom landed softly, dropping his right shoulder, which broke the first man's grip on his arm as another sailor approached from the side. He launched a right-handed, open-heeled strike to that man's forehead, snapping his head back and stopping him in his tracks. He dropped to his knees, joining Quigley on the deck. Recoiling swiftly, Tom drove his right elbow back hard against the seaman who had grabbed his arm, shattering his nose. The man flopped back against the bulkhead, holding his face as blood gushed between his fingers.

Tom twisted around, adopting the taekwondo tiger-fighting stance. His movements were easy and smooth, and the other two uninjured sailors in Quigley's clique lost their stomach to fight. Berger came rushing down to see what all the commotion was about. After interrogating us, he herded Quigley and his wounded mates to sick bay, where they received an unpleasant visit from Captain Craven.

After Craven dressed down Quigley and his gang, he called Tom and me to his cabin. When we entered, he was seated behind his desk, smoking a foul-smelling cigar, and writing on a piece of parchment, while Berger lounged in a chair to the side. We stood there for several minutes, wondering what would happen to us.

Finally, Craven set his quill pen down, looking at us through half-lidded eyes. "Gents," he began, "though ye be new to me crew, I cannot hold ye inviolate to the Articles of the Ship to which ye both be signatories." He paused, and memories of Nigel's fate played unpleasantly through my mind. "Fighting be strictly forbidden on board me ship, and if any curmudgeons insist, they are to be put ashore, to be concluding their hostilities in a duel." He stroked his beard while Tom and I glanced at each other.

"But given the conspiratorial nature of said attack on your persons and given that ye dispatched your assailants forthwith and with rapidity, I be of a mind to overlook your offense—this time—and absolve ye of guilt therein."

We inwardly heaved sighs of relief, because neither of us were experienced in facing a desperate, hostile enemy in a duel to the death. But we were concerned what would happen when these men recovered from their beating.

Craven brushed our concerns aside. "Don't be worrying about tangling with the likes of Quigley and his scabrous friends again. I have rendered me judgment, and they'll be marooned on yonder cay once we sail. Ye shan't be laying eyes on them again." He dismissed us with a wave. "On your way, gents, and be mindful of the Articles, be that plain enough?"

We agreed, turning to leave, but before I exited, Berger caught my eye, giving a slight approving tilt of his head. I could not know for certain, but we might have made an important ally on board this ship full of men accustomed to hard, violent living.

TWENTY

If I don't kill a man every now and then, they forget who I am.
—Blackbeard

Sarasota, FL
Monday, April 1, 2019
14 years, 3 months, 16 days since Reemergence

TransCaribe was located north of the Sarasota airport, occupying the first floor of a multi-story building off 301. We turned into the parking lot and slipped into an open parking space.

Our front door was electronically locked, so I swiped my employee ID, pulling the door open when the access pad winked green. The expansive lobby was impressive: nautically themed, with oversized couches and chairs spaced throughout. There were also the prerequisite framed photos of people accomplishing incredible feats, with titles like Attitude, Teamwork, and Excellence.

Valerie, our effervescent receptionist, smiled radiantly as we walked in. “Good morning, Mr. Petrie! Who do we have here?”

“Good morning, Valerie. This is my daughter Riley. She’s job-shadowing me for the day.”

“Wonderful! Well, if there’s anything you need, Miss Riley, you just ask me!”

We turned right, into the ‘Bullpen’, a large open area populated by cubicles with four-foot walls and ringed by offices. This was the heart of our operation, where the people who routed and rated the shipments TransCaribe handled worked. As a Director, I was granted a corner office, with wide windows overlooking both the bullpen and a pond behind our building.

I proudly introduced Riley to my staff, who were impressed with her poise. Afterward, she roamed around, gawking at display cases built into the walls and bookcases. These featured detailed replicas of different types of cargo ships, each three to five feet in length. She stopped to examine each display as we headed to my office, cooing in admiration.

“Daddy, do you have any models of pirate ships?”

Oh, no! my mind screamed. Import Specialist Miles Roland loved pirates, too, and his work area was just down the aisle from my office. His sense of humor was exasperating, and he was sure to use Riley’s love of pirates to tweak me.

I tried to avoid his cubicle, failed. “Hi, Riley, I’m Miles,” he called to her. She shook his hand tentatively. “Did I hear that you like pirates?”

“Oh my gosh, yes!” she exclaimed. She covered her mouth with both hands in embarrassment, but Miles merely laughed.

“Don’t be embarrassed, Riley, everyone loves pirates!” He cast a spurious glance at me, “Well, almost everyone.” She giggled, eyes squinting in merriment. "Say, do you know what I have here in my office?"

"What is it?" Riley asked in wonder as he produced a ship-in-the-bottle about eighteen inches long, setting it on his bookshelf.

"That, matey, is a model of Blackbeard's fearsome flagship, *Queen Anne's Revenge*! Have ye heard of her?" he drawled, in the worst pirate voice *ever*.

"Yes, I read about it at Pirate Golf! His real name was Edward Teach, right?" People were poking their heads up to see what was going on, all caught up in the hoopla.

Does anyone work around here?

"Arrgh, that's right, matey! And with forty guns, what a fearsome ship she was!" He paused for effect, then said, "Didya know that Blackbeard once blockaded the entire city of Charles Town until they paid him a ransom?"

That was true, but the city ended up giving him medical supplies and not much else.

"He did?" Riley said, her eyes wide as cup saucers.

"Aye, that he did! He was a bold one, Captain Blackbeard!" Miles leaned even closer to the enthralled Riley. "Rumor has it when ships saw *Queen Anne's Revenge* approaching, the crews cried for their mommies!"

That might also have been true. The more feared a pirate captain was, the more likely their intended victims were to surrender without firing a shot. Blackbeard's reputation spoke for itself.

"Have you seen the *Pirates of the Caribbean* movies, Mr. Roland?" she asked excitedly.

He gave her a pitifully sad look. "No, I wasn't allowed to see them."

"Really? Why not?"

"Because my mom never let me see movies that were rated *arrgh*!" Riley howled, and the rest of the office laughed along with her.

"My Uncle Tom says that he and my dad were pirates once," she proclaimed proudly.

"You don't say?" He gave me a sly glance. "Your dad was a pirate? He doesn't seem the type." I started to interject but he kept steaming along. "Hmm, Roger Petrie, a pirate…" Riley was biting her lip to keep from laughing. "He does limp from time to time, doesn't he?" She nodded. "Most likely that's due to extreme old age, but it *could* be due to some terrible battle fought on a pirate ship."

That was true, too, but he could not possibly know that.

He kept pressing. "Does he have a peg leg? And where does he keep his parrot?"

Riley covered her mouth with her hands, her shoulders shaking with mirth. Miles was enjoying himself, going on to tell her fables of Black Bart and Sam Bellamy and all the incredible things they accomplished. "You know, Riley, one of the stars of *Curse of the Black Pearl* said that pirates were the rock stars of the eighteenth century."

That was *not* true, unless you could be hanged for being a member of Aerosmith, KISS, or the Stones. Or even associating with them.

"Don't listen to him, Riley. Being a real pirate was nothing like that at all," I asserted, to no avail.

Corinne, one of my Customer Service reps, shot me a disapproving look. "Roger, why do you have to be such a wet blanket? Let the girl make up her own mind what she wants to believe." She regarded Riley warmly. "Don't listen to him, dear. He hasn't been anywhere to know about these things, anyway."

"Never been anywhere? I was in the Navy and Merchant Marine for ten years!" I protested vigorously.

"Well, whoop-di-do!" Jacklyn, another CSR, exclaimed, followed by whoops of glee from my fellow associates, to my embarrassment.

I walked up to the edge of Miles' cubicle. "Say, do you know what next week is, Miles? No? It's Performance Appraisal week. I wonder how yours is going to turn out?"

"Ahem!" came a throat-clearing cough. We all turned, and there stood our boss, Branch Manager David Fuentes. He was scowling, hands on his hips. "While I appreciate good spirits as much as the next person, it's my understanding that this is a place of business, right?" We all nodded wordlessly. "Then shall we attend to such business?"

"Yes, sir," everyone mumbled, turning back to their work. He gave the bullpen a last, satisfied look, including some sort of half-smile, half-grimace to Riley, then headed back to his office.

"Wow," Riley whispered to me as we entered my office. She sat in an armchair, while I walked around to my chair.

"What, sweetie?" I said as I shuffled papers around.

"That must have been what it was like to work for Blackbeard, being scolded when you weren't doing your work! That was so scary!" I marveled at her ability to turn even an episode of office discipline into something about pirates.

"Well, Mr. Fuentes is pretty strict, but he wouldn't shoot us for dereliction of duty like Blackbeard would." Riley's face fell, and I regretted saying that. Tom constantly berated me for being too pragmatic, but I did not want her to idolize pirates. Tom went so overboard in romanticizing pirate life that I felt compelled to counterbalance his influence. We *had* known *real* pirates, and their behavior should not be idolized by anyone.

Sighing, I opened a file on my desk and got to work. "Sweetie, Daddy has to do some work now." I knew she had brought a couple of books to occupy herself when I was busy. "You can listen if it will help with your school assignment. Otherwise, can you read for a bit? All the fun we were having earlier put me behind on some things."

She smiled. "Yes, Daddy, I'll try not to bother you."

Later in the day, my phone rang, interrupting us for the umpteenth time. As I spoke to my client, I noticed her staring wistfully at the model of the *Queen Anne's Revenge* resting on Miles' shelf. What must she be imagining?

Good thing she had never met Blackbeard in real life, because a lot of her fantasies would have been shattered. He was as brutal as they came, even more so than Benjamin Craven had been. Most pirate captains were nasty, cruel men, and woe to anyone who fell into their clutches.

If you only knew, my sweet, innocent child! I thought to myself. *If you only knew...*

TWENTY-ONE

"I am a free prince, and I have as much authority to make war on the whole world, as he who has a hundred sail of ships at sea."
—Black Sam Bellamy

From the Personal Journal of Roger M. Petrie
Aboard the Renegade
December 6, 1720

Finally, careening operations were over.

We unfastened the various lines and halyards, returning *Renegade* to an even keel. As the tide came in, her hull creaked and cracked, and finally she began to float. Tom and I supervised using the *Belvedere's* jib crane to haul her into deeper water. Next came reloading her with everything we had removed, a long, arduous task even using modern cargo loading gear. As pallets of equipment and supplies were set on Renegade's deck, a chain gang of sailors unloaded them, either stacking and lashing various crates on deck, or lowering them to the cargo hold. Tom stayed on deck, and I went below to help secure what was being loaded. By noon I was utterly exhausted, but I still laid my back into the work.

*****

Going below, I ran into Tom on the cargo deck. We both had bandanas about our faces, to filter out the smell. We had pumped the bilges clean during the careen, but it still stank to high heaven.

Making sure we were alone, I grabbed his arm firmly, causing him to swing around in surprise.

"Why are you trying so hard to help Captain Craven?" I hissed.

"Because the better I make him look, the more secure my position—OUR position—in the crew is. The real question is, why aren't you?" he rasped, removing my hand from his arm.

"Because he's a frigging pirate, that's why!"

"For real? I hadn't noticed. And keep your voice down, you fool!" We looked around to make double-sure there were no eavesdroppers. "What do you suggest we do, Roger? It's the year 1720, man, and I don't see a lot of options—"

"We only have their word for that, Tom. This could all be a big hoax."

"A big hoax, you say," he replied skeptically. "To what purpose?"

"I don't know, selling our cargo on the black market, or maybe they plan to sell *Belvedere* for scrap."

"I hardly think so," he scoffed. "Our cargo is specialized and wouldn't fetch more than salvage, and neither would *Belvedere* herself. I highly doubt this is a heist."

"Do you have any better ideas?"

"Just what I said, bro. I evaluated the situation and reached the most logical conclusion," he reasoned.

"And that conclusion is…?"

"It's the 1720s, Roger."

"What evidence do you have to back that up?"

He sighed, leaning against a bulkhead. "We're positioned close to heavy trade routes, right? So, where's the traffic? Where are the oil tankers out of Mexico and Venezuela? Where are the container ships and bulk carriers? We haven't seen one plane or patrol craft, which is crazy because drug runners use these backwater passages all the time." He poked me in the shoulder to emphasize his point. "We never raised anyone on the radio or SatPhone, did we? And the GPS went dead, almost as if the entire satellite constellation was missing."

I exhaled, frustrated. I had come to the same, mind-numbing conclusion myself, but I was holding out slim hope that this was all a giant hoax or bad dream.

"Tom, I *know* there's no logical explanation for all this. We'll find one, eventually. But for now, all I know is we should be focusing on finding a way to get off this ship."

"Get off this ship?" he asked incredulously. "And then what, Roger? Apply for asylum at the nearest US Embassy? Flag down the Coast Guard? Fix the *Belvedere* and motor away? None of those scenarios is remotely possible. Or, maybe we could lead a mutiny so we can become the 'really nice' pirate gang?"

I pounced on that. "'Maybe' is right! Don't forget, we've stashed away the AR-15 and two pistols. Given the *right* scenario, we could overpower Craven's minions and commandeer the *Renegade.* I don't think they could withstand that kind of firepower."

"And then what?"

"Then we sail to a British port, offload these ruffians, and make a new life for ourselves."

He frowned. "Your knowledge of Caribbean history could use some updating."

"What are you talking about?"

"For starters, do you know how to captain a sailing ship? A brigantine schooner like this one has over one thousand rope lines in its rigging. Do you know what they're all for, or how to use them to your advantage? Do you know how to trim the sails, so we make headway oblique or perpendicular to the wind? Without capsizing, or stopping? Do you know how to maneuver a ship like this in an engagement with another ship? You were a fine captain of a diesel-powered ship, Roger, but that doesn't necessarily translate to a wind-powered craft."

"Point taken," I conceded. "What else?"

"Secondly, you're banking on us getting the drop on sixty-plus hardened pirates who are used to fighting and killing. We aren't, and if we made even one mistake, we'd suffer the same fate as Nigel." He held up his hand as I started to protest. "These guys are deadly serious, Roger. We signed the ship's Articles, but they wouldn't hesitate to slit our throats if the situation warranted."

He was raining buckets on my parade. "Okay, that's true, too—"

"Third, we can't simply sail into port with a pirate ship and walk off unscathed. We'd be arrested right along with Craven's bunch, and we'd have to prove we were forced into piracy before an Admiralty Court. If the judge had any doubts whatsoever, we'd hang as pirates alongside the real ones. And even if we escaped judgment, what exactly would we do to carve out a life here, in this time? Where could we go? We know next-to-nothing about life in this era, what the protocols are." He shook his head emphatically. "We're stuck here, Roger. We can't leave *Renegade*, for we've no place to go. We have to survive with what we have here."

"What we have here?" I asked, bitterness creeping into my voice.

"Yes. It may not be our first choice, but *Renegade* is our home for now, until we figure out how to get back to our time." He placed a hand on my shoulder. "And you need to watch yourself, Roger. They've already attacked us once, and there's scuttlebutt about your 'insolence' and 'intransigent attitude.' Ship discipline is different for pirates. You don't get defrocked or called to Captain's Mast out here, bro, you get fed to the sharks."

I was deflated, because Tom was right, on all counts. "I suppose I'll have to accept the fact that we're not getting out of here anytime soon."

"Please do. I don't want to lose any more *Belvedere* crewmen."

"I wish you weren't enjoying yourself so much, although I always suspected you were a scallywag at heart," I said half-jokingly.

"Hey, can I help it if I'm a mechanical genius? And you have to admit it's been fun incorporating our technology onto the *Renegade*." He hesitated, and then went on. "And what little kid hasn't dreamed about being a pirate? You and I are getting to live that out! I mean, could we ever be any cooler than we are now?"

"We haven't exactly done anything pirate-y, yet, Tom," I retorted, "and I haven't forgotten about Smythe and Tompkins, either. What happened to them wasn't cool at all. And are you ready to use force to subdue a ship's crew if they resist? Are you ready and willing to hack someone to death, or shoot them, in the name of piracy?"

He chewed on that for a second before responding. "Hey, we'll figure something out to mitigate the situation. We always do, right?" Dang his eternal optimism! He turned to leave. "Sorry to run out on you, but I need more cabling. It looks like we're going to be stuck here, so I'm going to make things as comfortable as I can. If it helps get us in Craven's good graces, well, that's icing on the cake." He chucked me on the arm. "As for enjoying what I'm doing, doesn't that old song say something about loving the one you're with?'"

I shook my head in dismay as he disappeared up the stairs, laughing and singing to himself.

*****

With careening complete, tensions aboard had noticeably eased. *Renegade* swung at anchor, waiting patiently to be released back to the sea.

Captain Craven was *not* waiting patiently, nor did he cease pacing the deck, casting worried glances both shoreward and seaward as he patrolled the weather deck. Occasionally, he would pull out his spyglass, sweeping the ocean from horizon to horizon, cursing under his breath.

While he was roaming around like a caged animal, we hurriedly tied up the stores—barrels of fresh water, coconuts, and fruit from the island—and salted away the fish caught in the bay, including both butchered and live sea turtles. At least there would be fresh meat and eggs to start our voyage, and *Renegade* was still home to a posse of live pigs, goats, and chickens. Those should last far longer than normal, thanks to the new food preservation systems Tom had engineered.

We were almost ready to set sail.

"Arrgh, just what we need!" Craven exclaimed, shutting his spyglass in disgust. "It's that cursed Jonathan Barnet and his band of pirate-hunting brigands! He be fresh off capturing Calico Jack, and now the scurvy scoundrel be looking to see me dancing with Jack Ketch!" He gestured towards a far-off ship. "That be his flagship, the *Falklands*!" He twirled around, his wrathful eye falling on bosun Patrick Carney. "Mr. Carney, what be the status of our shore parties?"

"All boats are aboard, Captain, but there still be men aboard the metal monster beside us."

"Blimey, that's no good!" he blurted out. "Mr. Vogel, get those swabs on board quickly now, or we'll leave 'em behind! We must raise anchor!"

"Aye, Captain," came the terse reply, and Vogel immediately dispatched two seamen to head over to *Belvedere* to gather the men still collecting supplies and materials for transport over to *Renegade*. I doubted Craven would wait long, and Tom was still there.

The incoming warship, a beautiful three-mast frigate, was still miles away, but moving in our direction. Moving at five knots, she would be upon us within the next three hours. With both anchors down and our sails lashed to their booms, a speedy getaway was out of the question.

Craven watched the approaching ship intently, growing more agitated by the minute. He hollered at the bosun, "What course of action would ye suggest, Mr. Carney?"

"I…I…uh, nothing comes to mind, Captain. Our anchors be set, our sails be lashed, our crew be exhausted, and that be a warship under full sail. She outguns us four to one. Begging the captain's pardon, but I think we should put ashore, or hide out in the metal beast beside us."

Craven rolled his eyes, then fixed him with a withering gaze. "And pray tell, Mr. Carney, how long do ye think we can hide from Barnet once he sinks our ship and burns our boats?" Carney shrunk back, mumbling incoherently, and Craven dismissed him with a backhand to the head.

Craven rounded on me and scowled, "Well, Mr. Petrie, any thoughts?"

His request caught me unawares. Honestly, I had zoned out, wondering if I was going to die here. Refocusing my attention, I saw that the Frigate was closing steadily. When she entered the lee of the island, she would lose wind and be forced to slow. The wind would be blowing to the west, directly over us and toward her, which gave me an idea.

Craven might have been thinking the same thing, watching his approaching doom. He turned, but before he uttered a word, I held up my hand. “Captain, I may have something for you.”

“I pray it be more plausible than Mr. Carney’s recommendation,” he growled.

“Aye, it has the benefit of having never been tried,” I answered. “At least not in this century. Have you ever heard of the Corbomite Maneuver?”

He raised an eyebrow at that. “What gibberish be ye speaking of, Petrie?”

“The Corbomite Maneuver. I saw it on an episode of *Star Trek*.”

Craven hesitated, then grabbed my shirt, his breath foul and putrid in my face. “Mr. Petrie, this be no time for foolish talk. Our lives hang in the balance, so we be needing a *sound plan* to be saving our necks from the gallows.” He let the threat sink in. “Now, what in thunder be ye prattling on about?”

I cleared my throat. “Sorry, Captain, but given our dire predicament, this might save all our necks.”

He frowned, but ultimately spread his hands in a helpless gesture. “Corbomite Maneuver, indeed,” he grunted. “What do ye require of me?”

“Okay!” I was enthused, as happy my head was still attached to my body as I was that Craven endorsed my idea. “Captain, here’s how it’s going to work…

TWENTY-TWO

"The average man will bristle if you say his father was dishonest, but he will brag a little if he discovers that his great-grandfather was a pirate."
—Anonymous

Sarasota, FL
Monday, April 1, 2019
14 years, 3 months, 16 days since Reemergence

My workday mercifully came to an end, meaning I would finally be free from Miles' influence.

Riley and I exited TransCaribe, climbing into the Edge. I was exhausted, but she was still energized from all she had learned from Miles. He had built Blackbeard up into some sort of heroic figure who fought for the common folk against the excesses of the British

Empire. But I knew he was the man who reputedly said, "Sometimes I need to kill someone, so they don't forget who I am."

Not a quintessential role model for young girls.

We pulled into our driveway, followed immediately by Tom. He was driving a sleek new Audi Q5 SUV, a stylish crossover painted a beautiful metallic blue. Riley squealed in excitement, jumping out and running to embrace him. He swung her around as she yelped in delight

"How's my favorite niece?" he teased.

"Great, now that you're here!" she whooped. "Uncle Tom, you're coming to my birthday party this Friday, aren't you?"

"Sure, I am! That is, if I'm invited. I haven't received a formal invitation yet." He smirked as she shot me a disapproving look.

"You have to come, Uncle Tom! My friends are all going to be there, and they want to hear pirate stories!" She flashed him her sad puppy-dog eyes for emphasis.

"They do, eh? How can I say no to you, Riley? You have me heart wrapped around your little finger."

She shrieked in delight. "Yay! I'm going to tell Mom!" She galloped through the garage into the kitchen, almost tearing the back door off in her excitement.

Tom and I walked up the driveway, heading for the villa's back door. "Pretty nice ride, Tom," I pointed out. "How many doubloons did you sell to pay for it?"

"You are so last year, bro. I told you I liquidated almost all my coins and jewelry years ago."

"I know, but I looked into that. There weren't records of valuable coin dumpage that I could find."

"I was very discreet, selling them in small lots to various dealers around the country. I've got a few baubles lying around, but most of my holdings are in mutual funds and CDs." He stopped and studied me for a minute. "Don't tell me you never cashed yours in?"

"Well, I haven't, you know—"

He clipped me on the shoulder. "Geez, didn't Dad teach you anything about personal finance? Are they still collecting dust in your storage units?"

"That's none of your business, Tom!" I blurted out, louder than I intended.

"What was that, honey?" Rebekah called from the kitchen. That is all I needed, for her to overhear our conversation.

"We'll finish this later!" I hissed, entering our villa.

*****

Supper was delicious: pan-seared chops, green bean casserole, parmesan potatoes, and a spinach salad. I was happy the subject of pirates was not broached, because today's events had put me in a foul mood.

My happiness was short-lived, however, because after dinner Tom pulled out a snap-together model pirate ship for him, Riley, and Drake to build. As he laid out the pieces to start construction, he grinned impishly.

"Guys, know what this ship reminds me of? *Renegade,* the ship your dad and I served on years ago. Although she had cleaner lines and a narrower beam than this ship," he explained, checking out the picture on the box. "Ah, it brings back such great memories."

As she was fitting two pieces of the ship's hull together, Riley asked, "Uncle Tom, what was it like on board the *Renegade*?"

His face lit up as he answered her. "Ah, Riley, she was such a beautiful ship. She was built of wood, so rich and dark. Oh, we spent many a day polishing her decks and railings, I'll tell you!" He stared off into the distance, speaking wistfully of the past. "She was swift as a dolphin, deadly as a shark, and nimble as a seal lion. When under full sail there wasn't a ship that could catch her, though many tried. And no ship could outrun or escape her, either. Right, Roger?"

As my mouth was full of sugar-free chocolate cake, I mumbled something unrecognizable as English and continued eating.

"Tell me more, Uncle Tom!" Riley yelped, face flushed in anticipation. Rebekah was not looking so excited, watching him with concern.

"Aye, she was unlike any other sailing vessel in the world. Through the quick thinking of your father, we transferred many of our creature comforts from our poor old cargo ship to the *Renegade*. We had electric lights, ventilation fans, and better bathroom facilities!" he roared. "When we first boarded, the bathroom situation was positively medieval. We fixed that right quick."

"Eww, gross!" both kids said in unison, prompting all of us to laugh, even Rebekah, though she quickly resumed her worried demeanor.

But Tom barreled on. "Most of the time, it was an incredible experience. There were times it was so tranquil, so beautiful, especially sailing on a moonless, starry night. We had good food and good music. There was always someone plucking a guitar or fiddle, though I couldn't repeat most of the songs they sang."

"Why not, Uncle Tom?" Riley asked.

He laughed. "Aye, they'd make your innocent ears burn, that's why! Most of the ditties the crew sang were not fit for children." He leaned back, stretching. "Anyway, we danced, we practiced sword fighting, and we played all sorts of games. Aye, it was a bonny life, it was."

Evidently, you could not tell a pirate tale without talking like one.

"Will I ever be able to sail on a real pirate ship like the *Renegade*?" Riley asked hopefully.

"I wish that you could, but I'm afraid that won't ever happen," he answered.

I snorted involuntarily. That would not have happened back then, either. Seafaring men were a superstitious lot, would never have let women on board. Boys as young as ten had served as cabin boys and powder monkeys, but women—non-passengers, anyway—generally were not allowed on ships. I shuddered to think of the fate of a pretty, naïve young girl like Riley amongst the *Renegade's* band of rogues. I had dealt with enough trouble from Khamisi and Bartlett on that score.

"Why can't I?" she whined.

"Because, my darling niece, pirate ships like *Renegade* don't exist anymore. Nowadays, pirates use motorboats and things like that. The romantic days of pirating aboard wooden sailing ships are long gone."

Drake was assembling the mainmast, and as he concentrated on that he quipped, "Well, if there aren't any more pirate ships, how did you get on the *Renegade*?"

Rebekah leaned forward, hands folded in front, smiling sweetly. "Yes, Tom, I would very much like to hear how you and my husband came to live aboard an ancient pirate ship."

Tom did not miss a beat. "Well, it's pretty technical, especially for the kids."

"I'm a college-educated woman, so try me," Rebekah responded.

"Okay, you asked for it." I did not know what he was going to say, but knowing him, it was sure to be a doozy. "Near as I can tell, Roger and I were involved in a time-space dilation event caused by a momentary flux in the earth's magnetic and gravitational fields, resulting in a quantum gravity compression that transported us back in time. Two years later, we encountered similar conditions, which brought us back to our time again." He proceeded to casually munch on a cookie, like he had given us his grocery list.

"Sounds good to me," Drake stated matter-of-factly, reaching for a cookie himself.

"I think I saw something like that on a Dr. Who episode!" Riley said, giving him an approving thumbs-up. When Rebekah looked skeptical, Riley huffed, "Mom, it's how the Doctor moves the Tardis through time. Everyone knows that."

Rebekah stared at Tom, ignoring the Dr. Who tangent. I guessed she was trying to decide if he was joking, serious, or losing his mind, or a combination of the three. I did not know what happened, how it happened, or why it happened. I was forced to deal with what was and leave the technical explanations to God. I wished that she would, too, but I knew her too well. She would not leave this alone until she got to the bottom of why Tom said what he did.

And that scared me to death.

*****

After dessert, the adults retired to the lanai, enjoying a late-night snack. Rebekah was noticeably on edge from our earlier discussion; it would take some deft maneuvering to steer clear of talk about pirates or time-space distortion events.

"You know, when we were younger, I envied your sense of humor," Tom remarked after I made one of my patented smart-alecky comments.

"Really? I always thought it was a curse."

"Why would you think that?" Rebekah asked.

"Because it took more to impress girls, that's why. Ladies' magazines put 'sense of humor' as one of the top trait's girls looked for in a guy. They forgot to mention the ancillary requirements, which are a fat wallet and cool car."

"That is such a crock, Roger!" Tom chuckled. "You didn't have the right kinds of moves like I did."

"Yeah, you were a regular Casanova," I scoffed. "But I can prove my thesis."

"Enlighten us," Tom challenged.

"Okay," I began, "there were four standard guys in high school, right? Smart Guy, Strong Guy, Good-Looking Guy, and Funny Guy."

"If you say so."

"You know so. Here's the scenario: technicians are working in the control room of a nuclear reactor. Suddenly, alarms go off, and the control board blinks red. Everybody panics. But then…in walks Strong Guy.

" 'Hi, I'm Strong Guy. How can I help?'

'Help us, Strong Guy! The coolant pumps have failed, and we can't turn the manual override valve! If we don't restore coolant flow, the reactor core will melt down and we'll be doomed!'

'I'll take care of it.' He descends into the bowels of the reactor, turns the valve, coolant starts flowing, and the world is saved from disaster. 'Oh, thank you, Strong Guy! You've saved the world!' "

Tom looks skeptical, so I push on. "Okay, same scenario. In walks Smart Guy.

'Hi, I'm Smart Guy, how can I help?'

'Help us, Smart Guy! The coolant system's failed, and the computer won't engage the backup pumps. If it can't be fixed, the reactor core will melt down and we'll be doomed!'

'Where's your master computer?' He goes to the keyboard, starts typing like mad, and soon the alarms stop, and coolant starts flowing again. 'I overrode your firewalls. Everything will be okay.'

'Thank you, Smart Guy, you've saved us all!' Again, the world is saved from disaster."

They both looked dubious, but I forged ahead. "Okay, same scenario; in walks Good-Looking Guy.

'Hi, I'm Good-Looking Guy, how can I help?'

'Help us, Good-Looking Guy! Our coolant pumps have failed, the core is melting down, and the computer override isn't functioning!'

'Gee, sorry folks. I'm not a nuclear scientist, so I'm afraid I can't help you.'

'That's okay, Good-Looking Guy. At least we'll have someone really attractive to look at while we die.' The world wasn't saved, but the technicians didn't mind as much because he was so good looking."

Rebekah covered her face with her hands. "Roger, oh my goodness, this is so ridiculous."

I was ready for that. "Okay, here's the big finale. Same scenario, people are panicking, and in walks Funny Guy.

'Hi, I'm Funny Guy, how can I help?'

'Our core is melting down and none of our emergency procedures are working. What can you do about it?'

'I'm glad you asked. Okay, a Priest, a Rabbi, and a TV Repairman walk into a bar…'

'We're about to die, and you're telling jokes? How inappropriate! Come on, gang, we may be doomed, but we can beat the crap out of Funny Guy to make ourselves feel better.' The world wasn't saved, and Funny Guy suffered serious contusions and broken bones before succumbing to radiation burns. That's why it's a curse to be labeled the Funny Guy." I sat back, satisfied I'd made my point.

Tom said, “Roger, that is without doubt the lamest joke I’ve ever heard.”

“It’s not near as lame as your pirate stories,” I shot back.

“You didn’t think they were so lame when you were living them out, bro,” he retorted smoothly.

Rebekah shot Tom an apprehensive look, then flicked her eyes at me.

“Yeah, about that. As we discussed before, Rebekah and I would appreciate it if you would refrain from storytelling tomorrow night during Riley’s party. We need to limit conversations about pirates for a while.”

Tom pointed to all the pirate paraphernalia Rebekah had laid out. “Clearly, you’re committed to that. Just like last year, and the year before.”

I gave Rebekah a *told-you-so* smirk, which was not well-received. “Yeah, we let her choose the theme, like always, so we’re stuck with it. But we can avoid getting her riled up with ridiculous tales of you and I being actual pirates. Give her your present and leave it at that. That’s all we ask.”

“Ridiculous tales, huh? Well, sometimes truth is stranger than fiction, isn’t it, Roger?” He got up to leave, obviously angry, which was happening more often these days.

After he had driven off, Rebekah and I prepared to call it a night. As we walked, she touched my arm lightly, clearly worried.

“Roger, what did Tom mean by his ‘truth is stranger than fiction’ comment? He acted like you knew what he was talking about.”

“I don’t know. He was mad I told him to cool it with the pirate stuff. Guess this is his way of letting me know.” That did not mollify Rebekah one bit.

*****

After Tom left, Rebekah and I sat on the lanai, windows rolled back, listening to the frogs and insects thrumming.

"Roger, are you ever concerned about Tom's mental well-being?" she asked.

"I worry about his state-of-mind all the time." When she did not laugh, I added, "Come on, Rebekah. You know he tested at genius level. Yes, he's eccentric, but he's not mentally unstable."

"Really?" she declared. "He just spoke about you two living on a pirate ship, like it actually happened. Like he's been doing with Riley. Mrs. Truitt made it plain what's become of that." She paused, frowning. "To top it off, he gave Riley that fake doubloon, and he informed me yesterday he's giving her a pirate cutlass and pistol for her birthday. It's like he's trying to *prove* to her that his stories are true."

"Hmm. I don't see it that way."

That did not please her one bit. "Okay, then what did you think of his explanation as to how you two went back in time? Did that seem normal to you?"

"I was confused, honestly. I always thought we'd used our Flux Capacitor," I quipped, hoping to defuse the argument.

Rebekah crossed her arms tightly, not a good sign. "I don't appreciate your flippancy, but I know this is a tender subject, him being your brother and all. I think we need to keep a close eye on him."

"He's over here all the time, how much closer can we get?" I argued.

She harrumphed but made no reply.

"Roger that," I said, aiming to deep-six this discussion. "Anything else?"

"One more thing," she said, giving me a penetrating look. "Speaking of outlandish pirate fantasies, is there something you want to tell me?"

"About what, hon?" I answered innocently, though my heart was pounding.

"Tom mentioned the name of a pirate ship tonight, the *Renegade*, wasn't it? The exact name you've called out during your recent nightmares. Am I supposed to believe that's a coincidence?"

"I'm sure he's mentioned that name before, Rebekah—it's probably why that stupid ship is running through my head. I'll be so glad when this pirate fixation ends!"

She was not convinced. Still brooding, she got up, heading for bed.

Once there, she went right to sleep. I was envious because sleep eluded me. Plus, Rebekah was highly intelligent. Once she took hold of something, she doggedly pursued it until she got to the bottom of it.

I had a foreboding in my bones this whole pirate thing was about to blow up, and no one would escape the collateral damage.

TWENTY-THREE

"No captain can do very wrong if he places his ship alongside that of the enemy."
—Horatio Nelson

From the Personal Journal of Roger M. Petrie
Aboard the Renegade
December 6, 1720

Craven was not enthralled with my plan.

My credibility, not to mention my life, now rode on the proper execution of an audacious course of action. The first thing I did was coordinate with Tom.

"Tom, we only have a few hours until that warship arrives, and we're all shot or hung. We need to create a diversion that will allow us to escape to the south."

"My, you've changed your tune."

"Evidently self-preservation is overriding my moral outrage for the moment," I snapped. "Now listen up."

"I'm all ears, bro. What did you have in mind?"

"Smoke and mirrors. We need to create a display that will temporarily ward off that frigate, while simultaneously escaping to the south."

"Why don't we tow *Renegade* out with the RIBs? That would be quick and easy."

"No time," I explained. "We're not quite ready to sail, and *Falklands* is approaching on a course that would allow her to turn and block us whichever way we steer. One of the pitfalls of anchoring deep within a horseshoe-shaped cay."

"Ah, a question of geometry."

"Exactly," I affirmed. "She has the advantage, could take the perfect intercept angle to cut us off whichever direction we head. We need to draw her in close, put her in such a disadvantageous position that either way she turns, she can't intercept us. Accomplishing that, we jet out of here using the RIBs. Her pursuit angle would be so poor she couldn't possibly stop us."

"I'm with you," he said.

"There's quite a bit on the *Belvedere* that's flammable or explosive, correct?" I queried.

"Yeah, there's diesel fuel, oil, CO2 and bottled oxygen, things like that," he said.

"Save the fire extinguishers—they'll come in handy on a wooden sailing ship. But we do have motorized lifeboats, oil drums, stuff like that?"

"Sure, but to what purpose? They'll blow us out of the water before we could get close enough with any incendiary devices."

"IF they thought we wanted to make a fight of it. What if we led them to believe we were scuttling both ships to avoid capture? Barnet would want to come close to make sure, right? If we can get him to turn *Falklands* into the wind, we might just be able to make our escape without him being able to follow."

Tom grinned, his eyes bright with excitement. "Brilliant, Roger! We make enough smoke to force them to turn away, then we take off in the opposite direction. I have a couple of other ideas, too."

"Well, let's get cracking, because whatever we can engineer needs to be ready in three hours or we're all dead."

"Scotty would be jealous I have that much time," he winked, and hurried over to *Belvedere.* That is one of the reasons I loved Tom; no matter how dire the situation, he remained unflappable, taking impending calamity as a challenge to overcome. I needed that moxie now more than ever.

*****

I recruited all former *Belvedere* shipmates not helping Tom, plus fifteen able-bodied seamen from *Renegade*, and started working on the tactical elements of my plan. We needed to first get Barnet's attention, then make him think we were committing suicide rather than be captured. Finally, we needed something to propel us out of harm's way before he could see and react. Piece of cake.

Craven was understandably curious about the specifics of my plan, so I filled him in as we went along.

"Captain, when the warship draws nigh, I need you to send them a message about our intentions."

"How will I be sending this signal, Mr. Petrie?"

"With this, Captain." I handed him a megaphone. "You press this front button, and your voice is magnified. Tell Barnet we imported a new explosive from *Belvedere*, that we're going to blow ourselves up rather than surrender. Tell him due to the power of this explosive, he'll need to maintain a safe distance from us if he wanted to survive. Then we'll provide some fireworks to convince him to draw off."

"And if he refuses to draw off, what then?" he countered. "He outguns us badly, Petrie, in every way."

"I have every confidence Barnet will back off, Captain, giving us the opening that we need to escape."

"I pray ye be thinking rightly, Mr. Petrie, because being cornered like Calico Jack vexes me greatly. If ye be successful, I promise ye and your crew no longer be on probation."

"As comforting as that is, Captain, let's get out of this mess first," I urged, "then you can commend me to your crew."

He clapped me on the back, smiling for the first time in a while.

"Aye, Mr. Petrie. Let's confound this bloody picaroon and be on our way!"

*****

There were now upward of sixty people pulling drums, piping, compressed air canisters, and anything else we could think of from the holds of the *Belvedere*. We oriented both ships so that we were perpendicular to the approaching warship, our starboard sides facing her. We filled containers with diesel fuel, alcohol, sulfur, pitch—anything combustible—and laid them in a line in front of both ships. I was concerned that Barnet could see our activity, but there was no way around it. After all, we would have to be preparing explosives if we were going to blow ourselves up, right?

"Mr. Petrie, what be the plan to get *Renegade* underway, if I may ask?" Craven asked.

"Two things, Captain," I answered. "First, we attached an anchor line to a gas-powered winch. When the pyrotechnics start, we'll fire an anchor from a bow gun toward open water. We'll winch ourselves underway, then our two RIBs will hopefully tow *Renegade* out of harm's way, where we can set the sails and make for open water." It would be dicey, but if everything worked correctly…

It *had* to work if we were to have any chance of outrunning the *Falklands* and her long-range guns.

*****

After three concerted hours of labor, I looked up to see the *Falklands* three miles distant and closing. Her guns, if I remembered my facts right, had a maximum range of a mile, but an effective range of two to three hundred yards. I thumbed the transmit switch on my walkie-talkie, devices that freaked out non-contemporary sailors, but would be indispensable now.

"Tom, it's been three hours, are you ready?" I experienced a sense of deja-vu, but like Captain Kirk, neither Tom nor I liked to lose.

"Copy that, Roger. I've still got some tweaks left, but we're ready. I've rigged up some nasty surprises for them."

"Great. You might throw some flaming things into the *Falklands*' path to convince them to change course away from us."

"Way ahead of you, bro!"

"Outstanding. Captain Craven's going to give his ultimatum here in a few minutes."

"Copy that. I'll be standing by for your signal."

"Affirmative." I clicked off the unit, heading along the starboard gunwale to inspect our preparations. There were a couple of motor lifeboats that sailors were filling with something sticky and black; one of Tom's surprises, probably. Once the action started, we had cut our stern anchors and winch forward on the bow anchor, starting our forward momentum, then engage the RIBs to jet us out of harm's way.

Falklands glided gracefully over the bay's placid waters, now less than two miles away. Through my binoculars I could see activity on her main deck, the crew readying for action. I assumed Jonathan Barnet was the nattily dressed bloke standing next to the ship's wheel. He looked very relaxed; his hands clasped behind his back. In his mind, I knew, he was convinced we were trapped with no possible means of escape.

He was about to learn otherwise.

Handing the megaphone to Craven, I said, "You're up, Captain."

He was perplexed by the baseball metaphor, so I corrected myself. "Sorry, Captain. It's time for your message to Barnet."

"Why didn't you say so, ye imprudent whelp!" he snarled. "Press this appendage here, ye say?" He pointed to the trigger, and I nodded. He pointed the megaphone at the warship and depressed the trigger.

"Jonathan Barnet, ye dastardly rapscallion!" he thundered, voice echoing across the bay. "Hold your distance, if ye value your life and that of your crew!" He licked his lips, and then continued. "You've caught us dead to rights, but we not be captured like stinking dogs, either! We'll be exiting this world in our time, our way!"

There was no answer, no indication that anyone on *Falklands* heard one word. With my encouragement, Craven gamely continued.

"See this metal monster be anchored beside us, Barnet? She has explosives far more powerful than anything ye can imagine aboard. They'll blast anything within two miles to kingdom come! We'll be lighting the fuse in a few minutes, Barnet— we'll take everything to the grave, and if that be including you and your abominable ship, so much the better!" Craven lowered the megaphone, glancing at me for reaction. "Petrie, do ye think this is doing a blasted thing?"

"Hard to say, Captain. One thing for sure, we'll know in a minute or two what their intentions are."

He gave one last shout. "Barnet, ye hearing me, ye slimy sea dog? Either heave to or meet your maker!" He put the megaphone down. "Mr. Petrie, let's hope your subterfuge be effective, else we'll all be swinging from a rope in Port Royal."

I swallowed, putting my hand to my neck. Tom's voice crackled over the walkie-talkie, and my resolve returned. "Roger, we're all set, waiting for your word."

Vogel gestured excitedly, pointing at the *Falklands.* "Captain, she's changing course!" Refocusing my glasses, I saw Vogel was right. She was reefing her sails, her bow swinging slightly to port. She was losing forward momentum, which would be difficult to regain when we made our run for it.

"Copy that, Tom." I licked my dry lips, taking a swig of rum to moisten my parched throat. "Corbomite Maneuver phase one, execute."

He clicked his radio twice in acknowledgment. Loud pops sounded as smoke bombs exploded all over *Belvedere's* main deck. Blooms of white-hot fire sent starbursts of embers soaring skyward, engulfing *Belvedere* in smoke.

After thirty seconds, Reynolds lit the long row of piping now floating less than a hundred yards in front of our pair of ships. These had been filled with diesel fuel, oil, tar, pitch, and sulfur, and a tongue of flame rapidly spread from east to west as the flammables ignited. The floating fire raft spewed forth clouds of dense, greasy smoke. It would not take long for this sooty smog to overtake the *Falklands*, which was now but a mile distant but veering away slowly.

I clicked the transmit button again. "Excellent, Tom. Commence phase two, now."

Two clicks, then barrels and containers on the deck of the *Belvedere* detonated. They had been laced with extremely prolific smoke-producing chemicals, resulting in dense plumes of oily smoke blowing outward toward the *Falklands.* She continued heeling port to avoid the dense smoke clouds, the exact reaction we were hoping for.

Fires were now burning at numerous points in front of *Renegade* and *Belvedere*, along with the continuous fire ring. *Belvedere's* deck teemed with small fires, adding their columns of dirty, dense smoke to the fray. The *Falklands* was now partially obscured, barely visible through the spreading haze to the west.

Time to put some teeth into our special effects.

"Tom, commence phase three," I squawked, then turned to Vogel. "Mr. Vogel, time to raise the bow anchor."

He left immediately, gathering eight able-bodied seamen to put the four bars into the capstan and commence the laborious procedure of weighing anchor. Simultaneously, bow chase gun crew number one was loading an anchor into the cannon. The anchor was tied to a large gas-powered winch by a one-inch thick hemp rope. Elevating the barrel to maximum height, the crew fired the weapon, which soared away in a high, parabolic arc, smacking into the bay five hundred yards away.

"Commencing phase three," Tom radioed. He sounded excited, in contrast to me; I was straining to not throw up my breakfast.

There was a *whang!* from *Belvedere's* deck, and a cluster of four fifty-five-gallon drums was slung from the jib crane toward the foundering warship, exploding in mid-air and showering a large area with burning fuel. It fell short of *Falklands*, but I imagined the blast caused a momentary panic. As instructed, Tom aimed these as best he could to intersect with her course. Fire was death to a wooden sailing ship, so *Falklands* frantically steered harder to port, almost heading away from us at this point.

If we could make her turn into the wind…

"Commencing phase four!" came Tom's call. The roar of gasoline engines echoed across the bay, as three of the motorized lifeboats propelled themselves away from *Belvedere*, crossing the still-burning tubing/piping arc and setting off for *Falklands*. These were coated in tar and pitch, burning brightly as they raced along. Aiming the unmanned boats was imprecise, and one of them skittered harmlessly to the left, roaring off to the west. The other two, however, powered dangerously close to the *Falklands*' starboard beam. The ship heeled even more to port, sails flapping in their yardarms as she turned almost full into the wind. This was our chance!

One of the lifeboats skipped off a wave and veered right, straight into *Falklands'* stern. Oil and pitch glommed onto her hull, and sheets of flame began licking upward. We stopped to watch the spectacle. Panicked crewmen were running frenetically away from the stricken stern, hampering men who endeavored to fight the fire.

Craven, Vogel, and I looked at each other, and then I shouted, "Recover shipmates, cleave the stern lines, engage the forward winch!"

Two pirates drew their cutlasses, swinging them viciously downward, chopping the ropes that held *Renegade's* rear anchors. Men still aboard *Belvedere* scampered into longboats lashed to her port side, away from all the fire and smoke. They motored or rowed their way to *Renegade's* port ladder, out of sight from the flaming warship. One of them towed a large raft, which Tom said was the rest of the equipment he needed to modernize *Renegade*. I had it secured to the stern, then returned to the helm.

At the bow, Gregg Reynolds fired up the gas winch. He let it warm up for thirty seconds, then disengaged the clutch. It wound up the line's slack, whining when it pulled taut as the anchor caught hold. There was a jolt, then slowly, almost imperceptibly, we began to move forward.

I turned to Vogel. “Mr. Vogel, prepare to make full sail when I give the word.” Vogel would be ‘squaring up the yards’, exposing the maximum square footage of our sails to the wind.

Renegade was gliding forward now, making headway to the southwest. *Falklands* was pointed north, still shrouded in smoke, her stern alight as flames greedily consumed it. Her crew would be too preoccupied with saving their ship to try and stop us now.

“Mr. Berger, cut the bow anchor line, engage the RIBs!” I shouted. To those near me, I said, “Might want to hold onto something, gents.”

Berger brought his cutlass down hard on bow gunwale, cleaving the line to the winch. He signaled to Cable and Samuels in the RIBs. Each RIB had two other crew on board for ballast. At Berger’s signal, they fired their engines and roared in front, taking up slack from the tow cables, then throttling up once they were taut.

There was a perceptible jolt. We started moving more rapidly now, water starting to kick up as *Renegade’s* bow cleaved the surface of the bay. We turned to study our adversary. The fire was spreading forward, now climbing the mizzenmast, devastating the vulnerable canvas, wood, and ropes. Poor buggers—without modern fire-fighting equipment, they most likely would lose their ship.

Bad for them, a good outcome for us.

Renegade had picked up enough speed to capture the wind, and Vogel and Rasmussen let the canvas out, sails billowing as they filled with air. We cut the tow lines and recovered the RIBs, securing them to our stern. Soon, we were sailing at a good eight-knot clip heading due west, leaving the now furiously burning *Falklands* in our wake. She fired her long nines at us, but we were out of effective cannon range. She discharged a broadside at *Belvedere* in impotent rage. I wondered if ancient cannons could penetrate her hull.

Vogel joined me in observing the warship's last few moments. I asked him the cannon question, and he rubbed his chin soberly, answering, "That's a right good question, Mr. Petrie. I suppose it depends on what manner of material her hull be made of. A twenty-four- or thirty-six-pound cannon can burst through three feet of oak planking at point-blank range, so I'm believing they might penetrate your ship."

We were almost out of sight when the eastern horizon glowed with twin bursts of light. One I supposed was the *Falklands*' powder magazine exploding. The other? Perhaps the B*elvedere's* fuel bunkers had ignited. Either way, both ships disappeared, two wispy columns of smoke denoting their watery graves.

Amongst *Belvedere's* former crew, not a dry eye was to be found. She was old, but she was *our* ship, and seeing her destroyed was heart-breaking. But the old girl had performed a meritorious service, her death giving us a new lease on life.

There was something to be said for that.

TWENTY-FOUR

"Every normal man must be tempted, at times, to spit on his hands, hoist the black flag, and start slitting throats."
—H.L. Mencken

Sarasota, FL
Friday, April 5, 2019
14 years, 3 months, 20 days since Reemergence

"Daddy, you're home!"

The now ten-year-old Riley launched herself into my arms as I entered the kitchen. I felt the familiar sharp twinge of pain in my left hip as I caught her, but I hid my discomfort as she giggled with delight.

"Your mother commanded me to be on time tonight, so here I am."

Rebekah came up and kissed me tenderly. "Wow, it's nice to see you can still follow orders, honey."

"Very funny. I'm going to go change, then I'll be out to help with whatever you need."

Seeing me limp away, she cooed, "What's the matter, baby, that old football injury giving you trouble?" I made a face, causing her to laugh at me. "I know! You were injured attacking a treasure ship with your pirate friends!" When I made no response, she said, "I mean, how long are you going to use that limp to play upon people's sympathies?"

"As long as it works!" I called, heading into our bedroom.

I have limped ever since returning to the twenty-first century, and it had nothing to do with football. The football injury story covered up the real reason I occasionally gimped around. I hated lying about it, but it was easier blaming my pain on a sports injury than confessing the real culprit was grapeshot lodged in my hip, fired from an ancient cannon.

Once in our bedroom, I laid out casual clothes to change into, washing my face to refresh myself. Changing into a polo shirt and jeans, I collapsed onto the bed, needing to rest for a moment. As I laid back, my head hit something solid. I reached back to retrieve the offending object; it was a small, plastic pirate cutlass, with a wide silver blade. I twirled it in my hands, finally resting it on my chest as I closed my eyes. Ah, just a few moments of blessed sleep…

"Let's go, me hearties!" Captain Craven yelled as we scampered across a wooden boarding plank to the deck of our prize, the Columbiana*. It was our second captured merchant ship since I joined Craven's crew, and I was terrified. Vogel still had not supplied me with a proper weapon, instead bequeathing me a rusty, two-foot-long sorry excuse for a blade. Not that I hoped I would have to use it.*

Tom and I joined the second assault wave. Craven and his most trusted cronies were already aboard, causing havoc. The clashing of steel and vulgar cursing met our ears as we jumped on deck. The merchantman's crew was small and ill-equipped, having no chance of repelling our attack. The battle was over quickly, the defeated sailors and their chastened captain lashed to the mizzenmast. I did not envy them their fates at Craven's hands. He showed little mercy to anyone who resisted him, having already thrown their dead comrades overboard.

I walked toward the raised forecastle. Rounding the foremast, I almost fainted in surprise when a sailor jumped out at me from behind a stack of crates, swinging a long sword savagely at my face. Fortunately, I had my sword drawn, and I reflexively ducked low and to the side, throwing my pitiful blade up in defense. His sword crashed against mine. My sword absorbed most of the blow, but his blade still managed to graze the right side of my face. Blood dripped down my neck, my face stinging from the wound. He swung again wildly, missing high as I ducked. His blade thunked solidly into the foremast, sticking fast. As he attempted to yank it loose, he took his eyes off me. Squatting down, I used the momentary respite to fire a side kick at his left knee. My right heel connected firmly, the man hollering in pain as he crumpled to the deck. Grabbing his knee, he crab-walked to the port gunwale as I freed his cutlass. Breathing heavily, adrenaline coursing through my veins, I walked up to him, pointing the cutlass at his face.

"What's your name, sailor?" I demanded, waving the blade before his eyes. The cutlass felt sturdy and sure in my hand, much more suited to pirating than my present weapon.

"S-S-Simons, sir," he replied, holding up his hands in surrender, his face a mask of pain and fear.

"What the devil were you thinking, Simons" I snarled. "If you'd killed me, my shipmates would have avenged me quickly."

"I-I-I know, sir, I simply desired to protect my ship and my friends," he whimpered, so pitiful that I felt a surge of sympathy for him. I had surely ruined his knee, for in this time there were no orthopedic surgeons, no physical therapists that could adequately repair the damage my kick had caused.

"Okay, Simons, go join your shipmates—" I started to say, intending to shepherd him to the mizzenmast, when Craven walked up.

"Roger, I see ye be acquiring a new blade. May I?"

"Certainly, Captain," I said, handing it to him hilt-first.

He inspected it carefully, running his finger down the edge, inspecting the hilt with its single, thin handguard. "Good balance, sharp edge, it should serve you well, Petrie." He held it waist-high, eyeing me as a malicious grin spread across his face.

"One thing about a new blade, Roger. It not be suitable for use until it be proven worthy. Let's be testing its mettle, shall we?" He shoved me back while whirling right, slashing downward at Simons as I looked on helplessly. The cutlass cleaved cleanly through his throat, blood fountaining from the gaping wound as he gurgled wretchedly, frothy red spittle bubbling from his lips.

Craven motioned, and Khamisi and Bartlett stepped forward, grabbing the man roughly and preparing to dump him overboard. As they hoisted him up, Craven undid his weapons belt, cackling, "You'll not be needing this anymore, ye slimy bilge rat!" He handed the belt to me as Simons' body was heaved over the side. Craven listened for the splash, laughing when it came.

He held the cutlass out to me, nodding approvingly as blood ran down the edge. "Now, Roger, your new blade be properly christened. Hahaha!" Noting my expression, he growled, "I told ye when ye signed on, Petrie, if anyone resists, we give them no quarter. Next time, be taking care of your own business, be that plain enough?" He smacked my arm, walking aft to supervise the pillaging of the ship, leaving me behind with a bloody cutlass and an anguished soul.

*****

I woke with a start, grabbing my neck, the dream still vivid in my mind. The toy cutlass fell off my chest; I snatched it up and threw it off the bed. Rubbing my eyes, I regained my bearings. Unfortunately, that included seeing Rebekah standing in the bedroom doorway, fear registering on her face.

"Roger, what is going on with you these days?" she asked in a hushed voice. "I don't think spicy food covers this one."

Rousting myself out of bed, I answered wearily, "Why would you say that, hon?"

"You called out Craven's name in your sleep again," she said, tears tracing tracks down her face, "and I think other people heard you." She wiped her eyes and quickly turned away.

What is going on with me I wondered.

TWENTY-FIVE

"I must down to the seas again, to the lonely sea and the sky, and all I ask is a tall ship and a star to steer her by."
—John Masefield

From the Personal Journal of Roger M. Petrie
Aboard the Renegade
December 7, 1720

December Seventh, the day that would live in infamy.

Two hundred and twenty-one years in the future, that is. There was no chance of *Renegade* being attacked by Japanese carrier aircraft today, but after sinking the *Falklands* off Tortola, the British would commit more resources to capture us. Craven wanted to be on the move, which was not a bad strategy. It was harder to hit a moving target, especially when your enemy is without the aid of modern warfighting intelligence assets like satellites, radar, reconnaissance aircraft, and submarines.

We headed for the island of Anegada to repair damage we had suffered, and to finish outfitting our ship with the modern technology and conveniences salvaged from *Belvedere*.

Tolliver and Tom got to work as soon as we anchored. Tolliver was an expert shipwright, seamlessly patching in new wood with old. He aided Tom's gang in adding PVC piping and inverted gallon jugs for rudimentary internal plumbing, running the PVC out the hull behind the bow. Voila, instant urinals. They also fashioned crude toilets from large bowls, replete with seawater flushing.

Hopefully, the modifications would cut down on the stench below deck.

Other changes included applying a polyurethane/polymer coating to the decks, masts, railings, and spars, and to the hull up to the gunwales. If the formulation was correct, the coating might be tough enough to absorb a hit from a smaller cannon. I hoped we would never have to put it to the test.

Tom also worked at improving the rigging lines, and how to incorporate more lines into our winch system. The fewer stations necessary to raise and lower sails, the more efficient our sailing operations would be.

Two days later, repairs and upgrades were complete. As we got underway, I participated in a unique meeting; Craven, Berger, Vogel, Carney, Spenser, Slocum, and Rasmussen all joined Tom and me in Craven's cabin. Compared with the normal onboard amenities, it was spacious and well-appointed, decorated with pieces of artwork, a writing desk, velour armchairs, and a bed with a thick mattress. At the center was a large wooden table, now covered with a map of the Caribbean.

Vogel was right—it *does* pay to be a ship captain, no matter what service you are in.

"Mssrs. Petrie," Berger explained to us, "pursuant to the Articles of the Ship, every crewman has an equal vote as to our affairs. What we be aspiring to do be to strategize our next courses of action, make those known to the crew, and put them to a vote. Majority wins, and that be the task we set to. We then be laying our course to that which was agreeable to our crew."

I could not fathom anyone challenging Craven on a command decision, but it complied with the democratic ideals set forth in the Articles.

We discussed sailing south along the Leeward islands to Puerto Rico, where plentiful shipping could be found, or setting our sights on something bigger: the Spanish treasure fleets that sailed from Havana, up the east coast of Florida, then out across the Atlantic to Spain. After eleven galleons sank in a hurricane in 1715, they were waiting until later in the year to sail. Ships that lagged behind would be our target. Galleons were well-armed, and often escorted by smaller warships; nevertheless, they represented our best chance to score a rich prize, the stuff of legends.

Craven presented these alternatives to the crew, and they voted to attack Spanish treasure ships in the Florida Keys. We would lay a circuitous course, skirting the northern shores of Puerto Rico and Hispaniola, north to the Bahamas, then west to the Keys. The plan was risky, as Royal Navy squadrons were based in Tortuga and Freeport, but Craven was emboldened by *Renegade's* increased fighting abilities, so the plan was ratified by the crew and the real planning began in earnest.

Craven pointed to the map. "Gents, here we be, and here the course I be recommending. We'll surely find worthy prizes on the way past Hispaniola and up by Freeport."

Berger looked worried. "There be plenty of pirate-hunters plying those waters, Captain, not to mention the blasted Royal Navy. We likely stirred up a hornet's nest sinking the *Falklands*. This be a perilous journey we be undertaking."

Craven growled, "All our journeys be perilous, Mr. Berger; we be pirates, after all. This course be giving us a chance to score a prize on the way. If we were of a mind to avoid naval vessels completely, we'd have to circumnavigate the entire Caribbean."

"Aye, 'tis true, Captain. With the instruments now in our possession via our new mates, we be having thc advantage now," Berger responded.

"Then we're agreed! Mr. Vogel, Mr. Slocum, please lay a course as determined. Keep a weather eye on the horizon, for quarry and foe alike. I've a hunger in me bosom for Spanish silver!"

*****

Though *Renegade* was ostensibly organized democratically, Craven ruled it with an iron fist. During the day he stalked the deck, inspecting the rigging, the rails, the booms, and the cannons. His face was set in a perpetual scowl, no matter how well the ship was operating. He had a way of issuing a scathing rebuke without saying a word, staring you down with his left eye wide, right eye squinting, lips downturned in a nasty snarl. Other times, he would break into an ugly grin, like when our musicians played an especially lewd ditty or when he was recounting past conquests to us over drinks.

Some of my *Belvedere* mates and I were gathered around a barrel holding Samuel's latest watered-down rum concoction. Craven and Vogel were strolling down the deck, and they moved over to join our group.

"Good evening, gents," Vogel hailed us. "What be the nature of your conclave tonight?"

"We were just discussing ship capture techniques, and how to deal with intransigent crew." I answered warily. We did not really want their input, but there was not much we could do about it.

"Is that so?" Vogel said. "Well, we be well versed on what actions be necessary to break the will of men who deign to resist." Craven chuckled wickedly as Vogel continued, "Captain, perhaps ye wouldst regale our new crew with one of your favorite ploys."

I braced myself for what was coming, because I had quickly learned Craven reveled in terrifying sailors.

"Aye, this be me favorite!" he cackled. "Upon subduing a vessel, I be gathering her officers around the mainmast. After plundering their ship, I allow them to be believing I'll leave them in peace, and in one piece!" He and Vogel laughed. "Then, I act like I be leaving. Suddenly, I'll whirl around, slashing with me blade at the nearest scurvy swab. Sometimes he be sliced open, but ofttimes he be losing a limb!" More laughing, and my men and I chortled uncomfortably, trying not to hurl at the mental images this conjured. "Aye, they be left to tell the tale, lads, of the terror wrought by the bloodthirsty raiders of the *Renegade*!"

He thought this tactic was hilarious, and he would recount it often. Other crew would roar with laughter along with him at each retelling. I saw the twisted logic of such behavior, to spread terror and fear throughout the Caribbean. This made it easier for *Renegade* to capture prey, but it still made my stomach turn. I left the group and walked forward, to clear my head.

I meditated as I walked. One thing I had learned fast—always check the rigging, masts, and spars to see if anyone was up there before you walked beneath them. If guys were working eighty feet above the deck and nature called, they did not bother climbing down to relieve themselves. They also did not bother turning the other way if you walked under them, and it became sport to try and hit the new guys. Disgusting behavior, but not much we could do about it. Fighting was forbidden aboard ship, and we were hopelessly outnumbered.

I had also learned most of the pirate stereotypes I had gleaned from books and films were inaccurate. The one that held true was the amount of drinking that went on. I constantly came across groups of sailors drinking ale or rum, in various states of inebriation. The same was true below decks—when these men were idle, and sometimes when they were not, they had Black Jacks in their hands.

The busywork common aboard naval and merchant vessels, the constant cleaning and polishing, was absent here. The crew did the bare minimum necessary to keep the ship in fighting trim; most of the heavy work was done during careens, and the tropical climate demanded we careen every two months.

There was genuine comradery amongst the crew, held in place by their confidence in Captain Craven to provide for their needs. The *treasure* these men coveted turned out to be commodities like tobacco, liquor, and clothes, especially the finer fabrics. Most never believed they would ever strike it rich or capture Spanish treasure galleons, nor did they care. They were content to live free at sea, away from the rules and constraints of life on land.

I arrived at the forward hatch, preparing to descend to the cargo hold. If I were to survive on board this vessel, I would need to make myself as valuable as possible to captain and crew. I had heard several of the regular crew refer to me as *Sharkbait*, not a nickname that would cut it for long.

I would need to change minds and attitudes in a hurry if I ever wanted to see home again.

TWENTY-SIX

"Never in my life before have I experienced such beauty and fear at the same time"
—llen MacArthur, Sailor

Sarasota, FL
Friday Night, April 5, 2019
14 years, 3 months, 20 days since Reemergence

Time for Riley's party.

I did my best to melt into the background. I also tried to avoid Rebekah, because every time our eyes met, she teared up. The open layout of our villa bedeviled my efforts, but I did the best I could.

There were pirate party favors, of course; eye patches, earrings, and tiny black flags. I sighed heavily. Why couldn't she pick *Beauty and the Beast* or *Frozen* like any other normal girl? *Pirates, we've got to be pirates!* Year after year. It was enough to drive me to drink. Unfortunately, a cursory look around made it clear we did not have any Black Jacks.

*****

After cake and ice cream, it was time for presents. Riley sat at the head of the table, waiting expectantly for the goods. One by one, she opened packages and gift bags full of books, clothes, and makeup. Standard gift fare for a young girl. Tom stepped up to present his gift.

"Riley, I gave your gift a lot of thought. You're getting so big and mature! Then, it hit me—we share a common interest, so what I was going to give you became crystal clear!"

"What is it, Uncle Tom?" she whooped, her eyes wide in excitement.

"Aye, hold your horses, young lady!" She loved it when he slipped into pirate-speak. He retrieved a large, flat box about three feet long and six inches tall from inside our pantry. "Here you go, my favorite niece. I hope you like them."

"UNCLE TOM!" Riley yelped as she opened the box. Inside lay a leather baldric with a cutlass scabbard, and a flintlock pistol. Not toys, but what appeared to be genuine weapons. What on earth was he thinking?

He laid a hand on the belt, warning her, "Now, Riley, please understand that these are not toys or playthings. These are valuable keepsakes, and you have to promise me you will *be careful* with them."

Rebekah was aghast. I imagined she thought he was bringing her toys or cheap reproductions. As Riley hefted the cutlass, the kids were beside themselves with awe and excitement. She started to unsheathe it, but Tom stepped in quickly.

"Riley, let me hold these, okay? We don't want anyone accidentally getting hurt."

The kids protested at first, but they dutifully obeyed. The sword and pistol were successfully displayed without anyone losing an eye—though we did have plenty of eye patches available if anyone needed them.

"Okay, gang, why don't we go into the living room for some fun pirate games?" Rebekah asked, giving me a quick evil eye. Rebekah's mom Dana joined her and two other adults in leading some pirate games while Tom and I cleared the table and threw trash into a garbage bag.

"Okay, how mad do you think Rebekah is?" he whispered. "I told her what I was getting Riley, but she didn't look too pleased when she saw them."

"Pretty darn mad," I replied. "She thought you were getting toys or cheap knock-offs, not the real McCoys. Don't tell me they're yours from way back when?"

"Yep, the same ones Edward Vogel gave me."

I paused to gape at him in astonishment. "And you thought they would make an ideal gift for Riley why?"

"I didn't need them anymore. What was I going to do with them? I wanted to give them to someone who would truly appreciate them. Someone like Riley."

"She might be a little young to 'truly appreciate them'," I advised, "and how exactly is this helping her get over her pirate fixation? Now, she'll be more convinced than ever that your stories are true."

"My stories are your stories, Roger, and they *are* true. You need to give some serious thought about telling your family that."

"I'll tell them when the time is right!"

"I've heard that before. What happens if you go before Rebekah? There'll be a bunch of money left and no explanation for it. The government might even confiscate everything on suspicion you were a thief, and your wife and kids would end up with zilch. You need to think about that."

He left the kitchen, leaving me holding the bag. Literally.

*****

I stayed in the kitchen, content to finish washing the pans. Rebekah appeared, leaning against the doorway.

"May I help you?" I asked innocently.

"I think you've done enough."

"What does that mean?"

"You with your bad dream earlier today, plus your reactions to swords tonight. You turned pale when Riley unwrapped hers."

I remained silent, knowing in my gut Tom's recent switch to including me in his tales had triggered something deep inside, something I had taken meticulous care to keep buried.

"And Tom's gifts looked like real weapons!" she continued. "Honestly, who would give things like that to a ten-year-old girl?"

"Tom, evidently."

"Nice," she replied, annoyed at my flippancy. "Riley and her friends are waiting for him to tell them one of his ridiculous stories. She said that was her birthday wish, so how could I refuse?"

Really? I peeked around the corner, noting the children had arranged themselves in a semicircle around my recliner. Riley sat in front, about to jump out of her skin with excitement as Tom settled into the chair. Children gravitated to Tom; I think his large size fascinated them.

"What is going on in here?" he growled in a cartoonish pirate brogue, eyes twinkling with mischief. "It looks like you all be desiring something from me. Pray tell, what would that be?"

"Uncle Tom, tell us a story about when you and Daddy were pirates!" Riley exclaimed. The other kids echoed her request, egging him on.

"A tale of when your dad and I were pirates, eh?" He stroked his chin thoughtfully. "Aye, I can gratify that craving for ye, little lady." Leaning forward, he continued in a low growl, "Didst I ever tell ye about the time we were cornered in Tombstone Cay by that dastardly British Admiral Brannigan?"

"No, Uncle Tom!"

"Well, shiver me timbers, I can't believe it!" He rocked back, to the delight of his audience. "Then sit back, me mateys, whilst I regale you with the tale of how me brother and I escaped certain death!" He thrust his left arm in my direction. "Aye, escape death we did, thanks to our magnificent pirate ship, *Renegade!*"

I risked a sideways glance at Rebekah. She was seated in the lanai, arms crossed, looking very unhappy. She loves parties, giving presents, and all the attendant hoopla, but not tonight. Tom telling pirate stories was exactly what we had not wanted, though I doubted we could have stopped it. When Riley and Tom got together, the conversation eventually turned to piracy. Regardless, Rebekah shot me an aggravated look as Tom sat back and began to spin another outrageous yarn to a young, eager audience.

TWENTY-SEVEN

"Only the devil and I know the whereabouts of my treasure, and the one of us who lives the longest should take it all."
—Blackbeard

Sarasota, FL
Friday Night, April 5, 2019
14 years, 3 months, 20 days since Reemergence

Tom cast a serious pirate glare at every kid before starting his story.

"Well, mateys, there we were, me brother and I, dueling the British and Spanish and taking their bounty, living off plunder and the sea. One time, our stores be depleted, so the cap'n decided to beach our ship for repair and resupply."

"Who was the captain, Mr. Petrie?" Kyrie asked.

"Oh, he was a gallant fellow, the cap'n!" he laughed. "The Red Raider be his name, and he was as fierce a fighter as Blackbeard himself. Whenever we fought, he donned a bright red coat he plundered from the blasted British, from whence he got his name." He stole a glance at me, eyes twinkling with amusement. "He flew a flag of red and black; swarthy captains cried in fear when they saw his colors, knowing the wrath of the Red Raider was upon them!" The kids voiced the appropriate amount of awe.

"Anyway, there was a certain British admiral, Sir Alec Brannigan, who wanted me brother and me bad. He chased us round the Caribbean, to the very shores of Africa and back, he did. But the cap'n, he wasn't so easily captured. He twasn't the Scourge of the Spanish Main for nothing." Tom paused for effect, then went on. "Anyway, we put into Tombstone Cay to resupply and repair."

Seeing several confused expressions, Tom explained, "Oh, me hearties, a sailing ship needed constant mending. The sails were always ripping, the rigging became frayed, and things in the water constantly ate away at our hull."

Rebekah caught my eye, rolling hers in exasperation. Guess she was not into Tom's story as much as the kids. He did not notice but kept the tale rolling along.

"Tombstone Cay, such a beautiful island, full of coconuts, flowing with bright clear water. We thought no one was the wiser, but a British spy learned of our whereabouts and got word to Sir Alec. After us he came in his blasted warship *Ark Royal*. A right powerful ship she was, mounting eighty guns to our twenty." It had been one hundred twenty guns to fourteen, but who was I to quibble? "And he had a hundred marines aboard, ready to board and capture the *Renegade*!" Several kids booed at this "Yes, boo, me hearties!"

"So, there we were, sitting at anchor, being approached by a huge warship under full sail. What were we to do? Aye, things looked very bad for us at that moment."

"What did you do?" several voices echoed.

"I'll tell you what we did, me hearties! Me brother thought up this brilliant plan, he did! We made Sir Alec believe our ship was on fire, and while he was wondering what was happening, we snuck off under cover of the smoke! Me brother figured that *Renegade*, being the swiftest, most maneuverable pirate ship afloat, would be able to outrun our enemy and live to fight another day. And we did!"

The kids cheered because we were able to escape, encouraging Tom to pour it on. "Ah, 'twas a blessed sight, me hearties, to see us running with the wind, leaving those English blighters wallowing around in a cloud of smoke! When they finally saw that we be escaping, we were long gone. Sir Alec, he gave a good effort, but it was all for naught." Tom leaned forward, finishing up with his usual flare. "Aye, there's nothing that a fast ship and courageous Captain can't do, me hearties, you do well to remember that! And that be how me brother and I escaped certain death at Tombstone Cay!"

Tom sat back, looking pleased with himself. The children were mesmerized by his tale, eyes round with wonder and mouths open in awe. Riley was beside herself, laughing and clapping at his newest story. Then, after a moment or two of silence, every kid began peppering Tom with questions.

"Mr. Petrie, did pirates have parrots or monkeys?"

"Sure, some did, but not as pets. Me mates would grab them from ports we visited, because they could sell them for a goodly amount of silver."

"Mr. Petrie, did pirates really say things like 'Arrgh, matey!' 'Shiver me timbers!' and 'Yo ho, yo ho, it's a pirate's life for me'?"

"Of course, we did, mateys! It was how we could tell who be a real pirate, and who be a landlubber!" he answered smugly, the children squealing in delight.

"Mr. Petrie, where did you bury your treasure?"

Tom thought about that one for a moment. "Ah, me treasure. Those baubles, jewels, and beautiful, shiny coins." His face suddenly switched from friendly to a menacing squint, and he rumbled, "Hold on, mateys! We worked and slaved by the sweat of our brows to gather our treasure hoard. I can't go about telling our deepest, darkest secrets to any old scallywag, can I?"

The kids were enthralled, giving Tom their rapt attention. "But, mateys, I can tell ya if you take the Pirate Oath! Will ya raise yer right hands and swear here and now that you'll take me secrets with you to the grave?"

"Yes, we swear!" was the communal response.

"Aye, I reckon you've proved your worth, me hearties. You now be honorary crew of the *Renegade*!" More cheers. "Yes, hooray. And a great honor it is!" He paused to take a swig of water, then pressed on. "Most pirates found some desert island to bury their plunder. But as for me brother and I…well, we wanted someplace no one would ever look, someplace safe that would hold our booty until we were ready to claim it again!"

"Where, where, where?" came the chorus of cries.

"Why, under the swimming pool of course!" he answered, pointing to the pool across the yard. The kids shrieked and howled, rushing to the sliding glass door to eyeball the supposed resting place of untold wealth.

I was sure the homeowner's association was going to be very pleased with Tom when they came by the pool later in the week and a dozen kids were digging at the foundation. There was one kid, however, who seemed more skeptical than the others. When I saw who it was, I was not surprised.

"Mr. Petrie, did you ever make anyone walk the plank?"

"Aye, but only if they really deserved it, like if they were a spy for the Crown or wouldn't surrender their treasure! We'd walk 'em to the end at the point of our swords, until they told us what we wanted to know. Didn't we, Roger?"

Rebekah fixed me with an exasperated look, imploring me to do something to wrap this craziness up. "Sorry, kids, no more questions," I said, to a smattering of boos. "I know, but the party's over, and your parents are waiting to take you home."

Rebekah handed me an armload of gift bags to pass out, full of gold-wrapped chocolate coins, small treasure chests with trinkets inside, bandanas and eye patches to wear, and other similar pirate-themed knickknacks.

The crowd cleared out as parents and children exited our villa. We said our goodbyes as moms and dads arrived to pick up their children. It had been a decent party, and Riley seemed overjoyed, which was the whole point.

*****

Bobby Sutton was the last kid to be picked up. He was the one who had looked aggravated during Tom's story time. He had a sharp, inquisitive mind, and he never met an argument he did not like. We sat on our front courtyard glider, waiting for his parents.

If they were anything like me, I would be taking my sweet time in reclaiming him, too.

"Mr. Petrie, I have a question."

"What is it, Bobby?"

"Does Riley really think you used to be a pirate?"

"Umm, I don't know, maybe," I answered noncommittally, not really engaged in this conversation. "Why do you ask?"

"Well, I mean, you and my dad are about the same age, right? He's forty-six now."

"Yeah, I think that's about right."

"Well, Mr. Petrie, I don't want to sound disrespectful, but for you to have been on the *Renegade*…well, you'd have to be over three hundred years old. And you don't look it."

"Thanks, I appreciate that." This kid was sharp.

"So, either you and your brother invented a time machine, or he made up the whole thing, right?"

"I suppose you're right, Bobby. As far as I know there's no such thing as time travel." There was, I simply did not know how it worked, and I was not about to debate it with a ten-year-old.

"So, does Riley really believe it, or does she go along with it to make your brother feel good?"

Not a bad question. "I think it's fun for her to imagine Tom and me as pirates, and he likes to indulge her fantasies. It's harmless, I guess."

"I guess," he muttered.

On impulse I said, "You know, Bobby, there's one question you haven't asked me."

He perked up. "What's that, Mr. Petrie?"

"You asked if *Riley* thought I was a real pirate. You never asked *me* if I was one."

That surprised him, I saw. He was about to reply when his mom pulled into our driveway. I stood up, and he reluctantly lifted himself off the glider, opening the courtyard gate. Once through, he turned and said, "Hey, it was a great party, Mr. Petrie, even if I don't believe all that pirate stuff."

"Thanks, Bobby, it was good talking to you." On a whim, I flipped him a coin I had in my pocket. "Here's a bit of pirate booty for ya, matey!" I growled in my best pirate voice, winking as I turned to go inside.

"Mr. Petrie? This is pretty heavy; are you sure it's okay if I keep it?"

"Don't sweat it, Bobby. Those are common coins where I used to work. Have a good night."

I missed the thoughtful look he gave me as he turned the coin over in his hand.

TWENTY-EIGHT

"I wanted freedom, open air, and adventure. I found it on the sea."
—Alaine Gerbault, Sailor

From the Personal Journal of Roger M. Petrie
Aboard the Renegade
Mid-December 1720

"Thanks to ye for resupplying me vessel!" Captain Craven shouted to the dejected-looking townspeople of Yauco as we cast off.

"Fortunate for us we came in a fair breeze, and your hospitality touched me heart, so much so we might be visiting ye again early next year, hahaha!" From their forlorn expressions, the people of Yauco did not share those sentiments.

We had set upon this small fishing village on the southwest coast of Puerto Rico to resupply our water and fresh bread and fruit. The town's fisherman had just brought in nets, so we scored several hundred pounds of fresh fish as well.

Once back to sea, my work detail set about lowering our new supplies into the cargo hold. We pulled open the large lattice hatch set amidships, loaded the liquor, spices, cloth, and foodstuff on makeshift pallets, and cranked them down to the third deck using our block-and-tackle hauling apparatus.

I was positioning trunks of cloth on the port side when my jeans caught on a barrel behind me. Wrenching free, I heard my pants rip, the left back pocket now hanging. Cursing my clumsiness, I wondered what I was going to do. I only had one other pair of pants.

The issue of clothing was one we modern sailors had put off until now, preferring to wring every bit of utility out of what we had brought with us. Our clothes, though, were proving to be unsuitable for laboring in a tropical climate. The polyesters, cottons, and denim we were used to wearing were fine for a ship with air-conditioning, but on a sailing ship like *Renegade*, they were proving to be too hot and restrictive of movement. Not to mention we had to wear the same clothes day after day, and they were perpetually wet from sea spray, rain, and sweat. After three weeks on board, our clothes were filthy and stunk to high heaven. Washing them in the ocean had little effect on their funkiness.

It would have been difficult for an outsider to smell the difference between us and regular crew, a fact that grieved me greatly

I climbed up to the main deck, looking for help. I had befriended several regular seamen, who were more even keeled and less bloodthirsty: James, the freed slave; Armando, a dark, hulking Spaniard; Simpkins, a young, fresh-faced pilot; and Plue, a muscular blonde who worked under Tolliver. I knew my crew needed friends amongst the pirates if we were to survive, and these men had proved willing to help us and show us the ropes.

I found Plue and James sitting against the starboard rail mending sails. Plunking myself down between them, I explained my plight.

"Aye, rippin' yer pants be a daily hazard aboard!" Plue laughed.

"Dat be no problem, mon," James added. "We can teach ya to make new uns."

"You guys make your own clothes?"

"Ya, mon!" James laughed. "Sit tight 'n I'll fetch da material." He rousted himself up and disappeared down the forward hatch, reappearing moments later with a bolt of linen cloth.

I rubbed my chin as I waited, fingers grating across stubbly growth.

Personal hygiene had pretty much gone out the window in the three weeks I had been aboard *Renegade*. My hair had grown over my ears and down to my collar. My fingernails and toenails had long white edges, despite my efforts to whittle them down. I still used deodorant, and brushed my teeth, but once those supplies ran out, it would be primitive living for me.

"'ere ya go, mon," James said as he sat back down. "Be meas'rin' ya legs 'n belly, 'n we'll cut da cloth."

It was amazing that they could swiftly get correct measurements without a measuring tape, but they did, just by laying out the material. Most of the 'breeches' or 'slops', as they called their pants, were three-quarter length, with a wide bell. The officers wore knee breeches. Plue explained the shorter length allowed for ease of movement and comfort, but I insisted on ankle-length pants. They thought my request odd, but James cut out the material, and Plue set about stitching them up.

They worked fast. It took fifteen minutes from the cutting to the finished product, which tied at the top and tapered at the ankles. Plue folded the material over at the waist and ankles, strengthening them in both places. I tried them on, enduring more teasing at the sight of my multi-colored boxer-briefs. I did not know what pirates did for underwear, nor did I want to.

The pants fit well, and my initial impression was they would be more breathable and comfortable than my jeans. That was tempered somewhat by James telling me the pants needed to be waterproofed to last longer.

"How do you waterproof pants?" I asked.

"Well, mon, we use da tar 'n grease before we be wearin' dem, dat works best," James explained.

Tar and grease? That sounded smelly and unpleasant.

"Thanks, but we brought some stuff with us that might work better," I answered. There was a spray called Nikwax waterproofing we had brought over from *Belvedere,* so I used that. The pants would be less breathable once coated but would feel and smell a heck of a lot better than tar and grease.

After ditching my jeans, I put on socks and my Pumas. "Why ye be putting on shoes, mate?" Plue asked. "We be barefoot, mostly, unless we be attacking a ship or such. The deck be wet day and night, shoes never be dry."

I looked at the deck, which was covered with new coats of Tom's polyurethane. "It will be a while for me to get used to going barefoot," I said, which elicited questioning looks from Plue and James. "I don't want to get splinters in my feet, man."

They both laid their heads back and laughed uproariously at my sensitivities. "Aye, we'll have to be calling ye 'Tenderfoot' from here on out, Roger!" Plue proclaimed, slapping me on the back. I have been called worse; other pirates referred to me as *Sharkbait*, which I assumed was not complementary. Still, it would be difficult to develop a scary pirate persona with a nickname of *Tenderfoot*.

"Next, Roger, ye be needin' to cover yer head." Plue pointed to the sun. "In these parts th' sun'll burn yer skin to ash. If ye not wish yer flesh be peeling off yer head, I'd be putting something on right quick."

"That makes sense, I guess," I said, having already endured serious sunburns. James produced a red linen bandana for me to try. It fitted over my head like a doo rag, tied in the back, with two long strips hanging down over my shoulders. My family would have laughed at the picture, I am sure, but it made me feel more at ease with my surroundings.

I noticed their jewelry. "Does everyone wear an earring? Men in my era normally don't."

James responded, "Well, mon, wearin' da earring 'elps wit' seasickness, right? Pinch yer lobe, don't be upchuckin', mon. Dat 'ow it supposed to work, anyhows."

"Wearing an earring helps with seasickness? I've never heard of such a thing," I admitted.

James nodded. "Be da truth, mon. Oder men, dey think da gold be helpin' der eyesight, or be keepin' dem from drownin', too, tho' I ain't sure 'bout dat. I seen too many drown, mon, and dey be wearin' da gold."

"Wow, hard to believe people would put that much faith in an earring," I said.

"'Tis true. Our gunners be putting wax on ders," Plue continued, "and then stick the wax in der ears when they be firing so they don't be deaf!" He laughed, and then went on. "Plus, for most 'tis the only gold we got. If ye be cut down, yer jewelry pays for yer rites."

"So, earrings pay for your funerals?" I asked, amazed. "What happens if you're killed at sea, far away from land?"

James grinned. "Den we be takin' yer gold fer ourselfs, mon. Ya can ne'er 'ave 'nuff gold!"

"Do ye wants one, Roger? Mr. Vogel be taking it from yer share, if ye wants," Plue offered.

"Sure, why not," I heard myself say. "I don't want to be the odd man out." *Really?*

Plue left, returning ten minutes later with a golden hoop, an inch in diameter. Belatedly, I saw it was *not* a clip-on. I started to protest, then figured, what the heck.

"Brace yerself, Roger, this will sting mightily," Plue advised, dipping a sewing needle in rum to sterilize it. He deftly jabbed my left earlobe, then hooked the hoop in. My ear bled for a few minutes, and ached something fierce for a while, but to my surprise, I dug the way the earring flipped against my neck.

All I needed now was an eyepatch, a parrot, a peg leg, and a hook, and I would have this pirate thing down pat.

TWENTY-NINE

Yes, I do heartily repent. I repent I had not done more mischief; and that we did not cut the throats of them that took us, and I am extremely sorry that you aren't hanged as well as we."
—Anonymous Pirate when asked if he repented for his crimes.

Sarasota, FL
Friday Night, April 5, 2019
14 years, 3 months, 20 days since Reemergence

After the party, I put Drake and Riley to bed.

After turning out Drake's light, I coaxed Riley into her bed. She promptly burrowed under the covers. Honestly, I have never seen anyone who needed five blankets to be comfortable, especially living in Florida.

She said her prayers, and I asked, "Did you have a good birthday, sweetie?"

"It was great, Daddy. I know you and Mommy worked super hard to make it special for me." As I reached to turn off her nightstand light, she whispered softly, "Daddy?"

"Yes, sweetheart?"

"Did you like Uncle Tom's story tonight?"

That was unexpected. "Yeah, it was one of his better ones."

"I loved it," she rejoined. "He sure doesn't like that Sir Alec! I'm glad you both escaped from him."

I answered carefully, so as not to squash her fantasies. "Well, it was exciting for a while, but things worked out." *Good, noncommittal answer, Roger*.

"Yeah, I guess so." She sounded deflated by my lack of enthusiasm.

"Why do you ask, sweetie? He's always telling you stories."

She bit her lower lip. "Well, I notice when he's talking, you look so unhappy with him. Your face scrunches up, like you tasted something yucky."

"Really, I look like that?" She was observant, for sure.

"Yes, Daddy. I can't enjoy Uncle Tom's stories as much if I know they upset you."

My heart felt like it had been run through with a blade. "I had no idea you felt that way. Why didn't you tell me?"

"Because I didn't want you to be mad at me for asking him to keep telling me stuff."

"Why would I be mad…"

"Daddy, I'm not stupid; I know most pirates lived a long time ago. But it's so much fun to imagine you as pirates! And part of me thinks, why couldn't it have happened that way? I mean, would he be so specific if there wasn't *some* truth to it? Uncle Tom seems to know a lot about pirates, how they lived and talked, you know."

He should. He had lived as one long enough.

"Sweetie, I get irritated with Uncle Tom because you're obsessing over his stories lately. You've never been in trouble at school until this semester, and we must deal with that. Do you understand?"

She nodded her head dejectedly.

I was bothered about what she had said. Had I been so self-absorbed about Tom's foolishness that I had not taken bothered to ask my own daughter what she thought about the whole thing?

"Daddy, are you okay?"

"No, sweetie, I'm not," I answered truthfully.

She sat up in bed, concerned. "Are you feeling sick? Should I call Mommy?"

I stroked Riley's hair affectionately. "No, I'll be fine. I realized I haven't been fair to you, and I'm sorry. I didn't understand why Uncle Tom's stories meant so much to you. Will you forgive me for being such a selfish jerk?"

She giggled. "Of course, Daddy!" She sat up and gave me a hug.

"Goodnight, Riley. Remember, we have a big day tomorrow."

"Oh my gosh, I almost forgot! We're going to Disney World!"

"Yes, we are, and the last time you were there, you were a year old. You probably don't remember much."

"Oh, Daddy, you are so funny!"

"I keep telling Mom that I am the funny one." I pulled her covers up to her neck. "Love you, sweetie! Dream good dreams about pirates tonight."

Did I just say that?

THIRTY

"Damn ye, you are a sneaking puppy, and so are all those who will submit to be governed by laws which rich men have made for their own security."
—Black Sam Bellamy

From the Personal Journal of Roger M. Petrie
Aboard the Renegade
Late December 1720

I had to shade my eyes from the sun's glare as I climbed through the forward hatch onto the main deck.

We were cruising north of Puerto Rico, heading northwest toward Florida and the Bahamas. I spotted Doc Loechner leaning on the starboard gunwale forward of our beam cannons. The gunwale was rising and falling gently in the shallow swells, but Doc did not seem to notice. He was staring out to sea, looking older than his fifty-four years: His skin was wrinkled and leathery, age spots dotting his arms, silver hair thinning even more, it seemed. My nose wrinkled as I approached; he was smoking a pungent cigarette, a Black Jack of Bodie's latest concoction in his left hand. Smoking on board was not encouraged, because fire and wood did not mix well.

Doc did *not* look like he was having a good time.

"I'm not sure the American Medical Association would approve of this, Doc," I jested, pointing to his cigarette and cup.

He grunted, flicking ash into the waters below. "You're hilarious. I'm sure the Health Department would have serious problems with the cleanliness of my medical facilities, too."

"How are things in Sick Bay these days?"

He laughed harshly. "If you can call a splintery bench, a rickety chair, and two lice-infested bunks Sick Bay, then things are just swell."

"I'm not sure pirates ever used the term 'swell', Doc," I quipped, hoping to lighten his mood.

He merely stared out to sea, looking tired and old.

"How's being doctor for a pirate crew suiting you?"

He turned, squinting from the sun. "Are you kidding me, Roger? Why, caring for a bunch of brutish, foul-mouthed, foul-smelling louts with atrocious hygiene is every doctor's dream." He paused to take a drag on his cigarette. "Sorry about that. Anyway, I'm blowing through my stock of penicillin because those louts have the moral turpitude of rutting pigs. Without it, we'll see more virulent outbreaks of tropical diseases, and I won't be able to stop them. I suppose I could conjure up some homeopathic remedies, but they won't have the effectiveness of antibiotics. Once they're depleted, this job will be even less enjoyable."

I felt bad for him, because he had been forced to join *Renegade* due to his profession. Working aboard a sailing ship was dangerous work in the best of conditions; he dealt with a constant stream of cuts, scrapes, and sprains, not to mention more serious injuries caused by storms and battles. A man fell out of the rigging at least once a week, twice resulting in death. He also had to deal with tropical diseases like Scurvy, Cholera, and Malaria, which had wiped out large numbers of eighteenth-century sailors.

"I'm sorry, Doc, I know you didn't ask for this. We're all trying to make the best of the situation. Who knows, maybe we'll strike it rich soon, and we can all retire to Tahiti."

He regarded me with sad, bloodshot eyes. "Roger, my friend, that day cannot come soon enough." He flicked his cigarette overboard, watching the butt float away in our wake, then took a swig from his cup, regarding it thoughtfully. "Who knew a witch's brew like this would make life on board this floating asylum somewhat tolerable?" Turning to leave, he clapped me on the shoulder. "Aye, it's a pirate's life for us, eh?"

I watched my friend shuffle toward the rear hatch, feeling utterly powerless to help him.

*****

We sailed from the Antilles up the western edges of the Bahamas, surprising a merchant ship off Freeport. We found she carried valuable cargo bound for a sugar plantation owner. Craven and his minions put down resistance brutally by hacking away with boarding axes.

The fighting was brutal, the issue never in doubt, the results sickening—to me, anyway.

We sailed to Smuggler's Cove, Tortola, to sell our captured wares, unloading the spices and liquor at a warehouse on the outskirts of town. It was backbreaking work—I had thought I was in decent shape when *Renegade* first appeared, but the last weeks of manual labor proved I had been in pitiful condition. I had operated near exhaustion for much of our time here, just now feeling my strength and stamina were improving.

We unloaded the heavy barrels, trunks, and hogsheads onto a remote wharf, then transferred them to wagons. We walked alongside them down rutted, muddy avenues that passed for streets, clashing twice with ne'er-do-wells seeking to pilfer whatever they could. When we arrived at the warehouse, the mercantilist and his henchmen inspected the cargo, giving us a good price because the plundered wares were first-rate.

We did not linger in Smuggler's Cove but returned immediately to our ship. As we sailed west, I lounged on the quarterdeck, speaking with Carney, the bosun. He was an agreeable guy, not cut from the same cloth as Craven and his bloodthirsty minions. In the middle of our conversation, Captain Craven came stomping down the weather deck toward the helm, motioning to me.

"Mr. Petrie, a word, if ye please."

We walked over to the starboard rail, both of us leaning on it. He did not say anything for a moment, staring out to sea. Then he turned to me, wearing one of the softer expressions I had seen. "Mr. Petrie," he rumbled, "I've not spake to ye about the *Falklands* affair, but ye handled yourself ably. Saved me crew and ship, ye did. For that I owe ye me thanks."

I was genuinely surprised by this. "Thank you, Captain. I'm glad things turned out well."

"Aye, that they did, Mr. Petrie." He rested his left elbow casually on the rail, looking relaxed for once. "I had me doubts, but your crew has proved to be worthy additions to me ship."

I glanced down, watching the water surging past our hull. "I appreciate that, Captain. It's been quite the learning experience for us all." He grunted his confirmation, continuing to stand there looking at me.

Unnerved, I said, "Is there anything else, Captain?"

He nodded, growling, "Aye, there is, lad." He paused for several seconds before saying, "Ye don't be thinking much of me, do ye, Roger?"

His question disturbed me deeply. His volcanic temper was legendary amongst the crew. Though I have only been aboard a short while, I had witnessed it countless times. We may be having a genteel conversation now, but his mood could change at the slightest provocation.

"I'm not sure I understand your question, Captain."

He barked loudly, rolling his eyes. "The hell ye don't! I be seeing how ye regard me, especially during battle. Ye don't be hiding your emotions well, Roger, your face be reflecting what lays in your heart. Ye object to how we freebooters be comporting ourselves and have little taste for bloodletting."

I said nothing, my heart chilled by his words and about where this conversation was going.

"I be watching ye, ever since ye set foot aboard me ship. I tell ye, there be times I debated running ye through."

That chilled me even more. "Why would you consider doing that?"

"Ye be a proud man, Mr. Petrie. Ye have the loyalty and respect of your men. I be noticing that from whence we met. Ye acted quickly and with conviction back at Tortola. And ye be a learned man to boot, the sum of which bodes ill for me and me crew." I expressed surprise, which he chuckled at. "Don't be vexed by me words, Roger, many a gentleman of fortune be deposed by the likes of ye. Ye be working laboriously at your given tasks, yet always there be anger and resentment close at hand. Which makes keeping ye aboard a dangerous notion for me."

What could I say to that? If he was considering killing me, I was not going to give him the satisfaction of seeing me reduced to a whimpering coward. "It's your ship, Captain. But you are correct, sir, I don't approve of some of your methods, especially torturing and maiming innocent sailors. I make no apologies for valuing human life. If my morality condemns me, so be it."

Unexpectedly, he clapped my shoulder and laughed. "By thunder, ye be having some moxie! Most of me crew are not so forthright in me presence. I be finding that refreshing."

"May I ask, Captain, why you use the tactics you do?"

He turned contemplative. "We be outlaws, Roger. Our entire way of life be revolving around capturing plunder with minimal loss to me ship and crew. When we hoist the black flag, we desire our prize heave to without resisting, surrender the plunder without conflict, and sail on without casualties. The only way, Roger, that ships be surrendering be if they fear us. We cultivate that fear carefully. If we must battle to vanquish our prize, the cost to me ship and crew be heavy. That be why I leave survivors, to tell the tale of the cruel, bloodthirsty Captain Benjamin Craven. Only by fomenting terror amongst sailors can we be achieving our aims without losing our limbs, am I explicit?"

I nodded, saying nothing. I understood all too well, but that did not mean I approved. If I managed to stay alive here, I knew I would devote myself to changing our methods and tactics, to get the plunder without invoking violence, torture, and death. I wondered if Craven sensed this resolve in me.

Answering my question, he said, "I be discerning your displeasure, Roger, and ye be the kind of man who might seek to change that which he cannot abide. Ye also have shewn a keen, calculating mind, a savvy for tactical and strategic thinking. Those be valuable commodities to a ship captain, truly. So, I must be deciding, be it more dangerous for me to keep ye close, or cut ye loose?"

I returned his gaze. "That is a decision only you can make, Captain."

His eyes bored into mine. "Tell me, Mr. Petrie—wouldst ye depose me, if the opportunity presented itself?"

My knees almost buckled at his straightforwardness. After a moment's hesitation, I said, "No, Captain, I don't suppose I would. The inclination would beckon, certainly, but I was raised and trained to follow orders from my superiors and carry them out expediently. That part of me hasn't changed, from warship to cargo ship to pirate ship. I don't condone or seek to be a part of wanton bloodlust, but I won't hinder you, sir, not while you still command."

He studied me for a moment, then nodded, turning to look out to sea. "Now there be a true word as ever was heard spoke, Mr. Petrie. We have an accord, then—ye not be planning me demise, and I not be planning yours."

"Aye, Captain, an accord it is," I said, relieved to still have my head attached after an encounter with Craven. He grasped my forearm, to seal the accord.

"One last thing, Roger. As I bespake, you've proved your mettle, being quick and adaptable. Be reporting directly to Mr. Vogel—I need someone like ye, improving upon me abilities to keep me ship afloat, armed, and fed."

"Aye, Captain, I'll do that immediately."

I was stunned; one moment he was deciding whether to kill me or not, the next I was being promoted to Assistant Quartermaster, a huge leap in rank. The captain reigned supreme during battle, but in non-combat operations the quartermaster might be just as powerful.

The chain of command so familiar to me on board both my former ships was considerably more complicated on *Renegade.*

I started to say something to express my appreciation, but a frown darkened his face. “That be all, Mr. Petrie.”

He left to attend to other matters; apparently, our moment of emotional bonding was over.

THIRTY-ONE

"A smooth sea never made a skilled Pirate."
—Anonymous

Orlando, FL
Saturday, April 6, 2019
14 years, 3 months, 21 days since Reemergence

Saturday morning came early.

Especially at the hour Rebekah wanted to leave for Orlando, even though it was only a little over an hour from our house to Kissimmee. Rebekah's mom Dana and my sister Chloe had spent the night at our place, and Tom came rambling in at seven. The seven of us crammed into our minivan, with Rebekah bringing along a cooler full of drinks and backpack full of snacks.

The drive was pleasant, the children growing more excited as we turned onto the main Disney avenue. I chose preferred parking, because my hip was bothering me more than usual and our walk would be shorter. We rode the bus from the Transportation Center to the Magic Kingdom, its line shorter than the ferry's or Monorail's.

Rebekah was bright-eyed and eager as we stood in line with our tickets. This was our first visit to Disney since 2008, and it was her favorite vacation spot on earth.

She had something special planned for Riley and Drake but would not tell me what. We did the deal, hitting up Tomorrowland (including Space Mountain and the Space Ranger Spin, my favorites), then traversed across the park to Frontierland, then Adventureland, where we climbed the Swiss Family Robinson Tree House and braved the dangers of the Jungle River Cruise.

We finally rolled up to the Pirates of the Caribbean ride. It was my favorite Disney ride as a kid, but after my actual pirating experiences, the ride now hit a little too close to home.

Tom sidled up next to me. "Pull yourself together, bro!"

"What are you talking about?"

"Ever since we headed for this ride you've been sweating like a pig, and you're white as a sheet! Man up, for crying out loud!"

Rebekah studied us curiously. "Everything all right, babe?" she asked. "You're looking a little peaked."

I gulped some water from my bottle, swishing the liquid around in my mouth. "I'm fine, honey, the heat got to me for a minute."

"Whatever you say," she responded, not reassured at all.

"Well, let's get to the ride then!" Tom exclaimed. "It's cool and dark, so Roger should be fine in there."

"We have something to do first," Rebekah interjected. "Kids, come with me, I've got a big surprise for you!"

Riley and Drake rushed to Rebekah's side, yammering at her as she walked past the entrance to the ride. *Where are we going*? I wondered. There was a door past the gift shop, and a sign above it announced *The Pirates League*. We went to the counter inside, where a lady in period dress named Constance greeted us. Rebekah gave her the kids' names, speaking loudly because our children were screaming and jumping up and down in their excitement.

"What is this, Rebekah?" I asked when she was done registering.

"I found it online. It's a special make-up experience where the kids get to choose an outfit, like a pirate captain, pirate princess, or a zombie. It looks cool, doesn't it?"

I sighed resignedly. Getting made up like a pirate…a perfect follow-up to the events of yesterday.

When they announced the kids' names, Riley about jumped out of her skin. "Is that us? Is that us?" she kept yelping, bouncing up and down. Each child was assigned a Pirate Master who was going to apply the actual make-up, and then they were shown different options on how they could be made up. Riley chose a pirate princess and Drake chose the zombie. They also went to a book-and-basket contraption that picked out new pirate names for them both.

It was fun watching them get seated and having face paint, eyeliner, and lipstick applied. The Pirate Masters, Angelika and Marisol, did a great job, looking like they truly enjoyed their work, talking and joking with the kids as they fashioned the kids' makeup. Drake and Riley each received a head bandana, an eye patch, a necklace with a facsimile of the gold coins from the first POTC movie, and a key to Captain Jack's treasure chest. It was a whole production, which we all really enjoyed.

I printed out a dog tag with Riley's new pirate name, Rosa Firecastle, and placed it over her head. I was impressed with the quality of the icons the kids received; they were not cheap plastic trinkets but solid pieces, which was very cool. Rebekah snapped oodles of pictures, and then we ventured into the gift shop for a quick look around.

Finally, it was time for the ride. I purposed to make the best of it. The line was short, so soon all seven of us were squeezing into one of the ride's boats; Tom, Chloe, and Dana were in front and Rebekah, Riley, Drake, and I were in the back. We slid into the water and off we went. I worried how the resurfacing of old feelings would affect me; guess I would find out soon enough.

The first dioramas involved skeletons, lightning flashing, and thunder rolling as one manned the ship's wheel in a storm. I remembered gripping the slick wood of the *Renegade's* as rain poured down in sheets and the howling wind ripped through the sails. We'd sailed through the outer bands of a hurricane once, lightning flashing in jagged bolts across our bows, raging waves crashing over the deck to soak me from head to toe, only the king spoke on the wheel letting me know what direction I was steering…

Rebekah put her hand on my shoulder. "Roger! Are you all right, babe?" I realized I was gripping the handrail in front so tightly my knuckles were white.

"Yeah, I'm fine. I don't know what came over me," I smiled, patting her leg, which did little to assuage her concern.

"I thought getting you out of the heat would do you good. Maybe I was wrong," she worried.

"Honey, I'm okay, I promise. Now sit back and let's enjoy the rest of the ride." I hoped that was possible.

A little while later, we rounded a corner to cannon blasts and salvo splashes, as a pirate ship and a fort exchanged fire. Did that bring back memories! I closed my eyes, recollections flooding my mind. I could smell the stench of cordite, feel the *Renegade's* deck shudder at the firing of her cannons. I could hear the clashing of steel as we battled enemy sailors in close quarters, see the blasts of splinters unleashed as cannonballs struck *Renegade.* I sat mesmerized, all the sights, sounds, and smells of battle swirling around in my head…

"Mr. Petrie, bring her 'round easy, line up with the shore guns!" Craven ordered.

"Aye, Captain, coming about now," I replied. After my first disastrous experience helming Renegade, *I had practiced under Slocum's tutelage, and my seamanship was markedly improving. Today we were attacking a small port on Martinique, garrisoned by a handful of French troops who were protected by a battery of guns high up in stone emplacements.*

"Mr. Spenser, ready on the port guns! Target the fort first, then the barracks."

"Aye, Captain, loading explosive shot now," Spenser reported back.

We were two miles out to sea, well out of range of the shore batteries but within range of our new brass, breech-loading cannons and their high-tech ammunition. Tacking north and south along the western shore of Martinique, the steady southwesterly wind kept Renegade *listing to the west. Our gunners would have to compensate for this as we cruised by our targets—our guns would ride high to the east, would have to be trained down to hit the fortifications.*

At Craven's command, our cannons began a steady bombarding of the upper fort. Once its guns were silenced, the three fat merchantmen sitting in the harbor would be ours for the taking.

Earth and rock blasted skyward as our high-explosive shells struck the fort's ramparts. The soldiers manning the fort's batteries gamely returned fire, their salvos falling far short.

Craven was emboldened by this feeble answering fire. "Bring her closer, Mr. Petrie, we far outrange these bilge-sucking lubbers!"

"Aye, sir, we'll close the distance on our next pass."

We crept closer to shore, continuing to pepper the fort with high-explosive shells. Their counterbattery fire was petering out, cannonballs still landing well short of our current course.

Craven ordered us closer still.

As we came about again, there were fiery blasts through the tree line closer to shore. Cannons! By the muzzle blasts, they were much *bigger than the ones higher up. Intense whistling sounds assaulted our ears, and large shot thundered into the sea all around us.*

"Captain, we're bracketed!" Berger yelled.

I was amazed to see Craven standing on the railing, holding a side stay and laughing hysterically. "The cursed French be hiding guns in the trees, using the fort to be drawing us close! A splendid trap, it is! Avast, me hearties, the fight beckons! Heave ahead and lay your backs into it, ye scurvy seadogs!"

The scene was unreal, as we scrambled to fire our guns as rapidly as possible, me doing my best to dodge cannonballs whizzing through the air, Craven roaring maniacally through it all…

*****

"Roger, what is the matter with you?" I was jerked back to the present as Rebekah tugged on my arm, real fear in her eyes. Tom, Drake, Dana, and Chloe were also regarding me curiously. Riley was oblivious, engrossed in the scenery of the ride.

"Wh-what's the problem, Rebekah?" I stammered.

"You had your eyes closed and you were yelling and ducking! What's gotten into you?" she demanded.

I brushed off her concerns, but her anxiety continued unabated. I squeezed her hand reassuringly and tried to relax for the rest of the ride, but the last part brought back memories as well, of the ports we had visited while on *Renegade*. Memories of dank alleyways covered in horse droppings, stumbling drunks, riotous bars and gambling houses, women of ill repute trying to separate us from our parceled shares, random shooting, and trying to remain unstained by the muck and mire.

All because you could not go to a more reputable port, lest you be arrested and hung for piracy. It was the darker side of pirate existence few people know about.

When we finally came to the end and I shakily exited the boat, I found myself being scrutinized by the other adults in our party. Tom thought it was humorous, but the ladies were not amused. I imagined the rest of the afternoon would be spent answering all their questions and trying to prove I was not suffering from heat exhaustion or a brain aneurysm.

Rebekah grabbed my arm and angrily guided me to an isolated spot in the gift shop by the restrooms. She wore a particularly unhappy expression as she lit into me.

"Would you care to explain what happened to you in there?" she forced out between clenched teeth.

I played the innocent card. "What are you talking about? I was anxious because I felt light-headed for a moment, but I'm fine now, everything's fine." That should allay her fears magnificently.

"Oh, bears, Roger! You're not fine, and everything's not fine!" she responded angrily. "I just watched you white-knuckle it through a children's ride! Are you aware you spent the last part of the ride looking from side to side with your mouth wide open? That you ducked whenever the cannons fired? Your daughter was oblivious, but Drake noticed; he doesn't miss much. And Tom, Chloe, and Mom all saw your histrionics. You owe me an explanation. It was almost like you were reliving past episodes in your memory, but that's not possible, right?"

She blanched, and I could tell an idea was formulating behind her eyes. "Tom's stories, they are only stories, right, Roger? He hasn't sucked you into his alternate reality, has he?" There was a silent plea behind those questions.

"Honey, please don't worry. You know I have bad reactions to foods or drinks sometimes." Which was true—I had IBS, which led to many uncomfortable digestive issues. That was not why I had freaked out, of course, but it sounded reasonable.

"Do we need to go to the clinic?" she persisted.

"No. Look, I haven't felt good all morning, but I didn't say anything because you were so excited for today, and I didn't want to ruin it for you. Come on, let's enjoy the rest of our day."

She looked dubious, but we went on and did the rest of the park, not leaving until after the fireworks, but her mood toward me remained frosty.

In my bones, I felt a reckoning was coming my way, sooner or later.

*****

The ride home was long and dreary. Rebekah stared out the window the whole way, still scared by what she had seen from me. Not a word passed between us.

When we arrived at our villa, Tom went home, Chloe and Dana went to the extra bedroom, and we put the kids to bed. I shuffled through my bedtime routine, ready for a good night's sleep.

Rebekah was reading in bed by the time I was ready to get under the covers. I told her about the conversation with Riley last night. I felt those feelings had only been strengthened with today's *Pirates League* experience.

"It was a lovely day—for the most part," she said pointedly. "I do worry we're sending her mixed messages. We don't want to belittle her imagination, but we can't overstimulate her, either."

"I agree."

"Do you?" she shot back. "Uncle Tom is a hero to her, and so are you, if you haven't noticed. We have to be careful, because Riley happens to love you both very much and enjoys fantasizing about you being pirates."

"Honey, I know!" I said, exasperated. "You don't have to belabor the point."

"I think I do," she retorted. "She's picked up on your unhappiness with Tom. That concerns me. And your reaction during the pirate ride frightened me, a lot. It's like you were reliving painful memories, which I know is stupid, but I know what I saw. What do you have against pirates, anyway?"

Seriously? "I don't have anything against them, but lately we can't make it through one day without the subject coming up. I mean, how much of one thing do we need? I wish everyone would stop treating them as some sort of heroes, because in real life, most of them were anything but!"

"And how exactly would you know that, Roger?" she asked pointedly. "Are you as much of an expert on them as Tom is?"

"What?" I asked, incredulous. "I know more about pirates than he does, and believe me, he plays loose with the facts!"

"Like what?"

"Here's the thing: we need for the kids to have role models who have the same morals and values we do, not ones who went around stealing things and terrorizing innocent people."

"I know that, Roger, but to her, pirates fill that void..."

"And they shouldn't!" I hollered, too loudly. "That's my whole point!"

"Oh, please! Riley's very capable of separating fact from fiction, and this obsession with pirates will pass soon enough. Before long she'll get interested in boys, and you'll wish she still loved pirates."

"I sincerely doubt that!" I fumed.

"Why are you still wanting to fight about this? My original point still stands; you need to be careful with her when talking about pirates and your brother."

"And my original point still stands. I've had it up to here with pirates in this house! I wish I'd never hear that blasted word again!"

"Roger!" Rebekah cried.

"No, I mean it, Rebekah, and I…" I stopped when Rebekah covered her mouth with her hand and pointed at our bedroom door. I swiveled around and saw Riley standing there, looking stricken. Her lower lip quivered as tears streamed down her cheeks, the baleful look in her eyes like daggers through my heart. She dashed back to her room, yelling at me before slamming her door.

Rebekah's eyes were watering, too. "Nicely done, Roger. You've just undone everything you think you accomplished last night." She threw back the covers, put on her slippers, and shuffled to Riley's door, pleading to be let in.

Later, I lay staring at the ceiling. Riley's last words repeated themselves over and over in my head:

"You lied to me, Daddy! Everything you said last night was a lie! I hate you!"

Yep, my credibility with her was buried deeper than any treasure had ever been.

THIRTY-TWO

"I returned to the sea, no matrimony for me, I be better off serving wit' me scurvy crew!"
—Pirate Ditty

Sarasota, FL
Sunday, April 7, 2019
14 years, 3 months, 22 days since Reemergence

After the spectacular blowup of the night before, emotions were raw in the Petrie household.

After lunch, Tom and I walked down to the Palm Isles' clubhouse. It boasted a nice veranda overlooking a lake, a prime vista for clearing my head. We leaned over the veranda's railing, listening to the soothing sounds of the twin fountains. Neither of us spoke, though I could feel he wanted to say something to me.

Finally, he turned to face me. “Dude, what is your problem? You cut Riley to the quick, man, and you act like you’re ashamed of our past, ashamed of me.” He paused, hurt. “*Are* you ashamed of me, Roger?”

“Of course not, Tom!” I did not sound convincing, even to myself. “I *am* reaching the end of my rope, though. Every day, no matter where I am, every conversation eventually turns to pirates. It feels like they’ve taken over my family, and I’m sick of it.”

“We were pirates once, you know,” he pointed out, “and not just any pirates, bro. We were the best the world had ever seen. We didn’t hurt people, and we never got caught. That’s a successful run in anyone’s book.”

I sighed heavily. “I *know* we were pirates once, Tom. We may not have killed anyone, but we beat them up, stole their belongings, and wrecked their ships. We affected commerce in the Caribbean and disrupted people’s livelihoods. That still haunts me, and the ride yesterday didn’t help. I’m pretty sure Rebekah thinks I’m crazy now.”

He snorted defiantly. “Your daughter loved that ride, you know. She said it was the happiest day of her life, getting made up like Princess Esmerelda and wearing her bandana and earring all day. I don’t think she’s taken off the key or medallion since.”

“I don’t need any lectures from you about my daughter!” I spat. “Your big mouth about everything we did is the reason we’re in this mess. She’s got all these wild ideas in her head about how fun and harmless pirating is, and it’s your fault. If she’d been there the day Craven died or been on the *Cantabria* to see him in action, she’d never want to hear another pirate story the rest of her life.”

He said nothing. Those days had been full of violence, bloodshed, and death. “Well, how many of our ‘exploits’ *have* you told her about?” he inquired.

"None!" I exploded. "Blimey, that's all she needs on top of your foolishness! Can you imagine what she'd be like if I fed into her fantasies? The less she and Rebekah know, the better."

"You believe Rebekah knows nothing, doesn't have an inkling about your dark secrets?" Tom probed.

"Sort of. She knows something's up, but she's not sure what. She sure doesn't suspect I was ever a real pirate."

"Uh-huh," he answered. "You know, one day you're going to have to explain to her where all the stuff you've got stashed around the city came from."

"Thanks, Dad," I scolded. "I've got a lawyer on retainer, so if anything happens to me, the loot gets liquidated and the proceeds will be distributed to Rebekah."

Tom grunted disparagingly. "Yes, how neat that will be: 'Mrs. Petrie, we can't tell you where these millions of dollars came from, but they're from Roger's estate, so here you go.' Sounds like you've got everything all figured out."

"Well, Mr. Quartermaster, what would you suggest? Spill the beans and accept the consequences? Can you imagine the reactions of Rebekah, Riley, and our family? They'd either hate us for being criminals or throw us in the loony bin. I don't know which would be worse. You don't have the responsibilities I have, Tom."

"Spare me your 'the weight of the world is on my shoulders' routine, Roger," he said, annoyed. "It's wearing pretty thin."

"That's so easy for you to say, isn't it? You don't have what I have—"

"You're exactly right, Roger," he interrupted. "I don't have your nightmares, receding hairline, or fear of the future. Have you forgotten what pirate life was all about? Enjoying the moment, not worrying about the next day. You can't enjoy today because you're too worried about tomorrow, even though you've got more wealth than you could ever need. What's there to be afraid of?"

I didn't answer immediately, and we both stood looking out over the lake, listening to the splattering of the fountain. Finally, Tom spoke softly, "You weren't always like this, you know. Once upon a time you commanded a proud ship with sixty men who were willing to die for you, and you were confident, decisive, clever, just, and fair. What happened to that Roger Petrie?"

"Times change, Tom. People change, circumstances change," I sighed. "It's not that easy anymore."

He studied me for a moment. "It could be. You're only choosing to complicate things. You were a great captain, and a good man to boot."

"Maybe," I answered, "but I don't have the compulsion you do to sit around and say *ooh, aren't we so cool because we were pirates*. I haven't felt that way for a long time, and I can't divorce my conscience from my past actions. I can scarcely look at myself anymore, thanks to you."

He stabbed a finger at me. "You're feeling guilty! Guilty for surviving the *Belvedere*, and guilty for serving on the *Renegade*!" He made a disgusted sound. "I can't believe you're still harboring that junk after all these years."

"And you aren't?"

"No! What was I supposed to do?" he complained. "I was obliged to join Craven the same as you! I chose to embrace that new life because I didn't see any alternatives."

"There are always alternatives," I said, knowing that sounded ridiculous.

"Thank you, Mr. Spock, that really added some clarity!" he snorted derisively. "Roger, we were thrown back in time *three hundred years*. We had no money, no clothes, no contacts, and no prospects. The world was a far more lawless and dangerous place in 1720. Had we decided to eschew piracy, we would've been stranded on that other island, too, though I feel confident Craven would have just killed us. Either way, we weren't going to live long."

"Perhaps you forget that we left some shipmates behind—"

"Don't you dare!" he replied angrily. "They chose their fate same as us. We did the best we could for them, Roger, you know that. It killed me that we never found them."

His points were sound. Still, I was Roger Petrie, the reasonable one, right? "Aye, a lot of that's true, but I wish we had done more…"

He chuckled humorlessly. "Were we going to fix the *Belvedere*? Not in 1720. And if we hadn't joined Craven, what then? If we managed to get off the island, we would have ended up begging in the streets, right next to the poor sots we saw in every port. Is that the life you're trying to sell me on?" He paused, shaking with emotion. "Not to mention the most important fact of all, Roger—apart from *Renegade*, we never would have made it back to this time. You know that as well as I do."

That rang true, too. "Okay, we did the best we could by our crew. It's just…sometimes I wish you'd explain pirate life to Riley more realistically. You make it sound like one big frat party."

"What's the harm in allowing her a little fun and fantasy?" He ran a hand through his hair, clearly frustrated. "You know what really gets me? You and I shared an incredible experience together, one unprecedented in human existence, and you can't embrace that. I mean, how many people in the history of the world had the experiences we did? That's what blows my mind even today—we were *there*, man! We were *real pirates*! And once Craven and his officers died, we were the most benevolent pirate crew who ever sailed the Caribbean." He put his arm around my shoulders, hugging me close. "Do you hear what I'm saying, Roger? You were a *pirate captain*, and a bloody good one! You and I ruled the Caribbean, for however short a time that was. What else have we ever done that compares to that?" He was so earnest, so sincere in his arguments. "I can't help it, bro. I want to share that with people I care about. And Riley loves it, man, she loves it with all her heart."

"You can afford to be that way, Tom. What real obligations do you have? I have a family and a reputation to protect."

Tom looked at me uncomprehendingly. "Are you serious? You're that worried about your reputation? Your family is provided for, for generations to come! Who are you so thirsty for approval from? You certainly don't need to prove anything to Rebekah."

"You leave Rebekah out of this," I warned.

"Man, I can't believe you're playing it this way. She is so great, and you're cutting her out of a major part of your life." He shook his head sadly. "I hate to say it, but I pity you, man."

Red fury exploded in my mind. "*You* pity *me*? That's a laugh, coming from the likes of you!"

We became aware our heated argument had drawn a crowd; people stood in both doorways gawking at us, whispering excitedly. Several couples at either end of the veranda were watching and listening, having failed at trying to appear disinterested.

Tom sighed, turned, and murmured softly, "You know what your problem is, bro? You can't forgive yourself. That's why I pity you. You lived the adventure of a lifetime, but you try and deny that every single day. You have a great life now, in *this* time, but you won't allow yourself to live it! You have a gorgeous wife who loves you, a beautiful daughter who adores you, a son who is terrific, and you can't enjoy them because you're too busy feeling sorry for yourself. And because you feel you can't make amends for your past actions you have the audacity to project your guilt onto me." He clapped me on my shoulder. “Sorry, Roger, that’s one order of yours I won’t be following.” With that he spun on his heels and walked quickly inside the clubhouse, ignoring the gaggle of folks whispering and pointing.

I stayed at the railing a long time, pondering on his words and everything that had happened tonight. Was he right? Was all my angst about pirates and my former life due to unresolved guilt and shame?

How could Riley ever forgive me for what I said last night, if I could not forgive myself?

THIRTY-THREE

"When a man comes to like a sea life, he is not fit to live on land."
—Dr. Samuel Johnson, Writer

From the Personal Journal of Roger M Petrie
Aboard the Renegade
December 24, 1720

Ah, Christmas Eve 1720.

Alas, there was no Christmas tree, no gay display of lights, no presents, no turkey dinner. Dinner on the *Renegade* consisted of smoked beef and pork, shark, sauerkraut, citrus, and bread, all washed down with rum. My parents would have been appalled at the table manners of my shipmates, and their dinner conversations would have made my grandmothers blush. None of them washed their hands before eating, and no one used cloth napkins to wipe up their messes. The sight of these brutish men sitting around, eating with their hands, and stuffing their faces with abandon made me laugh.

Interestingly, simple foods I took for granted were valued as delicacies on board *Renegade*, because there had not been ways to store perishables. Things like bread, butter, and cheese. A more common food was hardtack, which I avoided like the plague. Weevils still managed to infest our hardtack stores, so no wormy biscuits for me, thanks.

We were making brisk headway, moving south from Florida, planning to sail west of the Bahamas to resume hunting in the Virgin Islands. After the sun dipped below the horizon—the ship dark except for the occasional hooded LED lantern—I walked along the starboard weather deck, gazing up at the sky. It was a cloudless, moonless night, allowing thousands of stars to blaze down upon us in all their glory. That sight never got old. Here and there, a shooting star would flare briefly, drawing a fiery trail across the expanse of the heavens.

When I compared walking the deck of *Renegade* with modern ships, I realized how different the experience was. On modern vessels, there was always background noise from machinery. The interior spaces constantly thrummed with mechanical and human commotion. In the engineering spaces, ear protection was mandatory because it was so loud. But here the shipboard sounds were softer, simpler, cleaner. I listened to the rush of the sea against the hull, the wind rustling the shrouds and stays, the flapping and snapping of the sails, the hull and decks creaking as *Renegade* yawed gently in the calm seas.

A guy could get used to this I thought.

Through the evening, several men played lively tunes as the crew sang and danced along. Like most of the shanties they sang, the songs were peppered with obscenities and terribly profane. They knew none of the traditional Christmas carols, for which I was thankful.

Closer to the bow, I came across a couple of guys singing while playing weathered guitars, and they were quite good:

A fair time ago, back in me past,
I be pledged to marry a bonny lass.
She 'ad hair of scarlet,
She 'twasn't no harlot,
Our love be destined to last and last.

For months on end, I be out to sea,
She swore she'd always be waitin' for me.
Me mates couldn't be sure,
and swore she 'twasn't that pure,
that she 'twasn't no model of chastity.

I be cut to the quick, but I had to know,
Was me wench a-courtin' another beau?
I burst in to find her,
Wit' a lubber beside her,
How could she be betrayin' me so?

At first, I knowed not what I should do,
Then I drew me cutlass and ran him through!
I returned to the sea,
No matrimony for me!
I be better off serving wit' me scurvy crew!

I briefly ruined their jam session, though, when I asked, "Can you guys play Dueling Banjos?" They were totally confused by this twentieth-century reference, looking at me like I was mad. I quickly got up and removed myself from their presence.

*****

December 25, 1720

Christmas Day broke bright and delightful, with clear skies, gentle winds, and warm temperatures. I checked my socks, which were soaking wet, but there were no gifts from Santa Claus, not even a lump of coal.

I was somewhat disappointed with that.

It had been four weeks since we former *Belvedere* sailors had been impressed into service aboard *Renegade*, and the regular crew was getting used to our modern idiosyncrasies—to a degree, at least. One benefit was my muscles were becoming lean and hard from the manual nature of my work. My belly had flattened, and I noticed straps of muscle were now lining my shoulders, and my bicep veins were now visible. That held true for the rest of my former crew, as our bodies hardened and toughened with the plentiful protein we consumed and the vigorous activity we engaged in.

Vogel finally deigned to issue us "proper weapons", so we each now sported a variety of blades. Tom and I strapped the Colt .45s to our legs, which our billowy breeches hid excellently. I was digging having a real cutlass sheathed to my belt, along with my Colt Bowie and fighting knives. It is totally an immature man-thing, but it is hard not to feel like an action hero walking around with umpteen blades clinking at your every step.

My one complaint was that the blade I had been issued was a small, rusty thing. I brought it up to Mr. Vogel, to no avail.

"Mr. Petrie, you've not exactly proven your prowess with a blade yet, lad. Once you demonstrate to Mr. Berger you be worthy of a better blade, I'll be providing you one. Not before."

And that was the end of that.

The eastern Caribbean would still be a target-rich environment, so our spirits were high on that Christmas day. The proverbial pot of gold still eluded us, but we had scored several nice prizes during

December, and I was satisfied thus far with my share of the loot. My share comprised of numerous pieces of eight, a bolt of red silk that I fashioned into sashes and bandanas, and rations of coffee and ale. From other pirate crews we ran into in port, we found we were making out pretty good compared to most.

We were gunning, however, for much, much more.

THIRTY-FOUR

"If the highest aim of a captain were to preserve his ship, he would keep it in port forever."
—Thomas Aquinas

Sarasota, FL
Saturday, April 20, 2019
14 years, 4 months, 4 days since Reemergence

Palm Isles was holding a block party on Sunday afternoon.

Tom had invited us to join him, which surprised me considering recent events, but it was a welcome reprieve to the tension festering in our house. Bonnie volunteered to babysit, so we took advantage of the opportunity.

Halfway through the night, I questioned why he had bothered. He was very standoffish, not engaging us in any appreciable way. From discussions with other people, I gathered that he was well-liked in this community, though snootier members regarded him like he was their crazy uncle. He paid his dues and gave generously at their charity events, so he continued in good standing.

I did not know most of the people here—not personally, anyway. Rebekah left me briefly to speak with some acquaintances. I meandered around the clubhouse, managing to avoid talking to anyone for over half an hour while munching on a plateful of peeled shrimp.

Eventually, Rebekah found me and introduced me to a striking blonde woman she had met moments earlier. She was tall—about five feet ten—with blue eyes and a charming southern accent.

"Roger, this is my new friend Charlotte Seymore. She transferred here last month from Dallas, and just moved in two weeks ago."

"Pleased to meet you, Charlotte," I said. "I love your accent. Where are you from, originally?"

"Georgia. I grew up in Marietta and moved to Columbus when I was in middle school."

"Columbus? Small world, isn't it? My brother, Tom, worked in Albany for a few years after graduating from Georgia Tech."

"I know, Rebekah mentioned that while pointing him out, though I met him briefly last month," she giggled.

"Ah, ever the matchmaker. Hope springs eternal," I said, popping a shrimp into my mouth.

Rebekah smiled at me, *too* sweetly. "Well, I'm so happily married to you, honey, that I want everyone else to experience the same kind of joy and happiness that I have."

Charlotte laughed. I liked her laugh; it was light and endearing. "So, Roger," she began in her delightful southern accent, "tell me more about Tom. He's been stealing glances at me all night."

"Listen, Charlotte, if you want the scoop on Tom, ask me, not Roger," Rebekah advised seriously. "They've had a falling out recently, so I'm not sure you'll get the straight skinny from him."

"I really like your wife, Roger. We only met tonight, yet I feel like I've known her forever!" They giggled and hugged like they were life-long BFFs. I sighed resignedly.

"Now Charlotte, Tom's quite a catch," Rebekah stated. "He's an engineer, so he's got a good job. He's very smart, has a great sense of humor, loves children, and he's cute! Plus, he's still got all his hair."

Charlotte twittered at that. My first impression was that she was fun, outgoing, and highly intelligent. She might be the one to give Tom a run for his money.

We spoke for another ten minutes or so, Rebekah and I continuing to sing Tom's praises. Charlotte beckoned us to a quiet corner of the room, out of the circulatory paths of the club's serial hobnobbers. When we were properly sequestered, she spoke softly, "But there is something that I wanted to ask about, because more than one person has brought it up to me."

Oh boy, I thought, *here it comes...*

"I wouldn't even worry about it if it wasn't so odd," she continued. *Lady, you have no idea.* "Several people told me to be careful of him, because...well, because he has some eccentricities that might be of concern."

Rebekah continued her innocent routine. "I can't imagine what they're talking about; he's always been perfectly charming around us. Isn't that so, Roger?" Wow, she was laying it on thick. Did she think if she paired Tom off, he would forget the whole pirate thing?

There was no chance of that.

She pressed on. "What eccentricities are they accusing Tom of having?"

"Well," Charlotte began cautiously, "some of the folks around here are of the opinion that Tom believes…at some point he is, or was, a pirate. Isn't that the funniest thing you've ever heard?"

I coughed to cover up my laugh, earning myself a sharp elbow in the ribs from Rebekah. "A pirate?" she said, her eyebrows raised. "Wouldn't that be exciting, if it were true?"

"Did you ask him about it?" I asked.

"Oh, heavens no! We've only met twice, briefly, and to start up with that—what a disaster that would be!"

"The people around here are pretty stuffy. They're probably jealous of his swashbuckling style and buccaneer attitude," I offered, drawing a laugh from Charlotte and a scowl from Rebekah.

I was beginning to enjoy this party.

"I thought it was some big joke I hadn't been let in on, but these people were serious!" Charlotte whispered. "It's so weird because he's gone out of his way to make me feel welcome. I need you to be honest with me—does this rumor hold any water?"

I cleared my throat, ignoring a warning look from Rebekah, and said, "Tom, a pirate, you say? Well, yes, I can tell you that Tom can be a bit of a rogue at heart."

Charlotte cocked her head inquisitively. "What do you mean by that, Roger?"

"Simply that he's fiercely independent. He's never been married —not for a lack of suitors—and he does what he wants when he wants. He wears his emotions on his sleeve, he's loyal, and he makes no apologies for living his life with gusto." I licked my fingers clean of cocktail sauce, adding, "And I'll tell you straight up, there's no one I'd want by my side in a crisis more than Tom." I spread my hands out in front of me. "I guess that's about it."

"No lack of suitors, huh?" Charlotte seemed put off by my assessment.

I laughed. "That's what you got out of my whole spiel? We have our differences, but I meant every word. He's not a lothario, if that's what you're thinking. He has high standards, has held out for what he wants."

Charlotte was relieved by that. "That's sweet, Roger. The two of you must be very close."

"Normally we are, yes," I said, causing her to regard me questioningly. "We're going through a rough patch right now, but besides Rebekah and our children, he's the most important person in my life. In fact, he saved my life on a couple of occasions. I'm very confident that eventually, we'll make things right between us."

After I had said this, I caught sight of Tom across the room. He was trying to appear nonchalant but was failing miserably. I motioned to Charlotte with my eyes. He nodded and smiled, catching my drift immediately. A sense of relief washed over me as Tom and I connected from opposite sides of the room.

Yes, eventually, things would be right between us.

THIRTY-FIVE

"In an honest service there is thin commons, low wages, and hard labor; in this (piracy), plenty and satiety, pleasure and ease, liberty and power; no, a merry life and a short one, shall be my motto."
—Bartholomew "Black Bart" Roberts

From the Personal Journal of Roger M Petrie
Aboard the Renegade
Late December 1720

I was inventorying forward stores on the cargo deck, bracing myself against the pitching of *Renegade's* bow.

We were running oblique to the wind—I could tell by the way the deck heaved unevenly beneath me. I could not stay down here for long. Even with a bandana over my mouth and nose, the stench emanating from the bilge was overpowering. I was finishing up when someone hailed me unceremoniously.

"Petrie, get your arse up on deck, quickly now!" Berger thundered.

Stumbling up the ladder, I came upon a scene of general mayhem. Sailors were engaged in mock combat all over the main deck. Tom stood to the side, giving instructions to hand-to-hand combat participants.

Berger was standing next to Tom. "Well, Roger, we be knowing your brother can handle himself in a fight. What about you?"

"Hey, I was there, too," I protested. "I can take care of myself."

"Ye don't say?" he snickered. "Let's be giving ye a chance to back that up, shall we?"

"To what purpose, Mr. Berger?" Stalling is always good, even if it only delays the inevitable.

"This be a buccaneer ship, Petrie. I need to be knowing if ye possess the skills necessary to protect our ship and vanquish our adversaries. Be that plain enough?"

Oh, it was painfully plain. Some crew were smarting on Quigley's behalf and were itching for payback. Who better to serve as their punching bag than Tom's brother? I was handed a wooden two-foot cutlass and spent the next two hours fending off enthusiastic attacks from all directions, earning grudging admiration but also multiple bruises, cuts, and scrapes.

Berger turned out to be an excellent teacher, stopping our sparring time and again to make specific points. He helped me greatly with my grip, footwork, and cutlass technique. He scolded me quite often, as well.

"Petrie, ye be waving your sword about like it be some sort of magic wand. That might work against a wee lass, but seasoned sailors be slicing ye to ribbons. Your cutlass be a weapon, lad! It be cleaving lines, smashing doors, perhaps saving your life. A cutlass be your best friend, Petrie, if ye learn to wield it properly. Now, let's have a go again, mates!"

So, we began sparring again, Berger yelling instructions constantly and reprimanding me when I got sloppy. I was beyond exhausted, and the longer we went, the sloppier I got. Finally, Berger called an end to our exercise.

"By Pleiades, I've seen crippled wenches fight more effectively! Captain Craven be plucking out 'is eyes should he observe your efforts! Watching ye blundering buffoons wield your weapons be enough to make me weep. Remove yourselves from me sight lest I keelhaul the lot of ye!"

Berger stomped off toward the bow, leaving the small gaggle of us standing amidships, sweat pouring down our faces, panting like rabid dogs. In the end, we collapsed on the deck, gulping down rum to quench our thirst.

*****

During this break in training, I walked aft and found Vogel sitting against the stern rail. He saw me and motioned that I join him.

"Ha, ye look like a drowned rat, Mr. Petrie! It's taken a while, but you seem to be acclimating yourself to life on our poor, backward vessel."

Not sure what kind of a conversation starter that was. "There have been challenges, to be sure, but a ship is a ship no matter what century you're living in."

He snorted in amusement. "Even a pirate ship, Petrie?"

"I thought this was a 'ship of fortune'."

"So it is!" he cackled. "It was a pity about Carmichael. Succumbed to his wounds right quick, he did."

Evan Carmichael, my bosun on *Belvedere*, had been pierced by three musket balls during the battle with *Falklands*. His wounds had proved fatal despite Doc's best efforts. It was sobering to consider our modern medicine had limits here.

I said nothing, staring up at the mainsail flapping in the wind. Vogel shrugged. "Aye, 'tis true, Roger. Piracy is not without its perils, eh?"

I had noticed death did not concern the crew much—pirates were used to dealing with it and dishing it out. Most knew piracy involved intrinsic risks, like dying from tropical diseases, which was quite common. Or being attacked by warships, which led to being captured and hung. Despite those risks, my shipmates remained realistic about their fate, rejoicing in their freedom, however short it might be. Weird to a man of my modern sensibilities.

Vogel resumed whittling. "Your former crew be fairly adjusted to life aboard, it seems. Especially that Tom fellow, he's an enthusiastic rapscallion, isn't he?" He gestured to me. "He's your brother, is he not?"

"Yes, he is. You're good; most people can't tell us apart."

He cackled again. "You two be as identical as a swordfish and a sea cow." I hoped Tom was the sea cow in this scenario. "He's heartily embraced freebooting, has made some right profitable improvements to *Renegade*, as I'm sure you're aware."

"Yes, I'm aware, and when I'm not aware, he delights in making me aware," I groaned, causing Vogel to laugh harder.

Tom *had* taken to pirating like a fish to water. He had initially been fearful, like us all, but had quickly embraced the life at hand, endearing himself to Captain Craven with his engineering prowess. Using cables, pulleys, and tools cannibalized from *Belvedere,* he had greatly enhanced the effectiveness of *Renegade's* hull and rigging. Modifications now allowed for storage and refrigeration of foodstuff, ventilation, and interior lighting the likes of which no eighteenth-century sailor had ever seen.

"I have to tell you, Mr. Vogel, life on board a pirate ship is much different than I imagined," I said.

He continued whittling. "How so, Mr. Petrie?"

"Well, I expected the crew to be gravelly-voiced peg-legged ruffians, with hooks for hands, eye patches on their heads, and parrots on their shoulders. Men beholden to a Brethren Court and adhering to the Pirate Code, burying their treasure on deserted islands, and leaving behind treasure maps with X marking the burial spot."

He burst out laughing. "Neptune's blood, Petrie, wherever did you get notions like that?"

"Mainly from Hollywood…" I began.

"Hollywood? I don't recall anyone from *Belvedere* by that name."

"What? Oh, Hollywood isn't a person, it's a…never mind." I gestured broadly to the crew working and playing on the deck. "I always pictured a pirate crew as a bunch of drunk English criminals being lorded over by a horrible tyrant, making terrified sailors walk the plank."

"Did this Hollywood fellow tell you that, too? He sounds daft."

I smiled. "Yes, he can be. Although he did get the 'pirates drink rum all day' bit right." I ducked as *Renegade* crested a wave, showering us with spray.

Wiping myself off, I asked, "So, you don't bury your treasure, I take it?"

He laughed again. "Bury treasure? Who'd be wanting to do that? And for what purpose?" He motioned to the crew. "Do'ye see this sorry lot, Mr. Petrie? Whatever shares they be parceled be spent soon as their feet hit dry land. I'd be fainting dead away if any of these scurvy salts had two coins to rub together once back on board."

Seeing my disbelief, he continued, "Freebooting be a bonny life indeed, Roger, but we do pine occasionally for creature comforts that be found only on land. When these grimy sots hit port, they seek out drink, women, and shelter. They come back once their booty be spent, which for some be a matter of hours!"

He howled at his own joke, then turned serious. "Most buccaneers never find riches, Roger, that be the truth of it. I be surprised if more than one ship in a hundred be carrying valuables at all. We still seek bounty foremost to survive. 'Give me today me daily bread', so to speak. I've heard of captains hoarding their booty, and true enough, greed be what brought Teach to ruin. But no, we don't go about burying our plunder. 'Twould be my misfortune, I probably wouldst forget where I buried it!"

That was some eye-opening information. "Mr. Vogel, you seem like an educated man. You could be gainfully employed wherever you chose, without threat of hanging be over your head. Why this life?"

Vogel put down his knife. "Why did I become a pirate, you mean?" He brushed wood shavings from his lap. "'Tis a complicated answer, I guess. I already be a seafaring man, privateering under Vane, so hunting plunder be in my blood. And here, there be freedom to chart my own life course, the chance to get rich. The sheer excitement of the chase…that beckons me, too. I've no idea what life be like where you come from, Roger, but in these parts, life for the common man be dull, monotonous, and a drudgery beyond anything ye can comprehend. No, we choose to live life merry, come what may. Aye, we know we be considered outlaws, but I'd rather live life short on my own terms than a multitude of years little more than property of someone else."

He resumed whittling. "Ask the poor wretches where we peddle our wares whether our deeds do them harm. We be selling our plunder at half the price they'd pay to the merchants. That be why we're welcome at a number of ports even now."

From my studies, I knew many pirates had considered themselves to be nautical Robin Hoods, robbing from the rich bureaucrats, selling the captured plunder in local markets cheaply, thereby bolstering local economies. It was quite illuminating to encounter this attitude first-hand.

"So, to our crew, this life is more attractive than a career in the Royal Navy."

"Excuse me, Petrie, but weren't you in the, what did you call it, the bloody US Navy?"

"Yeah, for six years—," I began.

"Sail, ho!" a lookout in the foremast cried, pointing to port.

Renegade yawed to port as fifty-plus men scrambled to the port rail to look. I grabbed my binoculars from a shelf underneath the chart table, aiming them in the specified direction. A ship swam into view. I could see she was a single-mast British Sloop-of-War, Union Jack flying from her topmast. She would be armed similarly to *Renegade*, but her gunners would be more highly trained, her commander more tactically adept. She was running with the wind on an intercept course, and I wondered if Craven would fight or flee.

I did not have to wait long to find out.

"Mr. Slocum, hard to starboard, show her our backsides!" Craven roared from the stern. "Mr. Rasmussen, full canvas, unfurl the topgallants! Mr. Spenser, load the port and aft cannon, in case she closes too far for me liking!"

"Aye, Captain!" they hollered in unison.

"Boom about!" Slocum shouted as he spun the wheel clockwise. *Renegade* heeled sharply to port, the fore-and-main booms swinging left, swooping over our heads until they were jerked to a halt by their lines.

The deck degenerated into a confused melee as sailors scrambled this way and that. Some scurried up ratlines to the topmasts, unfurling the topgallants over a hundred feet above the deck, always a harrowing task. Others ran to man the portside cannons, pulling on massive hemp ropes to draw the guns back to loading position, while others scooped up powder, cannonballs, and wadding, ready to load. Others grabbed up unsecured boxes, trunks, and any other loose articles and took them below.

I stood there like a statue, not knowing what to do. On board modern vessels, every sailor had a General Quarters and Abandon Ship station, somewhere they were required to be when the alarm sounded. Aboard *Renegade*, I had no such station, and served only to get in everyone else's way.

"Out o' me way, ye blundering blighter!" a spindly sailor yelled, shoving me into a hulking man headed in the opposite direction.

"Flog off, Sharkbait, ye bile-laden buffoon!" he bellowed, casting me aside, where I almost tripped a gun captain heading for the stern cannon.

"Petrie, ye feckless dolt, don't just stand there like a blasted figurehead!" He side-stepped me and continued aft.

Strong hands clutched my shoulders, propelling me forward. I turned to see Vogel scowling as we walked toward the bow. "Stand at bow lookout, Petrie, and try not to disable anyone on the way!" he snarled, giving me a shove, hastening back to the quarterdeck. Chastened, I slunk up to the bowsprit, holding fast to a forestay to balance myself.

After the riggers had run out our sails and jibs, *Renegade* surged forward on a broad reach to starboard. The Sloop had closed during our maneuvering, now two thousand yards off our port beam.

Crewmen were struggling with something on her forecastle, and I donned my binoculars to see what.

I shuddered as I watched them load a massive bombardment mortar they had bolted to the deck. The barrel was six feet long, its enormous maw a foot in diameter. The gun crew turned the mortar in our direction and elevated the barrel. That maw belched an impressive plume of flame as the mortar was fired. I had no idea what range the weapon had, but soon a whistling sound assailed our ears, followed by a tremendous impact directly in our wake not a hundred yards behind.

"Neptune's Blood!" Craven cursed, "what sort of devilish cannon be that?" Whipping around, he roared at Rasmussen. "I be needing every inch of sail, Mr. Rasmussen! Those blighters only be needing to strike us once with that confounded contraption to be scuttling us."

"Aye, Captain, we'll fly every stitch of our garments, if that be necessary!"

Craven cracked a smile. "Then let it be done, Mr. Rasmussen." Another sharp crack, another massive impact, this time to starboard. They were attempting to bracket us but hitting a moving target a nautical mile away was a daunting task for the most experienced gun crew. Not to mention that an eighty-foot Sloop was not the most stable gunnery platform. Still, these Brits had moxie, putting a cannon like that on a fast, maneuverable ship. Like Craven said, all they needed was one hit, and we most likely would be disabled or sunk.

Fortunately, we did not have to strip and set our clothes to the wind. *Renegade* slowly pulled away. The Sloop fired a salvo every two minutes, a good, steady clip for such an enormous gun. But their shot fell further and further behind, and the danger finally passed.

We collapsed on deck, spent. Bodie came up on deck, handing out sloshing Black Jacks of rum to trembling hands.

Another day, another close escape from certain death. Did anyone ever get used to living like this?

THIRTY-SIX

"It is when pirates count their booty that they become mere thieves."
—William Bolitho

St Armands Circle, FL
Saturday, April 20, 2019
14 years, 4 months, 4 days since Reemergence

Alex Sutton was *very* interested in the silver coin Roger Petrie had gifted his son Bobby, so he drove them both out to Templar's Jewelry & Fine Gifts.

The store was situated on St. Armands Circle west of Sarasota. St. Armands was an upscale development on Lido Key, describing itself as "a hub of elegant shopping and dining."

Stan Templar smiled warmly as the Suttons approached the back counter. "Hello, folks. What can I help you with today?"

Alex placed the coin on the glass. “Stan, Bobby received this as a gift, and we were hoping you could tell us something about it.”

“Well, I am a member of the American Numismatic Association,” Templar stated proudly as he picked up the coin. “I’ll be glad to inspect it for you.” Expecting it to be a worthless trinket from some vending machine, Templar was genuinely startled when he looked it over. It was hefty, thirty-two millimeters in diameter, with stampings on the front and back. He weighed it, then moved to his microscope, looking for the telltale signs of reproductions. His puzzlement increased as he saw no evidence of plating, bubbling, or edge seams. The imprints were crisp and clean, showing no signs of plating wear. This was unusual indeed!

“May I take this coin in the back room?” he asked. “I need to compare it to some references I have.”

“Sure, as long as you bring it back!” Alex smirked.

Templar sauntered to his back office. Here lay volumes sanctioned by the ANA to authenticate ancient currency. Flipping through one of them, he came to eighteenth-century Spanish coins. He compared descriptions and pictures against Bobby’s coin, then photographed it front and back and sent the pictures to a numismatist friend, asking for verification of his findings. A few moments later the friend texted him back, confirming he concurred with Templar’s analysis.

Templar returned to the counter, a quizzical expression on his weathered face. “Bobby,” he began, “may I ask where you acquired this coin?”

Bobby shrugged. “Sure, Mr. Petrie gave it to me. He said they were common where he used to work.”

Templar chuckled, muttering to himself. “Yes, they were very common, if you worked on treasure ships from the Spanish Main…”

“Is there a problem, Stan?” Alex asked.

Templar held up a hand. "Oh, no, Mr. Sutton, there is no problem at all. However, this is a fascinating coin Bobby has brought in today."

"Really? It looks like any old coin to me," Alex probed. "It's not even perfectly round."

"Ah, but this is *not* any old coin, Mr. Sutton. This is, in my opinion, a genuine 'Peso de a Ocho', what the Spanish used to call eight bits or more commonly, pieces of eight."

"Wait a minute, this is an actual piece of eight?" Sutton looked dubious.

"That is my belief, yes. It is in excellent, almost mint-like condition."

Alex inspected it more thoroughly. It had a coat of arms on one side, with "PHS" in raised letters. Turning it over, Sutton saw "HISPAIRUM REX" and "1714" stamped on it. Judging from Templar's reaction, this coin could be very valuable.

"Tell me more," he said.

"As I stated previously, this coin is specified as an Eight Reale coin, likely minted from silver mined from Spanish territory in Central and South America, called the Spanish Main," Templar explained. "Before the advent of modern coin presses, the Spanish heated sheets of gold and silver, hammered them flat, and then pounded dies into the sheets to make coins. That is why this coin's edges are irregular."

Alex frowned. "It has 1714 stamped on the back. Is that really when it was minted?"

"Correct," Templar affirmed. "This was minted under the auspices of King Phillip V, which is the PHS noted on the front. Anything minted before 1716 is considered quite rare, for pieces of eight anyway."

Sutton rubbed his chin thoughtfully. "How much is this worth today?"

"Ah, that's where it gets interesting! Treasure hunters the world over bring up specimens of Spanish coinage, but the majority are worn and poorly defined. This coin, because of its excellent condition, might be worth, oh, somewhere in the fifteen- to eighteen-hundred-dollar range to serious collectors. Maybe more. Part of the value is attached to where the coins were found. The more famous the shipwreck, the more value the coins have to certain collectors." He scratched an eyebrow in contemplation. "Some very unique specimens found near Puerto Rico were valued at over ten thousand dollars each, and a gold doubloon from the same area was valued at over one million dollars."

Sutton whistled, legitimately impressed. "Are you serious? This is worth over a thousand dollars, and maybe a lot more? Can you tell what shipwreck this is from?" He was hoping it was a famous one.

Templar consulted his notes. "I don't know for certain, but this coin bears remarkable resemblance to other silver coins recovered from a galleon called the *Nuestra de la Capistrano*, which sank in 1721."

Bobby flinched, and Alex noticed. "Bobby, have you heard that name before? Did you study it at school or something?"

Staring at his shoes, Bobby mumbled, "Yeah, Dad, Riley Petrie mentioned it in show-and-tell. She showed us a gold doubloon and said her dad and uncle stole it from the *Capistrano* back when they were pirates."

Alex smiled. "Stole this from a Spanish galleon, huh? That Riley, what an imagination she has!"

He stood up, to be met by Templar's stare. "It is quite a coincidence that this Riley mentioned the exact ship this genuine Piece of Eight might have come from."

Alex shrugged, looking down at Bobby again. "Bobby, if this coin is so valuable, why would Riley's dad give it to you?"

"Gee, Dad, I don't know. Her uncle was talking about pirates, you know, and I guess I bugged Mr. Petrie about it too much. I thought he was mad, but when I thanked him for the party, he flipped me this coin. Said they were common or something like that. That's all, I swear!"

Templar chuckled. "Pirates, eh? Well, pirates certainly plundered their share of Spanish gold and silver way back then."

"This is crazy. Where would a guy like Roger Petrie get ahold of coins like this?" Alex wanted to know.

Templar considered that. "Perhaps one of his clients is involved in marine salvage?"

"Maybe." Alex picked up the coin. "Hey, Stan, could you do me a favor? Could you write up some sort of certificate of authentication or something for this? I'd be happy to leave it with you if that's what you need."

"Certainly," Templar said, placing the coin in a small, sealed plastic bag. "I can have that ready for you in a week or so."

Sutton waved as he and Bobby headed out the door. "I appreciate that, Stan, thank you. Please call me when you're done."

And with that, they were gone.

*****

Templar stood at the counter for several minutes. "Common" coins? Preposterous! If Petrie were in possession of that many Eight Reale coins in superb condition, he would be a multi-millionaire. If he was that wealthy, he kept it well hidden.

He cackled at that. If Petrie were a pirate, of course he would keep his treasure buried!

THIRTY-SEVEN

"There can be only one Captain to a ship."
—Thomas John Barnardo

From the Personal Journal of Roger M. Petrie
Aboard the Renegade
January 1, 1721

New Year's Day 1721.

Not much of a celebration this year. There would be no fireworks, no big ball dropping, no watching Dick Clark's *New Year's Rockin' Eve*. We had captured eleven ships and raided four ill-defended towns since leaving *Belvedere,* the last capture having been a week prior. Supplies of fresh meat and fruits were beginning to run low, but our provision situation would have been much worse without the food preservation techniques engineered from modern technology.

After leaving St. Croix, we looped around Hispaniola, but our search for prey was continually hindered by naval patrols. Even the new and improved *Renegade* could not match the firepower sported by the Fourth, Fifth, and Sixth Rate warships currently being deployed in these waters. Tom had spoken about exchanging our iron muzzle-loading cannons for breech loading brass ones—with rifled barrels and explosive shot—at our next careen, but we would need to score some silver and gold to be able to afford that.

For now, we were five knots faster than most warships, and, with our shallow draft, we could traverse shallow waters where larger warships could not come. Captain Craven used these advantages to good effect, keeping us from being captured time and again. I heartily approved of his 'flee instead of fight' strategy.

I *really* wanted to avoid being hanged, if possible.

*****

January 5, 1721

We rounded the eastern end of Hispaniola and headed for Puerto Rico, hoping to catch the stray merchant ship who was seeking to avoid pirate attacks by using the one route no one else did. This course of action was my brainchild, and my credibility with Craven was now on the line.

"I hope you know what you're doing, bro," Tom whispered as we closed on the island. "If your plan goes south, Craven's going to be mighty upset."

"Thanks for that encouragement."

He fist-bumped me for luck. "Roger, I'm only telling you because I'm digging this pirate gig, and I don't want you screwing it up for me," he said as he walked away. I could not tell if he was joking—he for one seemed to be having a good time.

"Sail ho!" cried a forward lookout, pointing to a place off our starboard bow.

Everyone on the weather deck craned their necks in that direction. There it was! Barely visible against the Puerto Rican coast were the sails of a three-mast sailing ship, slowly travelling to the east against the trade winds. This was the first phase of piracy on the high seas: finding a target. It would be easier if we could utilize radar or reconnaissance aircraft, but you work with what you have.

This was a dangerous time for a pirate ship, I had learned—determining exactly what type of ship we were targeting. Craven's strategy was to shadow a ship until he could identify it as prey or not. You did not want to approach too recklessly only to have it turn out to be a warship or heavily armed merchantman.

We crept toward it cautiously, slowly closing the distance over the next two hours. Craven wanted some pursuit music, so guys with guitars and fiddles sat between the masts, playing lively tunes as we prepared for battle. At first, I found the constant music playing peculiar, but I grew to enjoy it. Stereos were in short supply in the eighteenth century, so live music proved to be a valuable tension-reducer and helped pass the time during work periods. It reminded me of Oddball in *Kelly's Heroes*, who said his tank platoon played music very loudly when they went into battle to calm them down.

Hard to argue with logic like that.

*****

Utilizing binoculars, we finally identified the ship type: an old Dutch Fluyt. She was sneaking across the Caribbean using a little-used route, hoping to make for the trades back to Europe. Unlike other merchant ships, Fluyts were not built for conversion in wartime to warships, so they were cheaper and easier to build. They could carry twice the load and half the crew as normal merchantmen, but having a small crew meant they were more vulnerable to capture. Their functional design also made them ungainly and slow. Finding an easy target like this was fortuitous, and Craven smelled blood.

Standing next to Slocum at the helm, he started barking orders. "Master Rigger, full sail, trim booms fore and aft!"

"Aye, Captain, trimming her down!" Master Rigger Rasmussen responded. He turned, relaying orders to his men. Riggers released the rigging winch brakes, turning their handles to draw in the jibs, mainsail, foresail, and topsails. Cranking the lines, they streamlined the booms to be more parallel to our keel. As the booms were drawn in, we were close hauling on a port tack to the east, paralleling the Fluyt's course but at much greater speed.

"Pilot, adjust your course five points to port every ten minutes, until she's abeam; let's ease up on her as a friend would."

"Aye, Captain!" Slocum responded.

"Mr. Vogel, please keep all but a few crew hidden until me signal; we don't want to be showing our true intentions too early, am I explicit?"

"Aye, Captain, we'll hide our scurvy seadogs 'til you give the word."

"Excellent! Mr. Rasmussen, when I give the signal, please strike that bloody English flag and hoist our colors."

"Aye, Captain."

Craven looked like a man possessed as he watched his ship eat up the distance between hunter and hunted. Cackling evilly, he watched as the other ship became aware of our presence, and it soon became evident they were not buying our friendly English ship routine. There was frantic activity on her main deck, people swarming and shouting at one another while gesturing wildly. I doubt there were more than a few flintlocks on the whole boat.

Craven turned, his eyes wild and bright. "Mr. Rasmussen, hoist the Jolly Roger!"

Rasmussen turned to the sailors manning the lanyard, including myself. "Strike the colors, lads, and raise the black flag!"

"Aye!" we yelled, and rapidly lowered the Union Jack that was flying from the main topmast. Unclipping it from the line, we fastened the Skull and Crossed Swords to the halyard. It struck me as patently absurd that I, a man who a month ago was sitting on the bridge of a modern diesel-engine steamer, was now standing on the deck of a bona fide pirate ship, preparing to hoist the Jolly Roger to signal our intent to attack another ship. *How incredibly insane was that?* Nevertheless, I grabbed hold of the line and yanked like everyone else, raising the black flag to the top mainmast. All the crew on deck gave a hearty cheer, and we watched the Fluyt to see if she would heave to or fight.

She swung to port, approaching the shore as close as she could. I thought that was a disastrous tactical move, but Vogel informed me that Fluyts were shallow draught vessels and could maneuver with naught but ten feet under their keel. Lookouts were positioned to make sure there were no armed escorts; it would not do to get within grappling range, only to be set upon by a warship. It did not appear there were any other ships about, so we could concentrate fully on capturing this ship.

We closed inexorably on our prey. Her name, painted on her fantail, was now visible: *CANTABRIA*. This was the first large open-ocean capture for us *Belvedere* crew, and my heart was pounding with excitement, anxiety, and abject fear. The thought crossed my mind that, *Roger, you could be maimed or killed trying to capture this ship.* The ludicrousness of a twenty-first-century man taking part in attacking an eighteenth-century Spanish ship hit me like a sledgehammer.

What are you doing out here my inner voice chided. *If these ancient mariners resist, are you ready to kill them? Run them through with your cutlass? Torture them for information on the whereabouts of their treasure? Does it matter that they lived two hundred and fifty years before you were born? Does that absolve you from guilt over anything you do in pursuit of riches?*

I looked around wildly, looking for a way to remove myself from this unconscionable situation. On the verge of panicking, Tom caught my eye. He was crouching by the mainmast, cutlass out. He held my gaze, giving a quick tilt of his head for encouragement and pounding his left fist on his chest. My breathing and heartbeat steadied. This was the life—the *only* life—I could live right now. Not knowing if I would ever return to my time, my priority had to be protecting my brother, my lifeline to sanity in this crazy, eighteenth-century world.

THIRTY-EIGHT

"No one would have crossed the ocean if he could have gotten off the ship in the storm."
—Charles Kettering

From the Personal Journal of Roger M. Petrie
Aboard the Renegade
January 25, 1721

"Dang, Roger, where'd you get that cutlass?" Tom exclaimed, joining me on the starboard rail. "That's not the one Vogel gave you."

I did indeed have a new blade, one much better suited to pirating than the rusty sword Vogel had issued to me. "Took it off a sailor from the *Columbiana* a couple of weeks ago, remember? He tried to remove my head with it, stuck it in a mast instead. I managed to liberate it…"

My voice trailed off as I remembered what happened afterward—Craven had asked to see my new blade, then used it to slit the throat of Simons, the man I had taken it from. "I informed ye when ye signed on anyone who be resisting us will be given no quarter" he had growled. Not the way I would have handled the situation.

Tom drew his own cutlass, comparing it to mine. "Mine's not as fancy, but close. Hey, watch this!" He twirled it rapidly in concentric figure eights, blade singing as he did so. "Not bad, huh?"

"Yeah, you're a regular Zorro." Pointing to the pistol tucked into his waistband, I added, "Looks like he gave you something else."

"Yeah. Completes my ensemble nicely, don't you think?" he said, replacing his cutlass in its sheath, drawing the flintlock to let me see it.

"You know how to use it, I suppose."

"Haven't had time to practice with it yet. Berger said he'd teach me later today."

Turning the pistol over, I noticed markings on the bottom of the grip. "What's this?"

"My initials. Just in case it decides to run off."

I realized I had it upside down. Rotating the gun, the markings came into stark relief:

TP

*****

Sarasota, FL
Tuesday, May 28, 2019
14 years, 5 months, 12 days since Reemergence

Taking time off work to do work seemed counterproductive to me.

Rebekah had accumulated a long 'honey-do' list, so I was taking Memorial Day week off to help. My family was still trying to make sense of what had been revealed at last Saturday night's dinner party, and I was still trying to find the courage to tell Rebekah the whole truth. Should be an interesting week.

"Where are the kids?" I asked while sitting down for breakfast.

"They're over at Bonnie's. There are some errands I want to run today, and they'll have more fun over there than being dragged all over Sarasota with us."

"All over Sarasota? Sounds adventurous."

She sat down beside me at the lanai table, smiling. "Yep. Eat a hearty breakfast because we have a lot to do. I made an appointment with a Jacob Littleton at Sotheby's at 10 o'clock. After that, we're meeting Stan Templar at eleven-thirty, then on to USF Sarasota-Manatee after lunch."

"How does any of that take care of your To-Do list?"

She managed to avoid looking at me, replying, "Number one on things to accomplish this week—for me—is getting some answers to our pirate mystery."

"I see. Still dang the torpedoes, full speed ahead for you."

"Yes, Roger. I know you think I'm being silly, but this whole thing is driving me crazy. I just want to find the truth, that's all."

"No matter who it hurts?"

She stopped chewing, fixing me with a worried gaze. "What does that mean? Who would be hurt?"

"Some things should remain buried, that's all I'm saying."

"I don't follow you."

"Uncovering the past is like pulling off a band-aid, hon. Always a good chance a scab will be ripped off in the process." I got up and put my dishes in the sink, leaving Rebekah gawking at me from the table.

We got into my Edge, Rebekah stuffing a long, narrow box into the back seat. I recognized it as the package Tom had given Riley for her birthday. She had fretted about the pistol and sword ever since; evidently, she was looking for answers, hoping this Jacob Littleton and Stan Templar could provide some.

Driving in silence, I headed south to University Parkway, then turned onto the Tamiami Trail toward downtown Sarasota. Bearing right, we crossed the bay on John Ringling Causeway. The drive was beautiful, high-rise condominiums on either side giving way to parks and palm trees. Bird Key was next, then St. Armands Circle.

Sotheby's had just opened for business when we arrived, ten minutes early for our ten o'clock appointment. The office was richly appointed—oil paintings hanging on every wall, Victorian-style chairs decorating the lobby. The receptionist greeted us warmly, bidding us sit down while she notified Littleton we were here. I took a seat in a luxurious armchair, admiring the décor while I waited.

A trim, older man dressed impeccably in a dark gray Armani suit appeared in an office doorway. "Mr. and Mrs. Petrie, welcome to Sotheby's! Won't you please come in?" he said in a high, classic British accent.

We rose and walked to his office, which was also decked out impressively. He took a seat behind a large, polished mahogany desk, motioning us to sit in the comfortable-looking armchairs in front of it. A rich, pleasant aroma of brewing coffee filled the space.

"Thank you for seeing us on such short notice, Mr. Littleton," Rebekah said, handing the box over to him.

"I admit I was intrigued by your message, Mrs. Petrie. Can you tell me again what you have you brought for me to examine today?"

"Two weapons my brother-in-law claims were used by eighteenth-century pirates. I'd like to know if he's pulling my leg."

"Oh my, authentic pirate implements. That would be exciting, wouldn't it?"

I did not bother answering him.

Littleton carefully opened the box on his desktop, laying the pistol aside, focusing his attention on the cutlass. He repeatedly turned the belt, scabbard, and sword over in his hands, inspecting every detail, from every angle.

Watching him go about his examination was fascinating. He had set a notepad and pen on his desk, picking these up while swinging a large, desk-mounted magnifying glass in front of him. Peering through it, he began writing notes, talking to himself as his inspection progressed. He turned the cutlass this way and that, running his fingertips over every surface.

"Single curved quillon, single un-scalloped shell, thirty-inch moderately curved clip-point blade with minimal nicking. Some rust evident in the ricasso and hilt, metals compatible with period metallurgy. Overall, item is in excellent condition considering its apparent age." He set it gently aside, picking up the pistol.

"Mr. Littleton," Rebekah interrupted, "you mentioned its apparent age. How old would you say this sword is?"

"That is undetermined at present. I need to consult some references to be sure. However, its design characteristics certainly fit the profile of a true period weapon, manufactured somewhere between the late seventeenth and early eighteenth centuries. Say, 1650 to 1750." He smiled wanly, adding, "Give or take. These implements were rarely date stamped, and this piece is more utilitarian than decorative. But I believe my approximation is accurate."

"How exactly do you determine authenticity in pieces like this?" I said, wondering if I would be able to refute anything he said to Rebekah.

Exhaling loudly, he said, "The ultimate determination of authenticity currently available is X-ray and neutron-imaging. Forgeries and reproductions simply cannot withstand the investigative powers of such tools. In a case such as this cutlass, radiation analysis might indicate whether the metals used are consistent with traditional forging methods."

"Can you do that here?" Rebekah asked hopefully.

"I'm afraid not, Mrs. Petrie," he replied with an apologetic smile. "I rely on traditional surface analysis."

"How does that work?" I asked pointedly.

"An excellent question. It is a skill learned and honed over many years. But there are ways to be reasonably sure a weapon is authentic. For instance, does the weapon exhibit characteristics of production techniques true to the era, or are there visible signs of bulk defects? Are there maker's marks or dates of manufacture? If so, are they deep impressions or shallow? Original weapons tend to have shallower, less technically perfect stampings."

He paused to take a sip of water. One thing was becoming abundantly clear—Jacob Littleton knew his stuff.

"If a weapon has no date stamping, another determining factor is the heft of a particular item; does it *feel* like it would be an effective weapon? Many sword reproductions and forgeries are heavier than the original article, out of balance, less flexible, or vital components feel loose or are poorly aligned. Also, is the piece constructed of materials native at the time of manufacture, or does it incorporate more contemporary woods, metals, and plastics? Does it appear worn, as an older weapon would, or is it too new, too perfect?"

"So, your initial impression is that this is an authentic cutlass?"

"That is correct." He ran his hand over the hilt and handguard. "You must tell me more about the original owner—who he was and what he did. This is likely a piece of history from a period and place that we simply have a deficiency of accurate information."

"How would we know who the original owner was?" I said.

Littleton reversed the cutlass, so the pommel was facing us. "See, here on the pommel, the owner engraved his initials."

I had seen those markings before, back on the *Renegade:* TP.

Rebekah shot me a glance. "TP? Tom Petrie, perhaps?"

"Don't be ridiculous, honey, those can't be his."

"So, you do know him?"

"We're still trying to figure that out," Rebekah answered, frowning in my direction. "Mr. Littleton, in your expert opinion, would pirates have carried something like this?"

"Oh, yes, short-blade cutlasses like this were perfect for close hand-to-hand combat and for chopping through heavy ropes and wood," he explained. "Precisely the sort of thing a brigand would need when searching a ship for valuable cargo."

"Interesting. Say, does the pistol have initials engraved on it, too?"

He retrieved the pistol, rotating it while looking for any telltale markings. "I believe so," he said, showing us the bottom of the pistol grip. "The same initials, TP."

"Is it as old as the cutlass?" Rebekah inquired.

"I have not examined it in detail yet, so let's do that now, shall we?"

Littleton picked up his notepad again, beginning a thorough examination of the pistol. He confirmed it was not loaded, then proceeded to examine it with his powerful magnifier, moving it in all directions as he inspected its mechanisms. As he had with the cutlass, he muttered to himself as he scribbled on his pad. Once, he swiveled around to the glass-doored bookcase behind him, consulting some sort of reference guide. He ran his hands over it one last time, then set it down before him on the desktop.

"Please understand that my inspection of these weapons today was cursory at best. To accurately ascertain their true ages would require a more intensive examination. However, based on what I've deduced thus far, I am satisfied that these are authentic weapons from the late seventeenth to early eighteenth centuries."

Rebekah was moved by his conclusion. "Mr. Littleton, I have one last question—could someone easily buy weapons like these on the open market or at collectors' conventions?"

"Certainly, but because of the price to be fetched for a genuine period piece, the number of forgeries and reproductions out there is daunting. Only savvy collectors and inspectors can tell the difference, and even they can be deceived by a very clever forger. You would have to search long and hard to find pieces like this, and they would not be cheap."

We sat looking at each other for a moment, Rebekah mulling over this information, me trying not to incriminate myself.

Breaking the awkward silence, Littleton asked, "Mrs. Petrie, you said you acquired these pieces from your brother-in-law?"

"Yes, he's an amateur collector of such things. He gifted them to his niece, who was excited to get them."

"I can imagine. These pieces are in excellent condition despite the normal wear-and-tear. It would be fascinating to know their history, who used them and where they have been."

"Yes, I would like to know that, too," she replied, shooting me an 'I told you so' glance. "Thank you so much, Mr. Littleton. "This has been most informative."

*****

Rebekah left me to collect the weapons from Littleton, waiting on the sidewalk outside for me to appear.

"Put the box in the car, Roger; we can walk to our next appointment. Templar's is just around the corner." Her attitude was markedly colder than it had been this morning.

"Yes, ma'am." That earned me a sharp, silent rebuke.

It would take a lot to make me wish I were at work instead of hanging out with my family, but this day was fast approaching that threshold. Setting the box in the Edge's back seat, I locked the car and hustled after her. I grabbed her hand when I caught up, thankful she did not pull it away.

"What did you think, Roger?" she said after a few moments.

"Proves the point everything sounds better when spoken with an English accent."

"You know what I mean! Mr. Littleton's conclusions were pretty interesting."

"He did seem to know the subject matter."

She stopped, tugging on my arm to make me follow suit. "Come on, Roger, don't play dumb. Are those articles Tom's or not?"

I exhaled, exasperated. "Yes, they were. Until he gave them to Riley."

"I'm not talking about Tom buying them at a yard sale. Did he have them aboard your ship?"

"I never saw them on the *Belvedere*."

"Roger!"

"You mean *Renegade*? A three-hundred-year old ship? Come on, Rebekah, do you really believe that?"

"I wouldn't have a few weeks ago, but the more I learn the more it seems Tom's wild pirate tales may be closer to the truth than I first thought. I know that sounds dumb, but you did tell me something you can't explain happened to you, right?"

"Right."

"Let's go talk to Stan Templar, then. Maybe he can shed more light on our situation."

THIRTY-NINE

"Aye, we know we be considered outlaws, but I'd rather live life short on my own terms than a multitude of years little more than property of someone else."
—Edward Vogel

Sarasota, FL
Tuesday, May 28, 2019
14 years, 5 months, 12 days since Reemergence

Templar's Jewelry was on the east side of South Boulevard of the Presidents, next to the 15 South Restaurant. The storefront was white, with a modern-looking silver marquis.

Stan Templar, looking wizened and elderly, was behind the main counter. "Ah, Mr. and Mrs. Petrie, so glad you could come in! I've been waiting to talk to Roger for some time."

"Thank you, Stan. It seems everyone wants to talk to Roger nowadays."

"Indeed. How may I be of service?"

Rebekah fished a coin out of her purse—I was shocked to see it matched the doubloon Tom had given Riley. Where on earth had she gotten it?

"We came into possession of this coin quite recently, Stan," she began, laying the coin in front of him, "and we were hoping you could tell us about it."

His eyebrows shot up as he picked up the doubloon, turning it over in his hands. Picking up a jeweler's loupe, he snapped the lens out and examined the coin intently.

"It certainly appears to be genuine. If you would be so kind as to have a seat over here, I'll examine it more closely."

The store had a sitting area set up on one side before a faux fireplace. Display cases full of shiny baubles framed the fireplace, with two single armchairs and a love seat arranged in a half-circle before it. Rebekah and I sat down to wait as he performed whatever tests he had planned.

Craning my neck to see, I watched as he examined the doubloon under a powerful microscope, then moved to another desk, consulting written and online resources, talking to someone on the phone. He took and eyedropper and dripped some sort of liquid on it, scribbling notes as he observed the results.

After half an hour, he called out, "Mr. and Mrs. Petrie, if you would come here, I have some results for you." We got up and joined him at the back counter.

"This coin, per my cursory analysis, also proves to be genuine. A surprisingly pristine example of a gold doubloon, no doubted mined and minted in Colombia or Mexico in the early 1700s. According to my friend at the Florida Museum of Natural History, Dr. Michael

Tropinsky, this matches other coins from a ship named the *Nuestra de la Capistrano*. She disappeared in early 1721 off southern Puerto Rico, apparently falling prey to piratical activities."

"'Piratical activities'?" Rebekah exclaimed. "Do he mention what pirate was responsible?"

"An interesting question, because the coin's value would increase if the pirate in question were extremely famous, such as Blackbeard."

"Was he famous?"

"He wasn't sure, but Michael favored a rather obscure figure named Craven. He was an acolyte of Calico Jack Rackham's, causing mischief in the early 1720s."

"Craven, you say?" she said, shooting me a knowing look.

"Yes. You act like that name means something to you."

"It might. To Roger, as well," she added, yanking my hand as she headed for the entrance. "Thank you, Stan, I really appreciate your time today."

On impulse, I cast a look behind me as I walked out the door. Templar stood transfixed, overt curiosity on his face as he watched me leave.

*****

Rebekah wanted Ruby Tuesday's for lunch, for their salad bar, among other things. That was fine with me—I was in the mood to mangle some red meat after everything that had happened today. So far. We still had a meeting with Desiree Costas at USF on the calendar, so my misery was not over yet.

A medium ribeye was just the thing to buoy my spirits, along with a loaded baked potato and fresh rolls.

"You inhaled your lunch pretty fast. I do feed you, you know," Rebekah remarked as I snatched another roll from the basket.

"You've been awfully quiet, Roger, about what we've learned so far today."

"Nothing to say, really. It's all seemed pretty straightforward."

"Didn't you tell Mrs. Truitt the doubloon was a fake?"

"Obviously, I was mistaken."

"By accident, or by choice?"

*****

After eating, we headed back west to the Tamiami Trail, passing the Sarasota International Airport, arriving at the University of South Florida a little after two o'clock. Desiree Costas' office was in Building C, part of the College of Liberal Arts and Social Sciences.

Her office was on the third floor, a somewhat small but comfortable affair. She was seated behind a dark walnut desk wedged into a corner. Desiree was a handsome, petite woman of Hispanic ethnicity, looking very professional in her short black hair and open-neck blue dress. She got up and shook our hands, her English slightly accented but crisp. She led us to a small table surrounded by four chairs in the opposite corner of the office.

"Welcome to USF, Mr. and Mrs. Petrie. Did you have any trouble finding me?"

"No, your directions were spot on," Rebekah answered. "I am anxious to hear what you've found out, Professor."

"Please, call me Desiree," she said amicably, pulling her dress hem over her knees. "It was refreshing to get a request for information on a pirate other than Blackbeard." Seeing my puzzlement, she added, "Rebekah asked about a Captain Craven, and a ship named the *Renegade*."

"She did, huh? Did you have any luck?"

"Yes, I did, though it wasn't easy. Records from that era are spotty at best, but I was able to piece together a profile. We know he served under Calico Jack, and that Jack gave him a vessel of his own, which he renamed *Renegade*. Craven is a mysterious figure, but what we do know is intriguing."

"How so?" Rebekah asked.

Desiree sat back, a manila folder in her lap. She donned a pair of reading glasses and opened the folder. "Craven and the *Renegade* operated at the tail end of the Caribbean's Golden Age of Piracy. Royal Navy records indicate they were active from late 1718 to November 1722, after many of the more famous buccaneers, like Calico Jack and Bartholomew Roberts, had been killed. According to Royal Navy Intelligence, Craven died in a battle with HMS *Essex* in July of 1721. Many of his senior officers died with him, and the crew voted in a new captain, known to us as the Red Raider." Costas gave me a curious look, like there was something she was not telling us.

"The Red Raider?"

"Yes. Interestingly, we recently learned his first name was Roger. Just like yours, Mr. Petrie."

"What are the odds?" I said flippantly, trying to cover up Rebekah's strong reaction to Desiree's statement.

"I know, right? But the exciting thing is the wreck of the *Renegade* was discovered early this year, only the third actual pirate ship every found. Schraeger Salvage made some very dramatic discoveries, one of which was a waterproof box containing journal pages from this Roger."

So that is where my old correspondence had gone.

"They were kind enough to give me several photocopies of letters contained within," Desiree continued. "Evidently this Roger was initially low down in the command hierarchy, but a series of events vaulted him to the captaincy. It's an extraordinary story, even though the details are still sketchy." She paused, then looked directly at me. "What's even more intriguing is the name on the records Schraeger recovered."

"Why is that?" Rebekah asked uncertainly.

Desiree pulled some laminated sheets from the folder before her, laying them out for us to see, pointing to some script at the top. "I think these headings speak for themselves, don't you?"

From the Personal Journal of Roger M. Petrie
Aboard the Renegade
Late December 1720

Rebekah's mouth opened and closed repeatedly, but no sound came out. She traced the name with her finger, then turned to me, mouthing "How?"

Desiree continued to gaze at me steadily. "What is your full name, Roger, if I may ask?"

Affecting a look of surprise at this revelation, I cleared my throat while squirming in my seat. "Um, it's Roger Michael Petrie."

"Interesting. Have you done a genealogy study lately? Petrie is not a rare surname, but I'd wager this Roger M. Petrie is a direct relative of yours."

Was he ever.

Rebekah finally found her voice again. "Desiree, uh, are there any pictures of this Red Raider?"

"Well, we are talking about an age before photography," she chuckled, "but there were drawings of various pirates from that era. I should have thought of that beforehand, sorry. Let me see if I have any of Craven or Roger."

She got up, moving to a bank of file cabinets lining the far wall. She opened the third drawer and started rummaging through it. After several minutes, she produced a charcoal sketch of Craven. Boy, did it capture his craggy features and frightening face perfectly.

"Eww, he's disgusting!" Rebekah exclaimed.

"He wasn't much to look at, but other sailors were terrified of him. He might have been bipolar, said to have suffered from dramatic mood swings. Who knows, he might have been killed by his own crew. That was an uncommon but not unheard-of fate for some of the more brutal or incompetent captains."

"And he was succeeded by this 'Red Raider'?"

"Yes, he was. They called him Red Raider because he loved to wear a redcoat captured from a British Royal Marine. Legend has it he only wore red accents, like bandanas and sashes, into battle."

"Why is that important?"

"Because at that time, red dye was the most expensive, so if you wanted to be pretentious, red was the color of choice. It was said that he was quite the flamboyant character." She rummaged in the drawer some more, talking as she looked for a portrait of the Red Raider.

"Roger the Red Raider is a fascinating figure. Records imply his pirate reign was partly defined by his compassion and humanity, and partly by his incredible success at capturing ships laden with treasure. He only commanded the *Renegade* for about a year before she was lost in a hurricane. Before that, there are substantiated reports that he and his crew gave generously to provide for homeless sailors, especially those who were injured or missing limbs. And he provided seed money for newly freed slaves to buy land. Maybe I'm a romantic, but that endears him to me."

I fidgeted in my seat as she talked, which did not go unnoticed by Rebekah. She was about to say something when Desiree shrieked in joy.

"Eureka! Here's the only sketch of Roger I have." She plopped it down in front of us.

It was another charcoal drawing, displaying a dapper-looking man with shoulder-length hair, neatly trimmed beard, wearing a greatcoat with brass buttons, a sash, beads, ankle breeches, and…strange black shoes, resembling modern athletic wear.

Rebekah lost her voice again, dividing her gaze between the drawing and me. "Roger!" she whispered, "he looks *just like you!* How is that possible?"

"The likeness is uncanny," Desiree agreed. "A long-lost relative?"

"It's a distinct possibility, obviously," I deadpanned, "though I'm not all that into genealogy."

She was going to reply, but eyed Rebekah with concern. "Rebekah, are you all right? My goodness, you look like you've seen a ghost!"

Rebekah did not laugh. "Desiree, may we take a picture of this drawing?" she eventually was able to say.

"Certainly, on one condition—you *must* come back and tell me how this Red Raider is related to Roger. I'm dying to know what you find out!"

"We'll see what we can do," I replied, helping Rebekah up from the table. "Thank you for your hospitality, Desiree. We really appreciate it."

"My pleasure. Remember our bargain! I look forward to seeing you again. Soon, I hope."

"We'll remember," Rebekah answered earnestly. "Believe me, we'll remember."

FORTY

But here is no arguing with such sniveling puppies who allow superiors to kick them about deck at pleasure."
—Black Sam Bellamy

Sarasota, FL
Tuesday, May 28, 2019
14 years, 5 months, 12 days since Reemergence

Rebekah collapsed onto our couch when we returned to our villa, totally drained by the day's revelations. She had not said much on the way home, but I knew there would be a reckoning sooner or later, with the testimonies of Desiree, Littleton, and Templar, the ancient weapons, the doubloon.

I had a feeling I would not slip out of this situation. I was right.

After eating a bite and hydrating, Rebekah was in a questioning mood:

"Can we recap what we've learned today, honey?"

"Sure, why not?"

"Okay. First, we know that the weapons Tom gave Riley were probably made in the 1700s. Next, Tom's doubloon proved to be genuine, probably taken from a ship the *Renegade* captured. Finally, we have Craven succeeded by someone who looked an awful lot like you, with similar handwriting."

"What?"

"I recognized your handwriting on the journal page, Roger. I didn't tell Desiree that, because I didn't want to give her more questions to ask. But it looked like yours. From December 1720. Mind telling me how that happened?"

BONG! Thankfully, the doorbell rang, interrupting our conversation.

"Expecting someone?" Rebekah said tersely, getting up to answer it.

"Not that I know of."

Rebekah had barely unlocked the door before someone pushed her aside and entered our home. It was Regina Sutton, Bobby's mother. She stood in our foyer, shifting her weight from one foot to the other while her eyes darted around warily. *She is a high-strung one* I thought.

"Hi, Rebekah, Roger," she said in a high, nasally voice. "Sorry it's so late. I would've called first, but I was on my way home and thought, what the heck, might as well drop by."

"No problem, Regina, come on in," Rebekah, offered, showing her to an armchair. "What's up?"

"Well, you know, Bobby was at Riley's birthday party last month. He told Alex about a strange encounter he had with Roger here, talking about pirates and all that stuff." She rolled her eyes to indicate what she thought of the subject. "Anyway, when I came to pick Bobby up, Roger flipped him a coin, saying something about pirate booty." She pulled out a stick of gum from her purse, shoving it into her mouth and chewing noisily.

"Did he now?" Rebekah replied, shooting me a questioning glance. "We did hand out a lot of pirate party favors that night, including chocolate coins. Roger must have given Bobby one of those."

Regina continued to smack her gum. "That's what I thought at first. But Alex was acting all weird, especially after I found it while doing the wash Thursday. When I confronted him with it, he confessed the whole thing."

"What 'whole thing'?"

"Oh, Alex had this big plan where he was going to auction it off. He said he was hoping to make a real killing on it."

I stifled a laugh. "Alex was going to hold an auction for a chocolate coin?"

Regina stomped impatiently. "No, no, no! Haven't you been listening to a word I've said? He was going to auction off the coin you flipped Bobby."

"What coin is that?" Rebekah said, frowning impatiently.

"This one." Regina reached into her purse, withdrawing something wrapped in Kleenex and handing it to Rebekah. When she unwrapped it, I was shocked to see it was not a candy coin at all, but an actual Piece of Eight. Belatedly I remembered pocketing a few of them after finding some in the attic. How could I have made such a stupid mistake? Not wanting to relay more than necessary, I kept my mouth shut.

"That's not one of our party favors," Rebekah observed. "Why did your husband think he was going to make a killing on it?"

"Oh, Stan Templar gave him some sort of Certificate of Authenticity, saying that this is a genuine Spanish silver coin, minted in 1714 or something." She pulled out a rolled-up paper, giving it to Rebekah as well.

"And you're sure this is the same coin Roger gave Bobby?" Rebekah asked, eyeballing me suspiciously while reading the paper.

"Yes, of course I'm sure! Stan said it was worth over a thousand dollars, or something ridiculous like that. Anyway, I didn't think it was right to hold onto it, so here it is."

"Worth a thousand dollars, huh? What a generous thing to give a little boy, Roger."

"I honestly thought I was tossing him candy, not this. My bad." Avoiding Rebekah's stare, I said to Regina, "Thanks, Regina, we appreciate you returning this to us."

She waved her hands. "No problem, Roger. Sounds like an honest mistake, you know?" She giggled at her little joke. "Besides, I like squashing some of Alex's big ideas. But I'd be careful throwing things like that around."

"I will, thanks."

Regina stood to leave, Rebekah accompanying her to the foyer. "Thanks again, Regina."

"Toodle-loo!" she called, waving her fingers as she swept out the door.

"Wow," I laughed when she was out of earshot. "She is something else." Pocketing the coin, I stood up and yawned. "Well, it's late, think I'll turn in for the night."

"Wait just a minute, mister!" Rebekah said sternly. "We aren't done here. Where did you get that Piece of Eight?"

"This old thing?" I replied nonchalantly, fishing it out of my pocket. "Tom, probably. He's got a bunch of these in his study."

"For real? Where does he keep them—next to his stash of doubloons, right below the ancient weapons display?"

"Funny. Very funny." I noticed she was not smiling. "What?"

"There's a lot of coincidences piling up around you and Tom, and I don't like it, Roger."

"Such as?"

"The ones I just mentioned, your recent erratic behavior, Tom adding you to his storytelling. Put it all together, and several frightening scenarios come to mind."

"What kind of scenarios?"

"I'm not comfortable saying them out loud. Yet. But someone or something is going crazy with all this stuff. I just hope it's not me."

FORTY-ONE

"Damn you villains, who are you? And from whence came you?"
—Blackbeard

From the Personal Journal of Roger M. Petrie
Aboard the Renegade
January 5, 1721

Cantabria was still under sail, which irritated Craven.

"They have but a wee crew, and they imperil themselves further by antagonizing me? They be playing with perdition's fire!" he roared, to the crew's delight. Berger explained why Craven was so energized; because Fluyts were designed to carry prodigious amounts of cargo, the likelihood of a major haul of sellable goods was great. Our crew was in good spirits, no doubt aided by the large amounts of rum they had recently consumed.

The Fluyt's sails were luffing badly in the westerly winds, and we overtook her easily. She still had not surrendered, which was perplexing. Talking to Mr. Vogel, I learned that if a merchantman didn't give up after the black flag was hoisted, either they thought there were enough hands aboard to repel an attack, or they were carrying valuable cargo that the captain was not willing to give up easily. His opinion was that the latter was the greater possibility.

"Master Gunner, fire a warning shot across her bow! If she still resists, disable her rigging!" Craven bellowed.

Spenser prepared a shot with the port forward four-pound chase gun. A cloth "cartridge" filled with gunpowder was rammed into the muzzle, followed by a cloth wad. The four-pound cannonball was rammed in next, followed by another cloth wad (to prevent the cannonball from rolling out the end by mistake). A gunner's mate punctured the powder cartridge with a sharp quill, then poured gunpowder into the touch hole in the cannon's breech. Loaded and primed, the gun crew heaved on lines attached to the forward gunwale, rolling the cannon into firing position. At Spenser's signal, a gunner touched the lit linstock to the touch hole. There was a showering of sparks, a delay of three or four seconds, and then…

BOOM!

Fire and smoke belched from the cannon's muzzle as it recoiled back on its carriage. The shot soared about eleven hundred yards, impacting the ocean slightly inshore and forty yards in front of the fleeing ship. Within seconds, it had achieved the desired effect. The Fluyt loosened her sails and lowered her ensign. Slocum commenced procedures to slow *Renegade* as well, steering into the wind as Rasmussen supervised backing the foresails and easing off on the mainsail. *Renegade* palpably slowed, Slocum continually turning the rudder into the wind as she lost forward momentum.

"Excellent work, Mr. Slocum! As she's bearing to starboard, bear to port so that we may conjoin our bows. Mr. Berger, prepare the boarding parties!"

Berger gathered the forty pirates who would board *Cantabria*, disarm her crew, and plunder her cargo hold. Tom numbered among the boarding crew, which surprised me. Surely, a man of his expertise should not be exposed to danger. On second thought, he had probably volunteered.

Berger addressed his crew. "Now listen up, ye mangy mongrels! We be boarding her bows, so be laying your courses from stem to stern on every deck! Waylay any disagreeable blokes and be watching your backs! Be quick, for the less time we be spending tethered to this monstrosity the better."

Craven called forward his boatswain, Patrick Carney. "Mr. Carney, keep a watch on this beast's weather deck, if ye please, and dispatch anyone resistant to our plundering, will ye?"

"Aye, Captain, we'll keep a weather eye out for any trouble!" Carney shouted.

As Slocum maneuvered *Renegade* to slide up against the Fluyt's bow, Craven drew his sword, holding it high. "Are ye ready, me hearties?" he thundered, answered by rapturous cheering. "Now, let's see what this behemoth be having to fill our holds and bellies!"

As I organized the cargo handling crew to receive any plundered wares, Tom appeared beside me, eyes bright and eager. "Don't you love it, Roger? Aye, it's a pirate's life for me, bucko!" he yelled joyfully, watching as *Renegade* closed quarters quickly with the hapless Fluyt. He was wearing a long-sleeved, pale linen shirt, with a bright blue sash tied around his waist and a blue striped bandana adorning his head. Since Tom was tall and muscular (*Renegade's* sailors looked to average about five-foot seven), he cut an imposing figure, one hand gripping the mainmast shroud, the other holding a formidable-looking cutlass.

Was this my normally mild-mannered brother, an engineer by trade? "Tom, remember what we talked about," I warned. "Do you have the implements ready?"

He flicked his head. I turned, and beheld Riley and Wolcott running toward us, holding odd-looking metal contraptions, and wearing canvas storage bags slung across their backs.

"They have the tear gas, too, Roger. We'll do everything possible to limit casualties and find whatever treasure lies within her holds without resorting to violence and torture." I nodded gratefully, as everyone readied to board our capture.

Cantabria rode low in the water, but her freeboard still towered above us. Several sailors threw grappling hooks that clanged into place around railings and guy lines, while others swung big axes, sinking them into her hull, and using them as leverage to hop onto her deck.

Captain Craven led the assault, and men climbed up ropes, using axes and pikes to walk up the sides of the Fluyt. I heard sounds of clashing blades, followed by the bark of a pistol, all amidst loud shouting and yelling. Someone was not readily surrendering, after all.

I heard Tom yell, "Fire in the hole!" They must be tossing the gas grenades down the hatches, to subdue anyone below.

The battle was short, lasting only a few minutes. After the noises had died down, Carney called out to me, "Mr. Petrie, you'd best get up on deck now; they'll be needing to haul out our bounty."

I looked up at the ropes lashed from *Renegade* to the Fluyt. Both ships were heaving up and down in the light swell. Extreme sports like wall-climbing, bungee-jumping, and rope ladders were more Tom's thing than mine, but I secured my weapons and grabbed an inch-thick hemp rope to begin the ten-foot climb up to *Cantabria's* main deck. It was a harrowing journey, the rope sliding horizontally and vertically with the ships' movements. I was in fairly good shape, but it took all my strength and concentration to hold on and inch my way up the rope, which angled upward at a sixty-degree incline. After only a few minutes, my muscles were burning, my body shaking with the effort. Several times I looked down, the sea sloshing up between the hulls in great foamy splashes, soaking my breeches and shoes. I spied the shadowy figure of a shark swimming below and almost lost my grip, but finally I remembered how I made it up the ropes in gym class. I hung upside down, wrapped my left leg around the rope, then clamped it between my feet. Pushing up with my right leg and reaching forward, I traversed the rope two feet per push. When I reached the *Cantabria's* gunwale, I heaved myself over it, crumpling to the deck with what I am sure was the epitome of grace.

*****

Once on deck, I almost slipped. Looking down, I was shocked to see pools of blood everywhere. Several bodies lay prone, having succumbed to their heinous wounds. *Cantabria's* officers were seated around the foremast, while her enlisted men were tied to the mizzenmast. The captain was bound to the mainmast, Craven standing in front of him cursing vilely and threatening him with gross bodily harm. Wisps of smoke were snaking up through the hatch covers, remnants of the tear gas attack. When I approached amidships, I could hear the captain refusing to disclose the whereabouts of any valuables on board.

Vogel had appropriated a Ship's Manifest, which listed over sixty tons of cargo, two tons of which consisted of "Peso de a Ochos" and "Quadruple-pistoles", terms with which I was not familiar.

He was quite jovial, slapping me on the back. “It means we struck the mother lode, Mr. Petrie! These be Spanish pieces of eight and doubloons, silver and gold, lad! We just need to divine where they be in this cursed ship’s hold.”

Fishing a small Maglite out of my backpack, I informed him, “I think we can be of assistance with that, Mr. Vogel.” He scowled at the metallic red flashlight, until I turned it on, showing him the brightness of the Xenon bulb.

“Blimey, Petrie!” He said that a lot, I had noticed. “I’ve never beheld a torch be bright as that!”

“Wait ‘til you see what else we’ve brought with us, Mr. Vogel,” I said, heading for the mainmast where Craven was holding court.

FORTY-TWO

"Lend us yer ears, ye newbie crew, ye interlopers aboard our ship. Ahoy, me hearties, 'ave a taste of rum, raise a Black Jack to yer lips!"
—Pirate Ditty

Sarasota, FL
Saturday Evening, June 1, 2019
14 years, 5 months, 16 days since Reemergence

Chloe, Rebekah, and I were having a dinner party, hosting the burgeoning romance between Tom and Charlotte.

Tom was clearly smitten with her; they spent most of dinner making googly eyes at each other when they thought we were not looking. The five of us ate on the lanai, our children being next door at Bonnie's. Rebekah cooked a wonderful meal of chicken alfredo, red potatoes, green beans, rolls, and watermelon.

Dinner started out pleasant enough. We teased the new couple all during the meal, causing Charlotte to blush several times. Everyone seemed to be having a good time. Everyone but Rebekah, who was in some sort of funk. She picked at her food, not really engaging in conversations, her mind obviously elsewhere.

"Rebekah, sweetie, is everything all right?" Charlotte asked. "You haven't said two words all night."

Rebekah looked around in surprise, probably unaware of her odd behavior. "I'm sorry, I just have a lot on my mind."

"Like what?" Chloe asked.

She sighed, pulling her napkin from her lap, laying it on the table. "I'm finding out the state of my family may not be what I first imagined."

I cocked my head at her. "That's a pretty cryptic remark."

She leveled her gaze at me. "It just disturbs me that, whenever I ask you about what's going on with this pirate thing, I get the runaround."

"What are you talking about?"

She folded her arms tightly. "Take Captain Craven for instance." Both Tom and I looked up at the mention of his name. "See that? You both reacted to his name! Desiree Costas at USF confirmed he's a historical figure who actually commanded a ship named the *Renegade* in the early eighteenth century." She paused, looking at us both. "Isn't that the pirate ship you supposedly served on?"

Tom slowly lowered his napkin. "Yes, that's right, Rebekah."

Chloe and Charlotte looked uncomfortable as Rebekah went on. "I've heard both those names more times than I care to count recently. How exactly are you two connected to a ship and captain from three hundred years ago?"

"Honey, there might have been a number of ships named *Renegade* back then," I protested weakly.

"Not captained by a man named Craven, there weren't." *Touché*. "Did you make his acquaintance, Tom?"

Tom met her gaze. "Yes, I knew Captain Craven. He was a brutal, cold-hearted son-of-a-…" he stopped short of cursing, "and I'm glad he's dead. Does that answer your question?"

Rebekah digested that information. "Interesting. I also learned that the Spanish galleon you told Riley the gold doubloon came from, uh, the *Capistrano*, right?"

"Yes, *Nuestra de la Capistrano* was her name," Tom replied woodenly.

"Right. Apparently, she was Craven's biggest conquest, one of the richest single prizes in pirate history. Scholars originally thought she sank in a storm. She didn't, though, did she?"

"No, she did not, though Craven died before the *Capistrano* was captured."

"How do you know that, Tom?" Rebekah exclaimed. "And please don't tell me because you and Roger were there!"

"I won't, then," he said, pushing back from the table. "This was a wonderful meal, Rebekah, thank you. I believe I'll take Charlotte home now. Suddenly, I'm pretty tired. Say good night to the kids for me, will you?"

"Leaving so soon? That's a shame, I was just getting started," Rebekah snapped, starting to clear the table.

Tom gave her a thoughtful look. "What *were* you hoping to accomplish tonight?"

She dumped an armload of dishes into the sink. "Ever since Riley's trouble at school, I've taken a closer look at the events of this spring. The doubloon, the shift in your stories, Roger's behavior, etcetera. I'm trying to sort all this out before I go crazy."

"I see," he replied. "I didn't know that."

Rebekah slapped the counter, startling us all. “I’m sure you didn’t, Tom. Before this spring, all your folktales were merely fun and games, stories I thought you made up for the entertainment of my children. But now, they’re not so harmless anymore. Suddenly, you two are at the heart of the action. Riley repeats them, so emphatically that she disrupts her class, twice!” She held up two fingers for emphasis. “Roger’s headaches and nightmares have returned, coinciding with your push to personalize these stories. He mentions this specific ship and captain, which both turn out to be real. As did the weapons you gave Riley. A disturbing picture is forming, one that concerns me greatly.”

I admired Tom, man, he was *cool* under pressure. “I’m impressed, Rebekah. You’ve obviously put a lot of thought into this—what conclusions would you draw, knowing what you know now?”

Rebekah was losing her cool. “This isn’t a game, Tom! This is serious business that’s affecting my family and my marriage!” That sent shivers up my spine. She bowed her head, her next sentence more entreaty than accusation. “There’s something untoward going on here, and I’m tired of it. There’s tension at home, tension at school, lies and half-truths being told. I want it to end, Tom. I want the truth.”

“I don’t think you’re quite ready for that, Rebekah, but you’re getting close,” he replied. “You’ll figure it out soon enough.”

We all were flummoxed by that statement. Rebekah narrowed her eyes. “Now that is a mysterious thing to say. You asked what conclusions I’ve drawn; there’s only a few worth considering, Tom. For one, you and Roger lived hundreds of years ago as pirates, which is crazy. For two, you’re suffering from schizophrenia with delusions of grandeur, so you’re both crazy. Or thirdly, you believe in reincarnation and these pirate adventures are repressed memories that you're remembering now, in which case I'm crazy." She took a breath before asking, "*Do* you believe in reincarnation, Tom? Are you thinking you lived on *Renegade* in a past life?"

He laughed quietly. "No, I don't believe in reincarnation, past lives, or communal memories. All I have is what I know to be true." With that, he beckoned Charlotte to follow him out. She, Rebekah, and Chloe hugged, shedding tears together. As I squeezed past them, the only intelligible words I heard were, "Get to the bottom of this", which sounded ominous.

Rebekah called out as I walked Tom out of the villa. "Tom, is it your contention that you and my husband actually sailed the Caribbean on the *Renegade* back in the 1720s?"

He gave her a sly smile. "That *would* be something, wouldn't it?"

*****

Once on the driveway, Tom whispered, "Roger, wake up, dude! Rebekah's getting close to the truth, and if she finds out from anybody but you, you may lose her. No treasure is worth that, bro."

"You really think she'd leave me because of this?" The very notion appalled me.

"Maybe. Look, she either thinks we're both crazy, or that there's some dark secret you're keeping from her. Either way she loses; she has a husband who is a mental case, a loss, or she has a husband she can't trust and who won't trust her, another loss. Look at how this is pulling you apart. Do you want to live like this for the rest of your life?"

We arrived at his car all too soon. While he opened the passenger door waiting for Charlotte, he patted my shoulder affectionately. "Roger, listen, I love you and your family. I know a lot of the recent tension is my fault, and I'm sorry about that. But please, do yourself a favor—trust Rebekah, tell her the truth. She might surprise you."

"Tom, it's more complicated than you realize. Rebekah's a strong-willed woman, and she might surprise me by having me committed."

"That's pretty unlikely. My counsel is to do the right thing and accept the consequences. I can't say it any plainer than that."

Charlotte arrived, stopping our conversation. She eyed me sadly as she climbed into the car. Tom shut her door, then hopped into the driver's seat. Starting the car, he gunned the engine, waved, then roared down my driveway. The Audi's tires chirped as it turned left onto Palm Pointe Drive.

I turned wearily, trudging toward our front door, dreading what was to come.

FORTY-THREE

"Heave to and strike your cursed colors, before I scupper the lot of ye!"
— Captain Benjamin Craven

From the Personal Journal of Roger Petrie
Aboard the Renegade
January 5, 1721

"I'll fly your bloody head as me banner, ye mangy knave, lest you loosen your tongue!" Craven bellowed, face crimson with rage.

The Spanish captain, Alvaro de Barcelo, stared back defiantly. Infuriated, Craven tore Barcelo's tunic, exposing his left shoulder and chest. With a nasty grimace, Craven slid the point of his dagger under Barcelo's collarbone. To his credit, Barcelo uttered not a sound. He closed his eyes and bit down hard on his lower lip, drawing blood. Craven cackled, slowly twisting his dagger as Barcelo grunted in pain. "I'll peel your skin like a mango, ye cursed Spaniard, and still pillage your sorry scow like ravens pick a skeleton clean!"

This aspect of piracy—the penchant for wanton violence and torture in the pursuit of riches—still turned my stomach. It would be difficult to plunder using more humane methods, but we modern sailors vowed secretly to try. Being eight men amongst sixty seasoned pirates, it was a tall order.

In that vein, Tom whispered to Craven, "Captain, I've a better way. We've instruments that will unveil where treasure will be found, I promise you." It was a dangerous thing to interrupt a cutthroat in the middle of operations, but Craven trusted Tom, so he withdrew from his prisoner to listen.

Tom outlined his plan, and Craven grudgingly gave his blessing. Tom motioned to Riley and Wolcott, who switched on the metal-detectors they were wearing. Tom, Cable, and I led the way, switching on flashlights and draping bandanas across our faces in case there were any stubborn pockets of tear gas remaining. We advanced, weapons drawn, and warily descended the forward hatchway.

This ship stank worse than *Renegade,* and that was saying something. She had three full decks but no cannon, with greasy bulkheads and slick floor paneling, damp with who knows what. Apparently, shipboard cleanliness was not a priority for this crew; my Pumas would need a thorough cleaning after this. We wound down to the forward holds, our Maglites brightly penetrating the gloom, followed by Craven and other *Renegade* sailors. The hold contained racks of barrels and wooden trunks fastened with leather straps, with the occasional pile of bags on pallets. The racks ran lengthwise down the keel, bisected every quarter length with a side aisle.

Riley and Wolcott moved in front, running their detectors over all the exposed trunks, cases, barrels, and bags. We all jumped when Riley's squealed, outing a barrel on a side rack buried underneath other barrels. Approaching the indicated barrel, I swung my cutlass hard, cleaving the lines that held it in place. Reversing my blade, I pounded the front panel with my pommel, eventually cracking through the bottom face. Fragrant cinnamon poured out, a momentary disappointment, but Riley's detector squealed incessantly. I eagerly tore off more of the barrel end. More spices poured out, revealing leather bags stashed at the far end. I reached back, snagging one with the point of my cutlass.

It was heavy, clinking tantalizingly as I dragged it forward. Finally, I reached in and grabbed it, drawing it out and dropping it heavily onto the floor. Craven shoved his way forward, drawing a dagger and cutting into the top of the leather. Shining my flashlight into the hole created, we were rewarded with the intoxicating yellowish glint of gold. Spanish doubloons! My heart was racing as Craven withdrew a handful, showing it to the crew assembled.

"Take a look, me hearties! The blasted Spanish be trying to sneak treasure out under our noses! Looks like their efforts be for naught, eh, lads?"

Hearty cheers rose from everyone, even me, as we gazed upon the shimmering doubloons. Reading about capturing treasure may be exciting, but there is nothing on earth like experiencing the real thing. With joyous shouts, we scoured the rest of the hold, finding more hidden trunks and barrels, the high-pitched whine of our metal detectors continually revealing new treasure troves for us to uncover.

*****

Back on the main deck, I supervised the fitting of block-and-tackles to the mainmast spars, attaching heavy lines to makeshift pallets and nets the crew had cobbled together down below. Twenty sailors grabbed two thick hawsers, hauling mightily, and lifting the cargo up above the main deck. We set all these on *Cantabria's* deck. We made sure the cargo—consisting of many tons of coins, beer, liquor, meats, cloth, and spices—was strapped securely, then utilized cables attached to *Renegade's* masts to slide these down onto her main deck. The transit cables were disengaged, new ropes were attached to *Renegade's* own winch system, and the cargo pallets were lowered into our hold. The valuables were kept under heavy guard on the main deck. Craven and his officers would divvy up the loot in his cabin.

Given the volume of booty we had found, the shares we would be awarded would be substantial, the stuff of pirate legends. I could not help but be excited about that prospect.

Vogel posited to Tom and me that this Fluyt was most likely a holdover from the earlier New Spain galleon fleet that had sailed in late fall, after hurricane season. The Spanish were aware pirates sought information on fleet sailing schedules, so they sent out decoy ships to confound them. Treasure was normally secured on their most heavily armed galleons, which sailed en masse. They had attempted to sneak *Cantabria* through on a different route, thinking she would not arouse suspicions as to the real nature of her cargo. Because she carried valuables, there should be an escort warship nearby for protection. However, we never laid eyes on it, and we were not going to hang around in case it showed up.

Before he turned to tend to other business, Vogel addressed us both. "Lads, you did well today by the captain and me. We would've wasted precious hours searching for plunder, and would probably have ended up killing the crew, with no promise of locating the bounty. The wealth we recovered, lads, be far beyond what we be dreaming of! Ah, 'tis a good day, it is!"

All around us, sailors were cracking open bottles and flasks of rum, Bodie sending up barrels to dip cups and tankards in. Tom and I drank from a batch that Samuels made, which was highly diluted and sweetly flavored, the alcohol content minimal. I remembered what Vogel said about a warship escort.

Should it appear, I wanted my wits about me.

*****

Later, Tom and I lounged against the stern rail, watching the sea flow by and ruminating on the day's events. We were two hours out from Puerto Rico, sailing southeast. The plan was to make for Smuggler's Cove on Tortola, still a notorious pirate haunt, and a place for the crew to let off some steam and spend their newfound wealth.

"Did you see the pile of coins we recovered?" he asked in wonder. "I've never seen anything like that in my life!" He clapped my shoulder. "We're rich, bro!"

"Um-hmm."

"Wow, your enthusiasm is overwhelming. Try to control yourself, will you?"

"Sarcasm noted."

"Did you hear what I said?"

I turned to face him. "Yes, I heard you. And yes, we're rich now. Because we just committed armed robbery. We held up a ship on the open ocean, Tom, and took what isn't ours. A crime for which the authorities would be only too happy to hang us for. Are you telling me you feel good about that?"

"Don't forget the Spanish raped the New World to mine and produce those valuables. Plus, we won't be born for two hundred and fifty years, Roger. We most likely will never return to our time. Given that, who really cares?"

"And that absolves us of all responsibility?" I asked bitterly.

"What other choices do we have? We've been at sea for two months, right? How many patrol planes have you seen? How many modern vessels have we come across? We're stuck here, and I'm choosing to make the best of it."

"And that entails being a true Caribbean pirate, taking what you want and forget the consequences?"

"If need be, Roger. My primary goal is to stay alive, so if actively participating in Craven's little venture is the best avenue for me to do that, I'm going to do it with all my heart."

I looked out to sea, watching the sun sink below the horizon. The explosion of colors as it faded from sight was breathtaking. "You realize, of course, that the average pirate was captured or killed after two years of operations."

"I am aware of that," Tom replied. "But none of them had the advantages we have."

I nodded, recognizing the logic of Tom's position. We both stared at the deepening twilight, not speaking for several minutes.

"Don't worry, bro, we'll figure things out eventually," he finally said, leaving for his bunk spot aft. "We always do."

The questions we had discussed weighed heavily on my mind as I trudged to my canvas bed on the prow. I found no relief in slumber—I dreamt of heaps of jewels, mountains of gold, and rolling around in piles of silver coins.

FORTY-FOUR

"Neither should a ship rely on one small anchor, nor should life rest on a single hope."
—Epictetus

Sarasota, FL
Saturday evening, June 1, 2019
14 years, 5 months, 16 days since Reemergence

It was still light out after Tom left.

Not wanting to be confronted by Rebekah yet, I grabbed two fishing poles and a tackle box from the front courtyard and headed out back. There was a good-sized lake behind our villa. It is a tranquil spot, an escape from the pressures of life.

My own *Fortress of Solitude*; tonight, I needed it badly.

It was warm, the air still, the lake's surface smooth—optimal conditions for fishing with my favorite surface lures.

Setting up at the lake's south end, I prepared two poles with Zebco 33 reels and strung on two surface lures, a Rebel Pop-R, and an Arbogast Hula Popper. Bass usually hit these lures hard in the spring, but even if I did not receive one bite, fishing was relaxing and soul-cleansing for me.

I cast the lures in opposite directions, setting the rod baited with the Hula Popper down while I retrieved the Rebel. The strike zone for surface lures was short, so having sharp hooks and quick reflexes was paramount for success.

The Pop-R was fifteen feet from shore, skirting the outside of a fountain ring, when a bass savagely attacked it. I whipped the rod tip back and was rewarded with the whizzing sound of line being stripped from my reel. I let him run for a minute, then set the drag and began hauling him up. Once to shore, I weighed it—just under four pounds. After extracting the lure, I made sure no gators were lying in wait, then returned the fish to the water. What a great start—I normally had to work much harder to catch the first fish of the day.

I was preparing to cast the Pop-R again when I heard the lanai's screen door bang. Riley came running out, making a beeline for me. Evidently, she and Drake were home from Bonnie's.

"Do you have an extra pole, Daddy? I want to fish, too!"

"Sure, sweetie. You can use this one, it's all set," I said, handing her the pole I'd just used. "The lure's already out there, Riley, so twitch your rod tip and slowly reel it in."

She gave me a *I know what I'm doing, old man* look, popped the drag, and started reeling.

"Remember to keep an eye out for Fred." Fred was the lake's resident seven-foot long alligator. He loved a free lunch, and surface lures normally caused him to come cruising in search of a meal. I spotted him to the north, cruising leisurely in our direction, his long tail undulating behind him. I reasoned he was far enough away that we could cast again before having to move.

I worked the Hula Popper along the east bank. After five pops, the flank of a largemouth flashed as it ambushed the lure from below. I set the hook, whipping my rod back violently. Fish on! My line sliced to the left, then eased slightly. The bass erupted from the lake, twisting violently in mid-air as he sought to dislodge my lure. Smacking back into the lake, he ran for another ten seconds, then launched into the air again. There was an unwelcome *twang!* and the lure shot free, coming to rest thirty feet from shore.

"Dang it!" I exclaimed. "Did you see that, Riley? That guy was a monster!"

While I was talking to her, Fred was zeroing in on my popper. When I realized what was happening, I started reeling madly, but the faster I reeled the faster Fred swam. I yanked back on my rod, popping the lure free of the water. Simultaneously, Fred launched himself in a desperate attempt to catch it. It was an incredible sight, this big alligator rushing through the water, jaws agape, body exposed so that we could see his light-colored underbelly. Fortunately, he missed, because the last thing I wanted was to hook a seven-foot gator.

Riley screamed, "Daddy, did you SEE that? Your lure almost got eaten by an alligator! I can't wait to tell Mommy about it!"

"Keep your voice down, Riley! And no, you can't tell Mommy, she'll never let you come fishing with me again!"

"Okay, I won't tell her...*this* time!" She laughed, then became very serious, tugging on my right arm and looking up at me with those huge hazel eyes.

"Daddy, are you mad at Uncle Tom?"

"We're having a bit of a squabble right now, sweetie, but we'll work it out, okay?"

She smiled slightly but did not hold it long. "I don't know. It seems all anyone does anymore is argue." She stopped to wipe her nose on her sleeve. "Do you think Uncle Tom will ever come to our house again? He left pretty early tonight."

"How do you know that?"

"We were on Bonnie's porch. He squealed his tires leaving."

I hated that she and Drake were exposed to our family's bickering. "I'm sorry you had to see that. We're working through some difficult issues, but everything will turn out okay because we all love each other."

She did not reply, tears forming in the corners of her eyes. She looked up and asked in a quivering voice, "Didn't you like being a pirate, Daddy?"

That caught me off guard. I thought we had convinced her last month that Tom's fantasies were not real. "Why would you ask me that?"

"Because that's what this arguing is all about…Uncle Tom's stories, right?" I nodded, and she kept going, "He loved being a pirate, you know. When he talks about it his whole face lights up. And he loved doing it with *you,* Daddy. He's so proud of you. I get the feeling that the biggest reason he loved it so much was that you were with him, sharing all the experiences he tells me about."

Out of the mouths of babes, indeed. "You think that's what he means?"

"Oh, yes, Daddy!" she enthused. "He knows what other people think about him, but he doesn't care. He said he's never been happier than when he was sailing on the *Renegade*. Sailing with *you*, Daddy."

What do you say to that? Something inside me crumbled at that moment. I knelt and wrapped my arms around her. I looked her in the face, for the first time in a long time not trying to dampen her spirits.

"I didn't know he felt that way, sweetie. I've always loved serving alongside Uncle Tom, too. He saved my hide on the *Renegade* more than once, I'll tell you," I said with a wink.

She pulled back, her mouth open, eyes wide in surprise. She hugged me again, fiercer than before. "I knew it, I just knew it!" She paused, then said, "You're not teasing me, are you, Daddy?"

I laughed softly. "No, sweetie, I'm not. I kept this secret for reasons I'll explain to you someday, but yes, Uncle Tom and I were real pirates, and we did sail together on the *Renegade.*"

"That is so AWESOME!" she yelped. "What was it like? Was it as cool as Uncle Tom says?"

"Sometimes. There's a lot to pirating, things that'll have to wait for another time. But yeah, there were times when it was pretty darn cool."

"But I can't tell anyone, can I?"

"Well, you've already told your class, right?" I jested. "But no, I'm afraid we can't discuss it seriously, Riley, with anyone, including Mom. She's not ready to believe yet, and neither is anyone else in our family. For now, we need to keep this between you, me, and Uncle Tom, okay?"

She kicked at a mound of grass, disappointed. "Okay, I guess that's best," she grumbled. Brightening, she said, "But at least now I know for sure, and that makes me really happy!"

I smiled at her delight. "Keeping a secret like this is tough, I know, though I wonder how much longer it's going to be a secret. I'm afraid the secret will be out sooner than later."

Riley noticed the sadness in my voice. She squeezed my hand, a radiant smile on her face. "Well, Daddy, if that happens, think of the stories we'll be able to tell!"

FORTY-FIVE

Piracy – Hostile takeover, without the messy paperwork.
—Anonymous

From the Personal Journal of Roger M. Petrie
Smuggler's Cove, Tortola
February 18, 1721

Craven parceled out shares from the plunder of the *Cantabria,* at least the coins and jewels we had recovered, and I was truly dumbfounded.

My share amounted to forty-two diamonds, eighty rubies and emeralds, nine hundred pieces of eight, and seven hundred doubloons. It was an incredible sum, easily worth over a million dollars in the twenty-first century. It was worth far less in 1721, and Berger advised me some of our crew could and would spend their entire share in one night ashore in a friendly port. I put most of mine away in a secure trunk, endeavoring to take it with me if the opportunity to return to 2002 ever presented itself.

After Craven was done, Vogel held an auction at the mainmast, holding up clothing we had captured and selling them to the highest bidder. It was comical, watching these brutish men spend their newfound wealth on garments worn by upper-crust Europeans, crudely swearing at each other over purchasing fancy clothes.

As Vogel oversaw the auction, *Renegade* sailed to Smuggler's Cove, Tortola. Arriving there the morning of February 18, we anchored a mile offshore, still protected by the bay but away from the busy wharves of the town. The port was moderately pirate-friendly; mercantilists in town purchased plundered goods, reselling them to the populace at a healthy discount off imported British goods. The local constabulary was persuaded to look the other way by sizable bribes from pirates like us. The British were not happy about this black-market operation, but at present could not field enough ships and manpower to stop it. From what I had read, it would be after 1730 when piracy would finally be curtailed.

Hopefully, I would be retired and living on a beach in Tahiti well before then.

We would be taking longboats into port, Craven reasoning our RIBs would cause too much commotion. Having recovered from the horror of a few days ago, I was fascinated watching the crew get ready for liberty, the chance to go ashore and spend their recently acquired shares of wealth. Normally, the regular crew never changed clothes until they were literally falling off their backs. But, we *Belvedere* survivors learned, they put away sets of clothes in sea trunks to wear whenever in port. These clothes amounted to whatever was in fashion that we pillaged from our conquests. Off went linen and canvas clothing, on went fine silks, satins, and cottons, with whatever ruffles, ribbons, and sashes they could find. Some of the crew even donned powdered wigs and overcoats, trying to emulate the fine English gentlemen we sometimes encountered. The crew took this very seriously; even Craven and his officers put on their Sunday best.

For myself, I dug into my ditty bag, pulling out a white long-sleeved linen shirt, blue cargo pants, dark socks, and my Ozark Mountain high-top hikers. Remembering the muddy dirt roads of our last port, I applied another coat of waterproofing to the hikers. Not quite the fastidiously dressed man-about-town as the regular crew, but comfortable. Not familiar with this port's amenities, I strapped a Colt 1911 to my left ankle, stored a couple of lockbacks and switchblades in my pants pockets, and strapped on my cutlass. Samuels and Doc were staying on board, having no desire to carouse on shore, so the rest of us modern sailors climbed aboard a longboat, coxswained by James, with two seamen manning the oars.

"Yo boys, dis be da first real port call for ya, eh mon?" he laughed, smiling hugely at the thought of us modern sailors walking the streets of an ancient, raucous port-of-call.

"Yeah, should be a humdinger of a night," I mumbled, causing him to laugh harder.

"Just be careful, mon, dees women know yer pockets be full, der sole aim be to relieve ya of what's in 'em!" he crowed.

I nodded sourly. For some reason I was not looking forward to this liberty call. Before we hit the beach, James, Armando, and Plue agreed to accompany us, to protect us from unforeseen threats.

As we neared the town, its skyline was dominated by a forest of masts, belonging to the numerous cargo ships tied up at wharves about the horseshoe-shaped port. There were many more ships moored in deeper water, swaying gently at anchor. Even at a distance, the town was alive with the sounds of music, laughter, cursing, brawling, and the occasional gunshot.

We tied up at a dock adjacent to what looked like the main street in town, Grande Street. The road was broad and unpaved, dry now but laced with wheel ruts from wagons, and there were piles of horse dung everywhere. The town itself teemed with hostels, taverns, gambling houses, and houses of ill-repute. The buildings were stark and functional, mainly two-story structures made of wood or brick. Many had porches or verandas overlooking the street, most full of garishly made-up women dressed in bright-colored, low-cut gowns. They waved handkerchiefs at us, calling out in soothing voices, promising pleasures untold. They reminded me of the Sirens of Greek mythology. Like those Sirens, we gave them a wide berth, knowing full well no good would come of fraternizing with them.

Our nostrils were assaulted by a variety of odors, most of them noxious. I was wearing my red bandana, having sprinkled some spices on it to negate some of the local smells. As we strolled down Grande, drunken characters would suddenly burst through doors of establishments, either stumbling out or being thrown out, causing us to veer to one side or the other to avoid their flopping bodies.

Let the good times roll!

I also noticed there were men sitting and lying everywhere, under porches, in back alleys, under stairways. James explained these were unemployed or disabled sailors, fated to eke out miserable existences begging for food and drink. It was a pitiful sight; most were emaciated, haggard-looking, and barely alive. Passersby either ignored or verbally abused them. Vogel had told me there were thousands of sailors out of work since the armistice in 1714, and viewing the human detritus littering Smuggler's Cove, I could believe it. There was nothing to be done for these poor sots this night, but I purposed to help improve their lives, if I ever got the chance.

James led our group one street west, to a rustic tavern named The Goat's Beard. He promised it was the most reputable eating establishment around. It did not look like much from the outside, a gray clapboard building with a cracked, faded sign. Upon entering, however, it had a warm ambiance, and inviting, meaty aromas tempted our salivating mouths. There were twelve wooden tables set about the place, with simple wooden chairs and benches. A large table sat in the back corner with enough seating for our party, which was attractive because it would protect our backs while affording an unobstructed view of the front door. It appeared there was a back way out through the kitchen, which might come in handy, too.

As we entered, a large, rotund man with bushy eyebrows accosted us. "Sorry, gents, but you'll need ta remove yer weapons if ya wish to be served."

I removed a small coin purse from my belt, jingling it in the proprietor's face. "Well, kind sir, we'd prefer to keep our weapons about us if you don't mind. If you do mind, we can always spend our gold somewhere else."

The man sputtered, close to throwing us out, when a short, lean woman with red, wildly curly hair pushed him gruffly aside. "Sorry, gov'ner, me mate takes leave of his senses at times. You're welcome to come in and sit a spell."

I bowed, tipping an imaginary hat to her. "Many thanks, m'lady, we hunger and thirst, and will reward you well for good food and service."

She smiled, waving us into the dining room, then turned and swatted her mate, chattering at him all the way back to the kitchen. We made for the back table, which was presently occupied by two rough-looking blokes. They were dressed in filthy clothes and smelled exceedingly bad, a combination of putrefying garbage and animal dung. They would need to go.

"Excuse me, gents, but it appears ye be reclinin' at our favorite table. It'd bode well for yer health if ye be findin' another place to eat," Plue said cheerfully. I noticed his smile did not reach his eyes.

One of the "gentlemen" looked at him with bloodshot eyes, face drawn in an ugly grimace. "Well, seein' as this here be *our* favorite table, looks like *you'll* be the ones needin' t' park yer ugly—"

He was interrupted as Armando brought his cutlass crashing down on the table. I am not sure they realized how big our party was, but once they took in James, Armando, and Tom—all large, well-muscled men—they relented and high-tailed it out of there. We settled around the table, scooting benches and chairs so no one's back faced the front door.

We ordered mutton, goat, and pork, along with bread, and ale to wash it down. The food was surprisingly good. We spent over an hour conversing, exchanging tales and lies, and toasting to our health. A couple of times, I noticed the proprietor regarding our group sullenly, busying himself with washing tankards and plates, but always glaring at us with baleful eyes.

This escaped the attention of my mates, who were thoroughly engrossed in enjoying themselves. A foreboding feeling began gnawing at my gut, a feeling that our good times might be coming to a premature end.

FORTY-SIX

"Freebootin' be a bonny life for brave, seafaring men, That is, if ye don't mind being shot at now and then!"
—Pirate Ditty

From the Personal Journal of Roger M. Petrie
Smuggler's Cove, Tortola
February 18, 1721

It was getting late, and we were considering leaving when the front door burst in.

To our unpleasant surprise, a blue-jacketed officer followed by six red-coated Royal Marines marched smartly through the dining room, stopping ten feet from our table. Other patrons scurried for cover or lunged out the now-open door; the British retinue ignored them. Each soldier carried a musket tipped with a trowel-shaped bayonet at port arms, while the officer had a sword sheathed at his left hip.

The officer, a prim, proper-looking young lad, took his hat off, waving it at us. "Good evening, sirs. I am First Lieutenant Abercrombie of HMS *Argonaut*. We were notified that vile pirates were frequenting the waterfront establishments of Smuggler's Cove this evening, especially filthy brigands of the *Renegade.* Governor Rogers will be elated at news of your capture, I'm sure. But for now, by edict of His Majesty King George I, I place all of you under arrest for the crime of piracy, pending transport to Port Royal, where you will be tried in Admiralty Court and most likely hanged. Please get up—carefully—and place your weapons on the table."

My pulse pounded in my ears, my throat was dry, and my palms were slick with sweat. This was a deadly turn of events, our evening of merriment forgotten, our lives now hanging in the balance. This was not a joke, or a bad gag at a costume party. These were sailors of the Royal Navy, a rightfully proud and well-trained service. We would need some quick thinking to save our necks from the gallows.

"Excuse me, Lieutenant," I said more calmly than I felt, "my mates and I are crew on the merchant ship *Orkney* anchored in the bay. We resent being labeled pirates with no good evidence."

Abercrombie looked confused for a moment as he considered my strange accent. He then smiled, putting his hands on either side of his shiny brass belt buckle. "I rather doubt that, sir. I have it on very good authority that all seated at this table are crew of Captain Craven's cursed vessel. Be assured, we will be dealing with him very shortly. But for now, we'll be placing your lot in irons."

He had it on good authority? Of course! The proprietor, the callow man with bushy eyebrows, had eavesdropped on our conversations all evening, and as the ale flowed, we had become louder and less cautious with our words. He must have alerted the

British to our presence, somehow. *Argonaut* probably landed several squads on the island, the ship herself rounding north of Tortola and advancing upon Smuggler's Cove. I wondered how many other bands of *Renegade* sailors were being likewise confronted.

It was time for action, because the alternative was to be led to the gallows, which for a contemporary man like me was unthinkable. An irreverent thought crossed my mind; if I died here, in this century, would Roger Petrie still be born in 1971, or would everything about me be erased from existence?

No matter, for I had no intention of dying here.

Catching Tom's eye, I mouthed, "Corbomite Maneuver." He nodded, understanding. We were dressed for liberty but were carrying enough armaments to deal with any sticky situations we might encounter. These included small versions of our tear gas and flash-bang grenades. I flicked my eyes to the table, then looked up for a brief instant. Almost imperceptible nods indicated we were all on the same page.

"Gentlemen, I grow weary of waiting. Are you coming peacefully or not? I've no problem executing the sentence immediately, if that's what you prefer," Abercrombie said irritably, his right hand sliding toward his sword.

I stood slowly, hands halfway in the air, not taking my eyes off him. "Lieutenant," I drawled as slowly as I could, while my mates prepared grenades under the table, "we appreciate your kind offer, but if it's all the same to you, we'll be going now."

Abercrombie was briefly surprised that we did not surrender immediately, which provided us with the time we needed. "NOW!" I cried, and eight grenades flew out, while we upended the table and ducked behind it, drawing bandanas across our faces. It was a heavy hardwood table, which hopefully would absorb any musket rounds. I had an image of Abercrombie pretentiously drawing his sword when four flash-bangs detonated, the bright flashes and sharp concussions stunning the Brits as the tear gas grenades went off, filling the small space with acrid smoke. There were heavy thumps as some of the soldiers hit the floor. This was followed by coughing and retching. They directed colorful curses at us through the coughing, disparaging our ship, parentage, and national origins. It would have been humorous in different circumstances.

While they stumbled about, we dove over the counter, dashing through the kitchen, out the back door, ending up in a filthy alley. Taverns, bars, and gambling houses all backed up against this alley, and from the looks of things, they all dumped their refuse in it. The poorly defined dirt roadway was covered with heaps of garbage, flowing with streams of grease, stale beer and ale, and who knows what else. The stench was nauseating, and we were momentarily disoriented, so distracting was the smell.

"'Dis way!" James yelled urgently, and we stomped through the slop, muck kicked up by our shoes sticking to our pants. We made a mad dash toward the alley's terminus at High Street. We just needed to turn right, intersect Grande, and take that all the way to the dock where our longboats were waiting.

As we reached the corner of the building on High Street, Abercrombie jumped in our way, sword drawn, backed by three redcoats. He pointed his sword at me, shouting in rage, "Stand down, you devilish rogues, or I'll run you through here and now!"

I scarcely knew what I was doing, but I drew my cutlass, determined that I would not be clapped in irons, to be carted off and hung. Berger had instructed me for many hours, so I was going to go out fighting. The rest of my band prepared to engage the three redcoats as I approached Abercrombie.

"En garde, then, Lieutenant, for we will not surrender to the likes of you!" I heard myself say in a cartoonish pirate brogue. I initiated rhythmic nose-mouth breathing, preparing my body for hand-to-hand combat. Somewhere in the back of my mind, I heard Berger's voice:

"Listen, Petrie, the secret to effectively using your blade be in always being aggressive, always moving, always attacking. Don't be simply parrying; be stifling your opponent's attacks, be using his leverage against him. Use your flat to be deflecting your opponent's edge, lad, then move in to strike!" I was thankful for his expertise and followed his instructions dutifully.

Apparently, Abercrombie had had similar teaching. He whirled, twirled, hacked, and thrusted like a dervish, his movements savage but deliberate. Our blades clanged repeatedly, neither able to secure an advantage. Footwork in the alley's tar-like muck was tricky, Abercrombie lighter on his feet than me. He circled with feline-like cunning and deliberation, looking for an opening.

Our blades met in front, and I heaved to the right, turning his torso, and disengaged, trying for a slashing down-cut. He recovered quickly, catching my right wrist in his left hand, then thrust forward. My blade was still in his clutches, so I snap-kicked him in the left thigh, simultaneously twisting my abdomen violently to my left. My kick knocked him back enough to prevent his blade from running me through. His sword-tip pierced my left side, my twisting maneuver thankfully keeping it from penetrating far. The pain was electric, the wound bleeding down my shirt. I wrenched my blade free, the both of us resuming our circling, Abercrombie smirking at my injury.

More blade clashing, then he dropped his right wrist, causing his blade to slide down mine, slashing my right forearm with the tip of his sword. The slice was shallow, but if I suffered enough of them my strength and stamina would be sapped. Soon, after more sleight-of-hand from Abercrombie, I sported slashes on my right shoulder and left forearm. I was tiring quickly, my breathing ragged, feet increasingly feeling like they were encased in concrete. Abercrombie realized this and started pressing in even harder.

I knew I would have to act quickly, or all would be lost.

Abercrombie launched a series of savage cutting and thrusting strikes. I struggled to evade and deflect them, barely keeping myself from being decapitated. Parrying a thrust, I landed the flat of my blade against his edge, knocking his rapier to my right. He drew up for a backslash, and there was my opening. I spun right inside of his right arm, my right elbow crashing into the right side of his face. He staggered back, defenses dropped for an instant, and I spun left, driving my left heel into his solar plexus. He dropped to his knees, and I spun again, whipping my right foot around in a standing round kick, cracking against his right temple. The sword dropped from his hand, and he crumpled to the ground. I kicked the sword away, lest he was playing possum.

The sounds of clashing blades still filled the cramped confines of the alley, and I glanced up from Abercrombie's prostrate form. The three Marines were still engaged with my men, wielding their bayonets skillfully despite being outnumbered. Looking down at Abercrombie, an idea hit me.

"Gentlemen, if I may have your attention!" I hollered. The combatants slowed, searching for the distracting sound. When they set eyes on me, everyone stopped fighting, still holding weapons at the ready. I had the redcoats' attention, for I was holding my cutlass to the throat of the unconscious Abercrombie. "You've acquitted yourselves well, Marines, but I request you drop your weapons, or I'll separate the Lieutenant's head from his neck." I do not know why I made such an audacious boast, for I had no intention of killing Abercrombie, but hopefully the lads would be motivated to throw down their arms.

Slowly, the three men lowered their muskets to the ground, radiating overt hostility all the while. "Excellent choice, lads. Now lay down flat on the ground, hands and arms out in front, please." It was a bold request, because the alley was filthy, but we did not need these guys jumping up and pursuing us, either.

I directed our guys to pick up the Marines' muskets, and we backed out of the alley onto High Street, making sure the coast was clear. We could hear shouting and intermittent gunfire echoing from other parts of town; we were not the only pirates confronted by the British tonight.

"Now, gents, we'll be taking the Lieutenant with us. Don't be following, or we'll return him to you in pieces, understand?" They nodded affirmation, not speaking but spitting nails at me with their expressions. A tough lot, these Marines. I would not want to tangle with them again.

We ran down High Street, turning onto Grande, Armando jogging along while transporting Abercrombie effortlessly in a fireman's carry. I contacted Doc via radio, requesting emergency assistance while breathlessly relaying the night's events. Reaching the end of Grande Street, we spied the dock where our longboats were still tethered. Armando unceremoniously dumped the Lieutenant on the side of the road, and we sprinted to the boats. A great number of shouts sounded behind us, and small parties of *Renegade* crew came running from other parts of town, pursued in the distance by squads of Marines. This was going to be one harrowing escape.

Our group piled into one of the longboats—Plue and James grabbing the oars while Armando and Tom cast off the lines—and we shoved off. Other boats were beginning to move, too, but a phalanx of Marines was double-timing it up Grande Street, closing on our position. Tom and I whipped out the Colt 1911's strapped to our ankles, laying down covering fire to allow our stragglers to dive into the last longboat and get underway. The Marines went to ground to avoid our barrage of pistol fire. We were not trying to hit anyone, but the rapid-fire of the forty-fives was awe-inspiring to eighteenth-century soldiers, giving us precious time to clear the area.

There was a roar of engines. I looked up to see Doc and Samuels driving toward us in the two RIBs, a couple of seamen riding with them. They swooshed into tight turns in front of us, throwing out lines to each boat.

"Tie these off, then hold on tight!" Samuels yelled over the thrumming Mercury engine. Once we gave him the thumbs-up, he rammed the throttle forward. The RIB responded instantly, water churning as the prop bit deep, taking up the slack in the tow lines instantly. The longboats jerked hard as the lines snapped taut, almost tossing multiple men into the drink as the RIBs took all six boats in tow. On shore, the Marines fired several desperate shots as we raced away toward our ship.

Renegade was a beehive of activity, Craven undoubtedly apprised of the unfolding situation by Doc. "Get those blasted boats aboard quickly, ye scurvy seadogs!" he yelled at seamen on deck. "Mr. Vogel, let out the reefs; prepare to get underway, quickly now!" Seamen scampered up the main-and-fore shrouds, unfurling the topsails, while others set the jibs, and still others wound the winches to set the fore-and-mainsails. We climbed topside on rope ladders, attaching lines to block-and-tackles, hurriedly hauling up and securing the boats.

"Mr. Carney, do we be having our full complement aboard?" Craven bellowed to the bosun.

"Nay, Captain. Lewiston and his mates still be missing."

"Those scabrous picaroons likely be shackled in irons now," Craven replied. "We won't be waiting for them, Mr. Carney. Cleave the stern lines, let's be making for the sea."

Evidently, *no man left behind* was not an adage that pirates adhered to.

Tom and I joined Craven, Berger, Vogel, and Carney at the wheel. Craven growled, "Gents, let's be heading for open water, quickly now!"

"Aye, Captain, one rapid getaway coming up," Tom yelled, heading for the bow winch.

He warmed up the engine, then engaged the winch, which was attached to the bow anchor line. The winch whined, straining to pull *Renegade* toward the anchor. Simultaneously, Samuels tied off a line from his RIB to *Renegade's* beak, gunning the motor when it was secured. With the winch at maximum torque and the RIB churning ahead, *Renegade* eased forward, slowly accelerating as we labored to get her hundred tons moving.

Soon, we were making a fair clip, clearing the bay's jetties, open water beyond them beckoning. The bow anchor was lifted free of the water, and soon after we hauled the RIB back on board. Once everything was secured, *Renegade* set sail under her own power.

We watched Smuggler's Cove recede from view, knowing how fortunate we were to have escaped with our lives.

FORTY-SEVEN

"As to hanging, it is no great hardship. For were it not for that, every cowardly fellow would turn pirate and so unfit the sea, that men of courage must starve."
—Mary Read, member of Calico Jack Rackham's crew

From the Personal Journal of Roger M. Petrie
Aboard the Renegade
February 18, 1721

Renegade rode the wind like a thoroughbred, her bows kicking up cascades of spray as she knifed through the dark waves.

Argonaut had appeared briefly after *Renegade* had put to sea, the ghostly outlines of her sails visible as she charged down Tortola's coast toward Smuggler's Cove. We turned our stern to her and ran out every inch of canvas we possessed, and she soon dropped out of sight.

As exhilarating as that was, I was almost too weary to notice. I elbowed my way zombie-like through men still amped from our narrow escape, seeking a quiet place near the bow to lie down. As I passed through, many sailors turned their heads my way.

Was it my imagination, or were some of them eyeballing me with newfound respect?

Tom caught up with me, clearly worried. I noticed my crisp white linen shirt and blue khakis were now soaked with blood and muck. *My dry-cleaning bill this week will be huge* I thought idly while looking for a place to rest my weary bones.

"Roger, you're hurt. Try to stop bleeding all over the place while I go get Doc, will you?" I nodded, my faculties hazy and dull. I collapsed against the port gunwale as Tom left.

Doc Loechner appeared shortly thereafter, eyeing me with consternation. "What happened to you?"

"Shore leave," I croaked.

He shook his head, bending down and opening his satchel. I gratefully accepted a cup of nutmeg-flavored rum from Tom as Doc attended to my wounds.

"Saw a little action tonight, did we, Roger?" Doc said, a bemused look on his face. He rolled up my shirt sleeves, cleaning my wounds and rubbing on antiseptic lotion. He applied butterfly bandages to the shallow slashes, covering the wounds with gauze and wrapping them with linen strips.

"Yeah. Evidently the waitress was dissatisfied with the tip I left her," I quipped, feeling better as the rum warmed my belly.

He chuckled, lifting my shirt to apply salve to my cut shoulder and abdominal wound. "Seems she was quite handy with a sword, this waitress. Maybe you shouldn't go about antagonizing the local help."

"Thanks, I'll keep that in mind next time."

Doc took on a more serious air as he finished up. "According to other members of your party, Lieutenant Abercrombie was an expert swordsman. You're lucky to be alive, my friend." He grabbed the railing and heaved himself to his feet, groaning. Seeing my amusement, he chided, "There will come a time, Roger Petrie, when you'll admit that piracy is a game for the young."

As soon as he left, Berger came by, squatting down by my side, eyes squinting in merriment. "Well, Mr. Petrie, I be terribly honored you apparently were paying attention to my swordplay lessons, all indications to the contrary."

"Yes, Mr. Berger, all your training fared me well tonight."

He regarded me with true admiration. "Aye, it did more than that, Roger. From what I be told, you squared off against a master and bested him. That be no small thing." Patting my cutlass, he continued, "A sturdy blade wielded by a capable man be a fearsome thing, Mr. Petrie. We may yet be making a proper freebooter of ye!" Berger laughed good-naturedly and took his leave.

More crew passed by after he left. Most just grunted, but some offered their take on my exploits.

Filipe said, "'Twas a good reckoning, Petrie, maybe yer not such a useless bag o' entrails after all."

"I guess we'll be needin' to stop callin' ye Sharkbait, eh?" Wilkins remarked.

Fisher offered, "Well, ye not be the bilge-sucking buffoon me mates made ye out to be."

Last to address me after those heartwarming adulations was Vogel. "Perhaps there be more to you than meets the eye, Roger Petrie."

I leaned back wearily, closing my eyes, letting the motion of the ship lull me to sleep. I was just about out when someone stomped up to where I lay. Opening one eye a slit, I beheld Captain Craven standing before me, hands on his hips.

"Well, Mr. Petrie," he began, "ye surprised me yet again. I wouldn't have given two bits for your chances against a proper swordsman, yet ye ultimately triumphed, then used him as ransom!" He laughed deeply. "That be inspired thinking, lad, truly commendable." He squatted down, thrusting out his right hand. "I daren't think this day would ever come, Roger, but methinks you've finally joined the brotherhood of pirates!" Merriment danced in his eyes as I grasped his forearm. "Ye took charge and delivered your mates intact. I knew ye had it in ye, ye just needed the proper motivation!" He rose, chuckling to himself as he walked away.

I was torn by any compliment Craven gave me. The Captain was as cutthroat as they came, but he could also be irritatingly charming at times. Besting Abercrombie was something I could be proud of, yet it was unsettling that it pleased Craven so. I sat there numbly as my soul and superego fought it out, laughing when a ridiculous thought struck me.

February 18, 1721—the day the legend of Roger Petrie was born.

FORTY-EIGHT

"So onward we sail on mighty Renegade, the far reaches of the Caribbean we roam, Treasure still be nothing next to a woman's sweet caress, Oh, Captain, please, we wanna go home!"
—Pirate Ditty

Sarasota, FL
Saturday Evening, June 1, 2019
14 years, 5 months, 16 days since Reemergence

When Riley and I returned to our villa, Chloe was in bed, leaving Rebekah sitting forlornly in the lanai.

My heart ached, as did my head. After sending Riley to bed, I sat down beside Rebekah, steeling myself for the conversation I knew was coming.

"What do you think Tom meant when he said I wasn't quite ready for the truth, Roger? What truth is he talking about?"

"Well, honey, you know Tom and his stories..."

She turned to face me. "Please don't patronize me. This whole pirate situation has become almost too painful for me to bear. Do you not agree with that?"

"Look, Rebekah..."

"Not to mention you've been acting weird lately," she continued testily. "I was hoping you'd help clarify some points tonight, but you had little to say, which was disappointing." She hugged a pillow, curling up in the chair.

"I know, and I'm sorry. But I talked to Tom tonight, hon, and he's as level-headed as he's ever been."

She pointed to the dining room table, exclaiming, "Level-headed, are you serious? He sat right there and said he knew Captain Craven!"

"I'm sure he meant 'knew of' Benjamin Craven, not knew him personally."

She stared at me, and I belatedly realized I had made a profound error, one that had not gone unnoticed.

"Interesting. I don't recall Craven's first name ever being mentioned. I didn't know it was Benjamin; would you care to tell me how you know that?"

"Come on, Rebekah," I backpedaled. "I'm sure his name has come up in past discussions."

She shook her head emphatically. "The only captain I've ever heard Tom mention is the Red Raider. But *you* have mentioned Captain Craven multiple times in your sleep. Did you make his acquaintance, too?"

"Of course not," I answered, hating having to lie.

"I don't know what you have to do with all this, Roger, but I promise you I will find out, with or without your help," she said firmly, trying to hold back her tears. "I'd rather you trust me so we could work through this together, but for some unknown reason, you don't."

Part of me wanted to break down and tell her everything, like I had with Riley, but the still, small voice in my head held me back. *There's too much at stake,* it said. *There's too much to lose,* it said. *Too many people would get hurt,* it said.

Sometimes I wished I would just shut up.

Rebekah studied me, granting me one last chance to come clean, a sadness in her eyes I had never seen before. Finally, she spoke, her words piercing my heart.

"Roger, you've been a wonderful husband and father. During our twelve years together, you have on occasion exasperated me, confounded me, and made me angry. But until today you have never, ever disappointed me. I can't tell you how heartbreaking that is."

Weeping, she got up and headed into our bedroom, slamming the door behind her. Guess that settled where I would be spending the night.

*****

As I lay on the sleeper sofa, I knew Rebekah would make good on her promise to uncover the truth, a truly frightening prospect. After serving under Craven and having been shot and stabbed with all manner of ancient weapons, that was saying a *lot*.

My mind and stomach were churning, making sleep impossible. Sitting up, I figured I had two choices: keep the status quo or tell Rebekah the truth. Knowing that my marriage, family, and more was at risk, I weighed the pros and cons of coming clean.

In the end, it all came down to one thing—I loved Rebekah, more than life itself. She was my rock, my best friend, the most amazing person I have ever known. If I could not trust her with my secrets and share my burdens with her, what was the use of being married to her at all? What would my life be like without her? Would the riches I had stashed around Sarasota bring me peace and contentment if I lost her?

The words of Jesus in Matthew 16 came to my mind: "*For what will it profit a man if he gains the whole world and forfeits his soul?*"

*****

Rebekah looked up in surprise as I entered the bedroom, shuffling over to the bed and sitting beside her. Her eyes were red and puffy from crying.

"What is it, Roger?" she asked wearily.

The words I had practiced quickly turned to mush in my brain as I looked into her eyes. But Tom was right. I *had* been a Pirate Captain, one who had been decisive, just, and fair. Time to channel that Roger Petrie again.

"Rebekah, my love, you were right in what you said to me tonight. I *haven't* been truthful with you, and for that I'm so very sorry. Maybe it's time to fix that."

She sat up, her eyes widening as she processed my words. "Roger, what are you saying?"

"Honey, we need to talk."

EPILOGUE

"All's well that ends well."
—Anonymous

"Now? It's late, Roger, and I'm worn out."

"Yes, now. I don't want to let this linger any longer. Never let the sun go down on your anger and all that."

"Okay." She propped a pillow behind her back, straightening the covers without looking at me. The issues raised earlier tonight still weighed on her mind.

I sat silent for a moment, trying to formulate my words. When I could not, she spoke up. "I don't know what you came in here to say, Roger, but I meant what I said earlier. I want…no, I *need* the truth. I need to hear it from you."

"I know." She looked tired, frustrated, fed up. I could sympathize, but how do you explain things like quantum gravity compression or time dilation to someone? Or travelling back and forth between centuries? How do you make someone else understand when you really do not understand it yourself?

"Oh, come on, Roger!" she snapped, her anger rising. "Tom's implication was clear: he believes you and he somehow ended up on a pirate ship back in the 1720's." I opened my mouth to say something, but she cut me off. "He believes you both knew this Captain Benjamin Craven personally. Things that are clearly impossible, but it certainly appeared that he believes all this to be true."

"It did sound that way, didn't it?"

"Yes, it did. And you danced around the subject all night." When I did not answer her, she went on, "Let me ask you this; do you remember things the way Tom does?"

Yowzah. She was smart, and it was useless to try and dodge her any longer. Matching wits with her was like tiptoeing through a minefield. One misstep, and *blooey*.

"I doubt anyone remembers things the way he does," I deflected.

"You know what I mean."

I sighed heavily. "Yes, I know exactly what you mean."

"Then why do you keep ducking me? I'm not asking complicated questions. I think I'm being pretty straightforward here."

"You are, honey."

She punched me lightly in the shoulder. "Then talk to me, Roger! That's what you came in her for, isn't it?"

"Believe me, Rebekah, I want to, I really do. It's just…"

She moved her head to meet my gaze. "It's just what?"

I moved my mouth, turning my head to the sea, trying to verbalize what I felt inside. "It's—difficult to explain, really."

"Why? It seems easy to me. Either you and your brother time-travelled to the 1700's or you didn't. You were either on board an ancient pirate ship or you weren't. You either knew Captain Craven or you didn't. What's so hard about that?"

"Because there's more to it."

She frowned, her face clouding over. "Dang it, Roger, man up and tell your wife what's going on!"

"I can't!"

"Why not?"

"Because I don't understand it myself!"

She dropped her arms, taking in what I had just said. "Wait…what?"

I threw my hands up in frustration. "I don't know what happened to us, honey, and I certainly can't explain it. One moment we're here, the next…"

I brushed my hair back, memories of death and destruction flooding my mind...

December 6, 1720 –

We were fighting for our lives.

The Falklands *had closed to within two miles of our position, our only escape route seemingly cut off. Utilizing combustible materials from the* Belvedere, *we had set up a screen of fire and smoke while we frantically readied our ship to make way.*

Forty-five minutes later, the battle was over. Falklands *was dead in the water, fire greedily consuming wood and canvas, her entire aft section ablaze where we had hit it with a motorboat loaded with tar and pitch.*

Renegade *slipped from the bay, leaving our burning adversary in our wake. There were some pings as our enemies futilely fired muskets at us, but soon we were out of range. We all breathed a sigh of relief, knowing how thin our margin of error had been. Port*

Royal's gallows would have to wait for another day to claim our lives.

Bodie handed out Black Jacks laden with spicy rum as we celebrated our defeat of the implacable Jonathan Barnet. I was in the middle of singing a song of thanksgiving when Tom tapped me on the shoulder, a hollow look in his eyes.

"Roger, you—you'd better come quick."

Dropping my cup on the deck, I hurried after Tom as he leapt through the rear hatchway. He led me to Sick Bay, where Doc Loechner, arms covered in blood, was ministering to a distraught young man lying on a bunk.

Drawing close, I was shocked to see it was Evan Carmichael. Evan had been a Bosun's Mate on the Belvedere, *a young man only twenty-three years old. I bent over as Doc pressed cloths to his chest. Jim Cable was somberly wiping his forehead with a wet cloth, comforting his friend.*

"Doc?" I asked quietly.

He looked up at me and shook his head. Evan's entire abdomen was blood-soaked, obscuring his wounds. Spotting me, he reached out a hand, grabbing hold of my shirt.

"Sorry, sir. In all the excitement—guess I forgot to duck." He tried to laugh but coughed instead, blood spurting out between his lips.

"Easy, Evan. Don't talk now. We need to get you patched up."

He gave me a knowing look. "Not going to happen, sir. But I want you to know—no regrets—would do it all over again."

"Evan—"

"Aaauuugghhh!" he gasped, his spine arching obscenely as his entire torso lifted off the bunk. After a few seconds, his body fell flat, his eyes open but unseeing. Choking back a sob, I reached out and tenderly closed them.

"Doc!"

He was washing his hands in a basin of water. "I did all I could. He took three musket balls to the chest and stomach. Pretty good shooting from that distance."

"Come on, Doc..."

"Roger, even if we had a modern ER there wouldn't have been much I could have done except make him comfortable. I can only do so much, my friend, with wounds like that. I'm sorry—I know you were fond of him."

"I'm sorry too, Doc, I know you did the best you could. It's just—Evan was such a good kid." I stood up, heart heavy in my chest.

It was chilling to learn that, in this era, modern medicine still had its limits.

*****

"The next, what?" Rebekah asked softly, touching my arm, returning me to the present.

"The next, good friends were dying," I whispered. "*My* ship, my first command, was burning, sinking, and I couldn't—" My voice cracked, and I was unable to finish my sentence.

She put a hand over her mouth, tears streaming down her face. "Roger, oh my gosh, I had no idea!"

I gave her a sad half-smile. "How could you? I've tried so hard to keep this from you. From everyone. I've never talked about this with anyone but Tom."

"But he makes it sound so, so—"

"Fun? Romantic? Adventurous? It was easier for him, I suppose."

"Why do you say that?"

I grabbed hold of her hands, gratified when she did not object. "Because Tom didn't have the burden of command. I did. Crewmen under my direct authority were killed, Rebekah, and it hurt."

"I'm so sorry! I didn't know—it was so painful for you."

"It was. Still is, in some ways. Tom's been able to move past the disturbing stuff. I haven't."

"Goodness, that must be hard." She bit her lip thoughtfully. "But I will say this—I don't like being lied to, Roger. You could've said something way before now."

"I know. I had reasons that sounded logical at the time. Most of all, I didn't want you to think you had a crazy man for a husband." I shrugged. "But you're right, I should have trusted you from the outset."

"Thank you for that." Tilting her head, she added, "I still have a lot of questions which need to be answered, but I'm beginning to understand your reticence better now."

"Thank you, Rebekah. For listening. For understanding—sort of, anyway. A lot of women wouldn't have put up with this craziness."

The smile she gave me was a beautiful sight to behold. "Probably not. You're lucky you're so cute."

"Well, I can't tell you what a relief it was to get this off my chest. Goodnight, my love." I leaned over to kiss her tenderly on the lips, getting ready to return to the couch.

"Roger?" she asked, pulling back the sheet.

"Yes, honey?"

"Why don't you come to bed?"

Stretching out under the covers, I felt a peace I had not felt in years. I hoped this was the beginning of a new chapter in our lives, where we could put Craven and the *Renegade* firmly behind us.

I hoped.

Roger and Tom Petrie's story will be completed in the exciting sequel "The Penitent Pirate."

MEET THE AUTHOR

ROBERT A. TAYLER was born in Kirkwood, MO, and raised in Indiana. A graduate of Indiana University, he minored in History, with a focus on military history. He began writing military fiction shortly after graduating, and Plundering the Past is his first completed work. He and his wife Jill have raised two terrific kids, and he now resides in the Indianapolis area, where he is working on the next Tide of Times novel.

On a personal note, Robert cherishes faith, family, and friends the most. He loves travelling, fishing, and is equally at home in the mountains or at the beach.

You can engage with him in many ways on social media:
Email – robertataylerbooks@gmail.com
Facebook – facebook.com/robertataylerauthor
Instagram – Instagram.com/robertataylerauthor
Twitter – twitter.com/robertatayler17

CPSIA information can be obtained
at www.ICGtesting.com
Printed in the USA
LVHW021154290323
742728LV00002B/328

9 781647 188498